THE SILVER LINING

AS GOOD AS IT GETS

ALEX J FISCHER

For my Family and Friends

1

"We're clear on the plan, right?" a head from the front passenger's seat of the van cabin asked. Its black hair blended into the darkness of the car as they sat at a stop light, and its masculine voice continued, "We get in there first, set up a perimeter, and wait for them to show up. After that, we do the deal and get the hell out."

Another male voice came from behind him. One arm rested around the other figure leaning into him. "Plan sounds great, Daniel old friend. How exactly are we going to be sure they'll actually hold up their side of the bargain though?"

"We can't, Rog, which is why we're going in strapped."

A bundle of black hair snuggling into Roger's shoulder turned to reveal red lipstick. "Didn't we agree there would be no weapons involved? If we break the terms, we're asking for an incident; and I don't think Daddy wants one with these people."

Daniel exhaled loudly and turned around to face the back. "Liz, if you believe they'll be coming in unarmed you're too naive for this business. Besides, weapons are the checks and balances of the life. You go in without any fire-power, and you're asking to be taken for all you've got."

Roger's free right hand reached to his left, grasped Elizabeth's small hands, and rubbed the back of them with his fingertips. "I don't like it, but your brother's right here, sweetie."

The driver up front stepped on the gas and angled his bald head toward the rear-view mirror. A low growl came from his throat.

Daniel looked to his left and slapped the figure's shoulder. "What's the matter, Axel? Jealous of the two lovebirds back there? I'd have thought you'd have been used to it by now."

A deep, gravelly voice came from the driver's seat. "No. I'm simply concerned it's just the four of us. If they come prepared, we could be in for a wild night."

"You heard the old man before we left. We can't have them paying for this and stealing the rest."

Axel grunted at the answer.

Elizabeth unbuckled her seat belt, scooted over, and curled up closer to her boyfriend. She climbed into his lap before speaking in a soft tone. Her blue eyes gazed up at him. "If that happens, we'll deal with it." She angled her head up and planted a kiss on Roger's jaw before continuing. "We'll set up a kill zone, which is why we're going in early. Right?"

Roger kept his focus toward the front of the van as he angled his left arm up around her shoulders. "That's the theory. Your brother and I will be going to find high ground inside, while you and Axel can watch our escape route."

"I'd rather go with you," she whined as she pawed at his chest.

Daniel cleared his throat before interrupting. "Sorry, Sis. You're getting better at the range, but you're no crack shot yet. If shit goes sideways we need to be on point, not to mention we don't want to end up trapped. You two need to keep the escape route open."

Elizabeth removed her hand from Roger's chest. "If they walk in and see you two up on the cat walks with guns, won't they get sketched out and bail?"

Daniel raised a hand to his chin and rubbed his stubble covered jaw. "Possibly, but that's why I'll be near a set of stairs. When the door opens, I'll descend with the briefcase."

"Unarmed?"

"That's a dumb question, Liz. I'll have my shotgun stashed below behind cover and my trusty 9mm on my person."

Roger turned to his right and gazed at the passing urban landscape. "I just hope we're getting there early enough. If they have the same idea, things could get complicated."

"You could just check the surveillance feeds before we head in, couldn't you?" Elizabeth asked.

His neck turned back and down toward her, her raven black hair in a ponytail obscuring his vision. "I could if someone," he directed his attention toward the front of the cabin directly at Daniel and raised his voice, "hadn't left my laptop uncharged all night after he used it."

Daniel raised his hands in front of him before his right snaked its way behind his head and scratched his neck. "My bad. A guy sometimes forgets after he's done."

"They usually don't when I explicitly tell them to connect it to the charger when they're done. I say this every time, and you never remember."

A snicker erupted from the driver's seat.

"Done with what?" Elizabeth's soft voice asked.

"I'd imagine you don't want to know, dear," Roger answered. "If his search history is any indication, I don't want to know either. You should clear that when you're done you know. I don't want to know your 'interests' in that department."

Daniel turned back around to face the front of the vehicle. "We're getting off topic. Now everyone understands the plan?"

The three other voices answered in unison. "Got it."

Daniel turned to his left. "How much further, Axe?"

The bald head turned to his right before redirecting his attention to the road. "It's Axel, sir, and we're a few minutes out."

"Yeah, but your name reminds me of a band, and 'Axe' just sounds cool."

Elizabeth's voice came from behind them. "No accounting for taste I guess." She rubbed her hands up Roger's body and came across two solid objects on the sides of his abdomen. "You are loaded aren't you, honey?"

"Fully. The last thing I want is to be caught without ammo. A guy has to be diligent when he runs around with your brother. You never know when you might need them."

A lone finger came up from the front passenger seat. "Oh, bite me. Things pop off a few times, and you never let a guy live it down."

I would not call that a few times. It's more like every other job. Contrary to your world view, not everything can be solved by a bullet or an explosion."

"Works well enough in my experience," Daniel fired back.

"And you wonder why we would ever be concerned with

the plans you come up with. It's a wonder." Roger lowered his voice and angled his head down, his forehead gently connecting with hers before speaking in a soft tone. "You do have your 44 don't you? I pray you don't need it, but better safe than sorry."

She slid further down and nuzzled her cheek into his chest. "Always do. You were the one who told me to always carry it around so I could get used to it. How did you word it? 'So it'd get so familiar it'd be like it's a part of me'."

"Close enough."

Daniel raised his voice from the front of the cabin. "What are you two talking about now? Sounded like something out of Tai Chi Children of Okinawa."

Elizabeth looked up at her boyfriend. "Is that where you got that from? I know he makes you watch a lot of his movies, but please tell me you didn't base my training regimen on some 80's movie."

Roger looked to his right. "I'm teaching you the way I was taught."

"How was that?"

"You already know."

Elizabeth rubbed her leg against his. "That pretty much answered the question," she replied as she looked out the same window that Roger was.

Axel's gruff voice asked, "I don't mean to interrupt, but we're nearly there. Where should we park?"

Daniel slapped the back of Axel's clean shaven white head. "Rookie, this is basic stuff. Look, you park around the back in front of the door. Make sure you back it in. That way we've got a quick getaway."

"Yes, sir. Sorry, sir." The man raised a muscle clad bare arm up and rubbed the back of his head.

Daniel's voice turned steely. "What's with the muscle shirt? Never heard a of a dress code, kid? It's a damned good thing you're not going to be up front. They'd take it as disrespect if they saw you and possibly start shooting. Always have a good suit on, rook." Daniel's voice softened a little. "Got me?"

"Yes, Mr. Morris. I'll do so in the future." He stepped on the brakes and turned the wheel in front of him.

"Take it easy on the kid. He'll learn," Roger said as he untangled himself from Elizabeth.

"Well, he'd better learn fast." Her voice emerged in the dark interior as she moved back to her own seat. "There's no easy interning in this life." She reached down the front of her pants and pulled out her .44. She opened the chamber and rotated it before flicking her wrist and closing it. "You'll be with me. Relax. We've got the easy job. Just make sure no one parks in front of this alleyway. Do you think you can manage that? I've got the other side."

"Yes, ma'am," came Axel's low voice as he gripped the car handle to his left.

"Speak up, boy. People have to know you've got a pair. You do, don't you?"

"Yes, ma'am," he answered in a louder voice as he lowered his head and got out of the car.

Roger elbowed her in the side with a smile. "I think you embarrassed him."

Daniel opened the front passenger's side door. "If that's the worst he gets, he should consider himself lucky."

Roger lunged forward and placed his left palm on Daniel's shoulder. "You did remember to bring your ear bud with you, didn't you?"

Daniel paused and rifled through his pockets before pulling out the small accessory. "Yeah, why?"

"Communication is going to get challenging if we get into a firefight, and I don't want to get stuck by my lonesome because I couldn't hear the call to retreat up in the rafters. We're just lucky Tanya sprung for the newest model with the built-in microphone, at my behest."

2

D aniel raised his left arm and looked at his watch. "Where are they? We've been here for three hours. They're an hour late."

Roger's voice was heard in his ear. "It could be a power play. Make us wait to show us who's boss."

A female voice interrupted them. "That or they forgot, and we're sitting on our collective asses for nothing. Hey, rookie! See anything over there?"

"You really need to mute your microphone when yelling, dear," Roger whined.

Elizabeth's brittle voice aired again. "Oops, sorry." Her breath returned to its normal throaty quality. "He sees one of their vehicles pulling into the opposite alley, so get ready in there."

"Roger," Daniel answered.

"What is it?" Roger asked.

"Are we seriously doing this bit?" Daniel asked. "It's nothing. Just acknowledging." He took a long exhale and paced back and forth on the grated platform.

"Roger wilco, good buddy," Roger's voice remarked with biting sarcasm.

Their back and forth was interrupted by the sound of a loud reverberating clanging from the door opposite to where they had come into the warehouse. The sound of numerous boots clattering followed. Five men clad in green sports jerseys entered their sight. Each one carried what looked like automatic rifles. The last one to enter appeared unarmed and carried only a large briefcase. Each of the four visibly armed men took cover throughout their side of the room. Two ducked behind nearby crates. The remaining rushed behind the support beams on the opposite side of the room, leaving the one unarmed man alone.

"He's probably their leader." Roger's voice came into Daniel's ear.

Daniel raised his hands as he called out. "Hey there. We were beginning to wonder if you were going to be a no show."

"Sorry about that," the man said with a heavy Brooklyn accent. "Traffic is a killer at this time of night. You know how it is in the Big Apple."

"Only too well," Daniel answered as he descended the stairs toward the ground level. "So, I can't help but notice the number of your colleagues packing heat."

"From where I'm standing, I see one of yours up there aiming at us. Guess that makes us even, Mr. Morris was it? You don't think your organization is the only one who knows how to set up cameras do you? Did you really think we'd come in unarmed without knowing you'd done the same? You and your family disappoint me. Underestimating us was quite a mistake."

Daniel reached the bottom floor and stood beside a large

shipping crate facing his business associates. His shotgun leaned against it just to his left.

"If you're thinking of making a reach for your shotgun, I'd advise against it. There may only be five of us in here, but there's ten more waiting outside ready to bust in at the first sign of trouble. That's a fight you can't win." His free pale hand reached up and made an adjustment to his bandana with a smug smile. "Even with all the stories of the Morris boy overcoming all odds in firefights, I wouldn't like your odds."

Roger's voice crackled to life in his ear. "Don't do it. I don't have a clear shot except on the leader.

"Seems you have me at a disadvantage, Mr.?" Daniel asked the man.

"Monroe. Joseph Monroe is my name. Now since we've established the status quo, how about we get down to business?"

"Fine by me," Daniel answered as he raised the brief-case, latch toward the other man. He had his left hand under the case and used the other to undo the latches and lift the lid revealing numerous disassembled parts of a rifle. "There's much more where this came from. This is just a taste. If you want them assembled that's extra, but we're all too happy to provide that service."

Monroe flicked his head to remove a lock of his brilliant scarlet hair from his vision as he approached. He stopped a few feet in front of Daniel, leaned forward, and inspected the parts. "Looks like some serious hardware you gentlemen are selling. This should help the cause back home."

"We don't do export. That's on you. How is the war going anyway?"

Monroe smirked as he straightened his posture and

raised his attention toward Daniel's chiseled jaw. "You know how it goes, give and take. Explosives just aren't getting the results we wanted, so we need some military grade hardware. Those bastard English are beginning to crack down hard on liberties, so we've got to arm ourselves. Am I right? Follow America's example with that first amendment."

"God bless America," Daniel said with a smile. "Home of the free market and the right to overthrow our own government if they become tyrannical."

"Afraid you boys may have missed the boat on that one, Mr. Morris, what with your surveillance state and all." Monroe knelt onto the ground and unlatched his own briefcase. "I am a bit disappointed however."

"In my country or the transaction at hand?"

"I'm afraid it's a bit of both. See, we were expecting a bit more hardware than one measly rifle."

The corners of Daniel's mouth curved down and his eyes narrowed at the man before him. "That will come next time. You know how business works. Get them hooked with a sample, and then both sides win once we know the landscape."

Elizabeth's voice sounded into his ear. "I've got a bad feeling about this, Danny. There's a group of men staring us down out here. It's getting tense."

Roger's quiet voice came next. "Keep it calm. He knows what he's doing. We're almost out of this."

Monroe stood up and kicked the briefcase at his feet to turn it around toward Daniel. An empty interior was revealed.

Daniel's eyes widened. "What is this? We don't do credit."

"You misunderstand me. First you bring guns into the

meet, which was expressly forbidden, and then you only bring one model for us. You thought this was acceptable?"

Daniel locked eyes with the man and stared him down. "Maybe you're new to this business, but trust isn't exactly in ample supply, especially on a first meeting like this. It's nothing personal."

"Regardless, I'm afraid I have my orders as well. A pity too. I quite enjoyed our little chat. Oh well, let's go boys!" He screamed as he ducked and made a mad dash to the side to a row of wooden crates.

As Monroe dove behind the cover, Roger's voice screamed in Daniel's ear. "Move now!" Acting on instinct, he put his back to the wall to his left and picked up his faithful shotgun. Immediately the deafening sound of gunshots echoed in the warehouse. The ricocheting of bullets off the shipping crate behind him caused a constant loud, reverberating, clanging noise.

His sister's screaming reached his ears, causing him to wince. "What the fuck happened in there? One minute everything's quiet, and the next we're under siege out here. Rookie, lay down suppressing fire right now. Aim for the car. We can't let them corner us. I've got another one down out here."

Daniel cocked the firearm in his possession before answering amid the cacophony of gunfire. "We had a misunderstanding."

"I'll say! Get out here right now. We can't hold much longer."

"Relax, Sis," Daniel poked his head around the corner for a second to see more men coming in on Monroe's side of the warehouse. He quickly ducked his head back behind cover and heard a whizzing noise in his left ear. "The majority of their reinforcements are coming in here from what I can see."

Roger's sarcastic voice met his ears. "Good for them, not so much for us. I've only winged a couple so far, and we're still heavily outnumbered. I count at least twelve in here. We can't make a run for it until we thin the numbers a little."

Daniel spoke as he pivoted around the corner, shotgun at the ready as the deafening symphony died down momentarily. "Then that's the plan." He aimed down the sights, the butt of the firearm pressing against his shoulder, and took aim at a man hiding behind a support beam to his right. He squeezed the trigger and saw the man's left ankle give out from under him along with a mist of red. Instincts took over, and without thought he got back to safety.

"That was brave down there. Stupid, but brave. You're lucky these jokers aren't disciplined. If they cycled their reloads, you'd be dead. Keep that to a minimum unless you want to go home in the trunk." Roger's scathing voice came over the ear buds.

"I had to do something. Can't leave all the fun to you up there."

"Look at the bright side. They don't have much of a shot down there at me since we got here first. The dumbasses thought numbers would be the be-all and end-all. Still, this is not going to end well if this keeps up. I've heard more than my fair share of whooshes up here. All I've got for cover is a thin beam and some metal handrails. Altitude is keeping me alive more than anything."

Elizabeth's voice interrupted them. "How about me and Axel circle around them? We've taken out three or four out here. If what he said was true, then their flank's exposed."

"You're sure about that, Liz?" Roger asked. "For that matter, how the hell did you take out that many?"

"They decided it'd be a good idea to drive down the road toward us, and the rookie got off a good shot at their driver. They were probably trying to corner us out here. They were easy pickings from our position. The point is, he's out of reinforcements. Right?"

Roger's voice answered. "I sure as hell hope he wasn't lying. Hear that Axel? You get to go point."

Axel's deep grunt and a subsequent, "Understood. We're going now," was his only response.

Elizabeth answered her brother. "You two just sit tight in there and keep your heads down. We'll be right there."

Daniel rolled his eyes and leaned his shotgun against his cover. He reached down the front of his jeans and pulled out his handgun. He extended his right arm and angled it around the corner before squeezing off a few shots. "Did I hit anything?"

Roger grunted before answering. "I think you hit the wall. That's not much help."

"Damn."

Elizabeth's breathy voice interrupted them. "We're ready, boys. Keep behind cover. We don't need either of you two trying to be heroes and getting clipped by friendly fire."

Daniel leaned to his right and placed his index finger into his right ear. "Hurry up then. The cops will be here soon."

He straightened up as he heard additional gunfire, followed by a marked decrease in decibels in the building.

Roger's excited voice cried out. "They're panicking down there and switching cover. You two get back to safety. Leave it to us now. There are only four left. Nice shooting, new guy. Bro, if you're going to take any more shots downstairs, now is prime time, buddy. You've got the better angle. You're flanking them. They're at your two o'clock."

"Got it," Daniel replied. He took a deep breath, pivoted around the corner, and saw the small group with their sides exposed. He took aim, exhaled, and squeezed the trigger multiple times resulting in numerous screams. Several forms lay writhing on the ground on top of a pool of blood expanding from underneath. "Nice work, everyone. Now you two get back to the van. We're getting out of here."

"Yes, sir," Axel and Elizabeth answered simultaneously.

"Now let's move," Daniel's commanding voice said. He picked up the rifle leaning at his side and walked toward the door they'd come in. He heard clanking coming from above him.

Along with the noises came a lone voice from the other side of the building. "Not so fast, you American trash," a strained wisp of a voice uttered just loud enough to be heard. A shot echoed throughout the building as Daniel's body lunged forward. An agonizing pain was coming from his left shoulder.

"One's still alive!" Roger yelled as three more shots rang out. "He's dead. You okay, buddy?" he asked as he descended the stairs. He turned around and saw Daniel on the ground. "Oh shit." He rushed over and knelt beside his friend. He lifted Daniel's uninjured arm over his shoulder and half carried him out the door. "Get the back doors open."

"Okay, why?" came Elizabeth's questioning voice. Any further retort was stifled as she saw them come into view from the open doorway.

"Axel, give him a hand while I get the doors."

He did as he was told. He wrapped his arms around the injured man's waist and lifted.

The trio approached the van and helped Daniel into the back seat. Roger turned to the young man beside him.

"You're driving again, kid. Take it slow. No need to draw attention."

"Yes, sir," he answered. He dashed around the front of the car and nearly jumped into the driver's seat.

Roger looked to his left to see his girlfriend staring at him. "Get in the other side. We have to keep him from moving too much."

"Okay," was all she said before she obeyed Roger and jogged around the vehicle to get beside her brother.

Roger followed suit and entered on the near side before closing his door and looking to his left at the two siblings beside him. Daniel clutched his shoulder and grit his teeth. He kept his eyes closed and had his head leaned back against the seat.

Elizabeth closed the door beside her and barked an order toward Axel in the front. "Get moving already. Get us home now." She directed her attention to her right toward her injured brother before looking at Roger on the other side. "Know any good doctors?" she asked.

Roger grunted as he attempted to rip a piece of his shirt off. "At this time of night? Our best bet would be to get him home and let someone dress this. We can get him to a doc in the morning. It should be fine. We need to do some basic first aid right now." A loud ripping sound made itself known and he handed the cloth over to the woman. "Press this hard against the wound." He raised his other hand over Daniel's mouth. "Sorry, buddy. You're not going to like this."

Elizabeth plucked the cloth out of his hand and did as she was instructed. It elicited a muffled cry of pain which escaped Roger's hand along with Daniel's body arching against the seat.

Roger glanced toward the front of the van to see Axel

looking into the rearview mirror. He turned his attention back to the road when he noticed he was seen.

"Don't worry, kid. He'll be fine so long as you get us home. Hell of a night's work, huh?"

Axel muttered just loud enough to be heard. "You can say that again." He looked to his left and his eyebrows raised. "Sir?"

"What is it, rookie?"

"I think we're being followed."

"By whom?

"No idea, but they're not being too subtle about it. They're right behind us," Axel said. A loud series of honks along with flashing lights came from behind them.

Roger twisted his neck and rotated his body to get a look out the back window. "How much you want to bet that's the McCrane clan? Bastards never know when to give up do they?"

"Orders, sir?"

Roger shifted his attention between the white van behind them and the two people beside him. "What do you think, Liz?"

"You're asking me? We can't lead them back to the safe-house, but we can't just let Danny bleed out either."

Roger bit his bottom lip as he continued scanning back and forth. "Honey, do we have a first aid kit and a few bottles of water in here?"

Elizabeth's eyes lit up. "They should be in the back."

Roger snapped his fingers. "Great, I've got a plan."

"Care to share with the rest of the class?"

"We'll deal with both problems back to back. Hey kid, we near anyplace that's abandoned?"

Axel answered in a snap. "There's a national forest north of here about half an hour away."

"Perfect. Go there. If they want to force the issue, we'll oblige them. He should be able to last that long given the location of the wound. Doesn't look like any arteries were hit. Bleeding's not too bad."

"May I ask what the plan is, sir?"

"You ever heard of a bait and switch?"

"Yes?"

Elizabeth placed a hand on her brother's shoulder. "Oh boy," she uttered as the car made its way north.

3

"I've managed to put some distance between us, sir. We should have enough time to get set up before they find us," Axel said as he made a final turn onto a dirt road surrounded by forest in every direction.

A buzzing sound came from Elizabeth. She removed one hand from her brother's shoulder and retrieved her phone from her pants pocket. She tapped the screen and exhaled.

"Anything important?" Roger asked.

"Just a message from Tanya." She shoved her phone back into her pocket. "She'll live if I don't read it asap; whereas others may need my attention in a more urgent manner." She placed her hand on her brother's covered wound and pressed down, resulting in a cry from beside her.

"So, before we stop out here in the middle of scenic nowhere, do you want to further elaborate?" Elizabeth asked.

"When we stop, we set up an ambush," Roger answered as he flicked open his .357 magnum.

"That's it? That's the big plan?"

He refilled the empty chambers as he spoke. "Maybe you'd rather have gotten into a shootout on the highway, but I wanted to avoid being on the six o'clock news. Plus, this way we have plenty of cover." He flicked the cylinder back.

"Okay, but what about Danny? This isn't exactly a sterile environment for a gaping wound."

"Look, we couldn't lead them straight back to headquarters. I'm doing my best. We'll put a blanket down on the ground or something. Any more concerns?" Roger asked.

Daniel groaned before voicing his thoughts. "It's a good plan. Do what he says, Sis, and that goes for you too, Axe. He's the second in command, so do what he says until I'm back in action."

"I guess that's settled," Roger added. He leaned forward and pointed over Axel's shoulder toward a small grass clearing surrounded by forest. "Park right up there. It'll give us plenty of cover and hiding spots." He turned back toward the rest of the party. "When we stop, make sure to hurry. We can't dawdle."

"Far be it from me," Daniel spoke with a strained voice.

"Now, Liz," Roger started as he turned to her, "you're going to-"

"If you think I'm going to stay behind, you've got another think coming. I want payback."

"If you'd let me finish - you're with me. Axel, you're staying with him. Also turn the radio up. I want any potential nearby campers to think we're jackasses rather than killers. Worst case scenario is they'll think we're setting off fireworks or something."

Daniel smiled as the car slowed down. "At least we've got one competent shooter going."

Elizabeth smacked her brother's forearm. "Screw you."

"Knock it off you two," Roger's louder voice said. "Let's

get going." The car screeched to a halt along the end of the unfinished road.

Roger and Elizabeth exited the vehicle while Axel turned the radio on and helped Daniel out of the car. The two men made their way into the forest in search of cover, while Roger and Elizabeth fell into step behind them.

Elizabeth reached over and leaned on Roger as they exited the relative light of the clearing into the unforgiving shadows of the forest.

Roger looked down as he felt her hands shaking. He saw her stoic face gazing into her brother's back. Her hand grasped his and squeezed. He placed his free hand over her shaking one and kept it steady. He leaned down and whispered in her ear. "He'll be fine. Just focus, and everything will be alright."

She shuddered before moving away. She looked away from him and stuttered. "I ... I don't need you to tell me that. I know. I'm not worried." She gave a shy glance back at him, her face alight with a blush "Thanks."

"Now as for your brother -" He raised his voice to gain the two men's attention in front of them. "He needs to hurry up already. Any tree big enough for you two is good."

Immediately following his command, the two men stumbled behind a large dead tree. A small thud was heard, followed by a low grunting noise.

Roger looked to his side. "Guess that's our cue. Now I want you to get to cover about twenty feet away to my side."

"Why?"

"Basic tactics. Two shooters side by side are a lot easier to hit, and the pressure they can output is greatly reduced since they can be suppressed easier. If you're further away, you can take another angle and set up a crossfire." He guided them over to a large oak tree. He grabbed her forearm and leaned in close, pinning her to the wood. "You stay behind this," he knocked on the wood over her shoulder, "and only start firing on my signal. You got me?"

"What's the signal?" Elizabeth asked as she pulled out her revolver.

"It's when I fire. Simple, right?"

He turned to move away when her free hand shot out and grabbed his wrist. She sniffled and looked up at him. "I don't know if I can kill someone, Rog. I mean, I've done a lot of heinous things, but straight up murder?"

He exhaled and turned around to fully face her. He placed both his hands on the sides of her face and rubbed her cheek with the back of his fingertips. "It's a hard thing, but think of it this way. If we don't take them out, they'll kill everyone here. That includes me, you, your brother, and even the new guy. You need to be able to protect your own, or your old man will never trust you to lead. Got it?"

"I got it," she replied with a huff. "You didn't have to bring up Daddy, but I got it."

"Just looking out for your future, dear," he answered with a smile. The sound of a distant roar interrupted him. "Now if you'll excuse me, I hear the sound of an engine in the distance, and I need to get to cover myself. Keep an eye on the clearing with the van. They'll stop out there I bet," he ordered before turning and taking off in a jog. The sound of snapping twigs, crickets, and the local wildlife were all that could be heard aside from the man-made racket approaching.

Within minutes a light could be seen approaching their now abandoned car. Roger could make out the same vehicle that had been following them coming to a stop behind their van. He reached into his holsters and readied his revolvers. He pivoted out of his cover and stood motionless in the dark, holding his weapons up in aim. He waited until the sound of loud thunks indicated that they had exited the relative safety of their car. Low voices could be heard but not made out. Soon the sound of crunching grass became audible, and he saw beams of light darting to and fro in the darkness.

Flashlights huh? he thought. *Good, it's a lot easier to shoot you when you mark yourself.* He pulled back the hammers and the revolvers clicked in readiness.

A loud unfamiliar voice broke the silence. "Hello? Anyone there?"

"Dumb bastards," Roger muttered to himself.

The beams of light approached closer until the figure holding them came into view. Words from Daniel came to the forefront of his mind in that moment. *Do not hesitate. Those who do, die first. Remember that lesson. It won't just be your life on the line in the future.* The words echoed inside his head. Without delay, he squeezed the triggers causing a deafening crack. His arms kicked back from the recoil. He could make out his target falling into the bushes, followed by a piercing scream and groaning.

A second figure ran up to the first and knelt beside him. The sound of another revolver firing caught his attention. A muzzle flash to his side was followed by a higher, more shrill voice crying out in pain.

Roger waited for any more interlopers to approach. After a few moments he exhaled. He moved out from his cover and towards Elizabeth, He approached from behind her and called out, "It's me. Don't fire."

"Is it over?" she asked.

"Not sure. I'm going to go check. I need you to back me up, okay? Just follow me. If anyone tries anything, you're going to have to..." he trailed off.

"I get it. Lead the way."

"Keep your head on a swivel out here. If there were more, they could have ducked into the surrounding woods, unlike their simple friends up there," he said as he moved forward toward their victims. As they came closer, the grunts and groans became louder along with the sound of rustling grass. The pair got within a stone's throw when Roger noticed they had dropped their flash lights, and they had rolled toward him. He bent down to pick one up and pointed at the other to signal Elizabeth. She picked up the other without question and moved in close to him.

He leaned in close to her ear and gave her instructions. "Shine it in their eyes. They don't need to know for certain who this is."

She nodded and followed suit. The large man had one hand grasped on his bloody wounds and another shielding his eyes. The larger of the two figures spoke first. "What the fuck is your problem? Are you trying to kill us, you psychopaths?"

Roger stomped right up to the man and moved his flash-light beam down the figure's torso. "You armed?"

"What? Yes, of course we are. We were going to-" the balding man coughed. Blood came from his mouth and made its way down to stain his white shirt. "We were here because of you."

Roger stared down at the smaller figure. "You? What's your story? Are you two alone tonight?"

The bigger one coughed again before reaching out and grabbing the other by the shoulder. "Don't tell him. He's gone crazy."

A quiet demure voice came from the smaller figure. "Yes. Our boy is in the back. We just wanted a family camping trip after work."

"Oh, we've shit the bed," Roger cursed to himself. "You mean to tell me you're not with the McCranes?"

"Honey?" the woman wheezed. "I'm scared." She grasped for the larger man's hand as her eyes opened wide and her gasping turned ragged. Her free hand banged into the dirt as her body convulsed.

"No!" the man yelled. He gritted his teeth, rolled onto his stomach, and inched his way over to the woman. He clutched her hand and whispered to her. The man reached with his other hand up to her face and brushed her brilliant cherry hair out of her face. Eventually her body stopped moving.

The man lay there with his head facing down for many silent moments before his voice turned low and even. "To answer your question, boy, no I'm not with the McCranes." He looked up at Roger, his attention unwavering as he stared him down. "I had no problems with you personally, but you just killed my girl. You'd better kill me now, because so help me, if I survive I'm gonna have you slaughtered for this - you and your little piss ant family you left," the man growled.

Elizabeth stood on her tiptoes and looked over Roger's shoulder and down at the man before looking back to him. "This could have gone better, honey," she said before pecking him on the cheek.

"You're not joking," Roger agreed under his breath. He raised a lone revolver up and leveled it at the man's forehead. He took a step backward and leaned away from the man in front of him. He glanced over at the couple's vehicle and back at him. "So, your boy's in there huh? Don't worry. He'll be fine - unlike you." His hand wobbled as his breath became unsteady. "Sorry about this. I sincerely am." He squeezed his index finger.

4

Roger announced their presence as they approached their two comrades further into the woods. "It's us. Don't shoot," Roger called out. "You two near here? We turned the radio off in case you were wondering."

A rustling sound caught his attention directly in front of him. A voice came from behind a large tree ahead. "Yeah, we're over here."

Elizabeth, Roger, and a diminutive figure holding his hand continued past the tree and turned around to see Daniel leaning against the tree with his uninjured hand applying direct pressure to his wound. Axel had his handgun out and was periodically looking around the tree beside him.

Roger cleared his throat. "At ease, but we have a problem. Like it's a really big one, and it's pretty much all my fault."

Elizabeth came out from behind Roger and moved in front of him toward her brother. She squatted down to get to his eye level. "He's talking about our uninvited guests from earlier. He's also wrong by the way," she said as she turned to glare at Roger before turning back. "He wasn't the only one who fired."

Daniel raised his free hand up to his eyes and massaged his temples. "I heard the racket. What exactly happened now? Who the hell is this anyway?" He pointed toward the small figure holding Roger's hand. He was hiding behind his leg and was facing toward the ground. He shuffled his feet and stayed quiet.

Roger side stepped, revealing a small boy with red hair. He looked up at the group for a moment before resuming his examination of the soil in front of him. "This is our guests' young son I believe."

Daniel stared at the boy, then looked up at Roger. "Shit, we're in it now, huh? Is his father...?" he trailed off, asking the obvious.

"He's indisposed over there, yes. Probably not going to be joining us tonight," Roger said.

Elizabeth spoke up after sweeping a strand of hair behind her ear. "He declared a blood feud before he lost consciousness."

Daniel slammed a fist down onto the ground. "So, to sum it up, we've started a war with the Irish when our orders were precisely not to. We also took out two people, and we've no clue who they were. Is that about the size of it?"

"Precisely, and if Daddy finds out how it happened..." she trailed off. She stood up and walked back over to Roger. "Then he's going to want someone to take responsibility, if you know what I mean.

Roger shifted his weight from one leg to the other. "If you're trying to be subtle, you're not doing a good job, dear. Just say it flat out. He'll kill me for this, won't he?"

"I won't let him," she answered with a tone of finality as she stood shoulder to shoulder with him.

"She's right," Daniel agreed. "We're not going to let that happen. After all, friends are in short supply in this lifestyle. We're not about to give you up without a fight."

"That's all well and good, but I have a question."

"What's that?"

Roger gestured behind him. "What exactly are we going to do with the kid anyway?"

"We'll figure that out later. We have more pressing concerns at the moment." He paused, then grunted. "For now, take that kid back and lock him in the back seat after you make damned sure it's clear of all the weapons. Stash them under the seats." He turned to the kid's face poking out behind Roger's leg. "Can't have you getting into trouble, now can we kid?"

The boy looked down at the dirt and shuffled his feet. "I won't be any trouble, mister. Honest."

Daniel made an affirmative 'Mm' sound as he switched around his position against the tree. He stretched out his feet in front of him. "You better not, kid. You know what happened earlier?"

"I think I heard guns. It was hard to tell with the music."

"That's right. Now don't give us a reason to use them again." His voice grew deeper and louder. "Do you understand me?"

"Yes."

He turned his attention back toward Roger and, with a wave of his hand, gave his orders. "Smart kid. Now take care of our guest, and let's get started cleaning this mess up, shall we?"

Roger motioned Elizabeth over and whispered when she got close. "Take him, would you? I need to get your brother ready for an impromptu field surgery. If you don't mind, grab the first aid kit from the back while you're at it. Okay?"

Elizabeth's thin red lips pressed together as she nodded. She reached out toward the boy's hand and grasped it before tugging on it. "Come on. You're with me, little guy. That goes for you too, Axel. You're with me on gun duty."

"I understand." He stood up from beside Daniel and moved beside Elizabeth.

The boy did little to argue and went along with his new handlers back toward the vehicles in the clearing.

"I hate to be the one to say this," Roger started, "but you know the kid's seen our faces now. He'll put it together that we killed his dad too if he has a lick of common sense - if he hasn't already."

Daniel sighed. "What exactly are you implying here?"

"I'm just saying he's a risk to all of us now."

"Do we even know who those people are? Are they connected to the McCranes?"

Roger shrugged. "They said no. Then again, who knows if they were lying?"

"Assuming it was a McCrane lackey, why would they have their kid with them following us?"

Roger looked over Daniel's shoulder into the stifling darkness. "No clue. Could have been a spur of the moment thing?"

"Yeah? Well until you come up with a solution, how about we focus on what we can fix? Like, oh say, my fracking shoulder?"

Rustling grass caught Roger's attention. He scanned to the right toward where the sound came from. The silhouettes of Elizabeth and Axel emerged from the darkness. She held a small red box in her right hand. She crossed her arms and bit her bottom lip. "Kids locked away safe along with the guns up front. Now how do we begin picking up the pieces?"

Roger walked over and took the box from her before turning around toward his patient. "We start by stabilizing our dear leader. I'm going to need a volunteer to help me with this. Any takers?" He looked over to Axel to see him still scanning the perimeter.

Elizabeth raised her hands in exasperation as she shrugged. "Fine, I'll do it. What do you need from me?"

"You're going to help me hold him down. He's not going to like this one bit. I might ask you to pass me something from time to time as well."

Elizabeth's mouth contorted into an impish grin. "Sort of like a nurse, huh? I have some experience with that."

Roger raised his hands and covered his increasingly reddened face. "Something like that."

Daniel cut in. "I'm right here you know."

Roger turned to Daniel and looked down toward him. "Alright, well let's get started. I'm going to need you to lie flat on the ground, so let's go."

Daniel growled as he slid down the tree trunk and gasped when his shoulder made contact with the soil underneath. "This good enough?" he asked in a strained voice.

"Technically yes, but you didn't let me finish. We're going to be moving you someplace where it's a bit lighter. Can't be treating blind, can I?"

Daniel rolled his eyes, turned toward Axel, and barked at him. "Get over here, Axe. I need you to help me up and to wherever this doctor and nurse need me."

The young man jumped up from his kneeling position and rushed straight over to lift him up. He slid Daniel's uninjured arm over his shoulders and looked at the other two. "Where we going?"

Roger pointed back toward the clearing with the vehicles. "We could use the headlights - so just put him down about ten feet in front of them, flat on the ground for now." He turned to Elizabeth. "You didn't put the kid in the front, did you?"

She placed her hands on her hips and pouted as the other two men made their way to the appointed spot. "No, I'm not an idiot."

He lifted his hands palm out in a placating motion. "Easy. I just wanted to make sure we weren't going to be doing this in front of the kid." His voice lowered to a ghost of a whisper. "He's seen enough tonight as it is." He raised his voice enough for her to hear. "Well, let's go nurse. Our patient awaits."

"I sure hope you take this more seriously than you're acting right now," she said as she crossed her arms in front of her and stomped off.

He reached up and scratched his nose as he made his way toward the rest of the group. "It's only my best friend, honey." He looked back at her staring at him. He exhaled and looked straight in her eyes. "Yeah, I'll do everything I can."

He emerged from the tree line to see Daniel lying on a lone blanket in front of the van with the first aid kit beside him. Axel could be seen on the other end of the vehicle with his weapon at the ready. Elizabeth had moved around him and was leaning against the engine block. Her index finger was tapping her other wrist as she waited.

He approached the group and announced the plan. "Alright, let's get started then."

Elizabeth kicked off her perch and came closer to the two men. "Where do you want me for this?"

"You're going to be right behind me, along with the kit. Your main job is to make sure I don't get kicked."

Elizabeth leaned forward with widened eyes. "What?"

"We have no anesthetics. He's going to be kicking as I work over here. You're sitting on his legs. You'll also be passing me what I need."

Daniel spoke up from underneath them. "Where are you going to be then?"

Roger answered by taking a step over his body. He lowered his body until he was sitting directly on Daniel's chest. "That answer your question?" He looked down at his friend's growling grimace. "Can't have you rolling around."

"What's to stop me from punching you?"

"You mean besides the fact your one arm will be in insurmountable pain? Well, nothing for the other I guess." He raised his hand in front of his mouth before calling out. "Hey, kid, come over here." His hands made a beckoning motion as he looked at Axel by the rear of the car. "Hurry up."

Axel jogged over and holstered his weapon. "Yes? What do I need to do?"

Roger pointed to Daniel's uninjured right arm. "Hold his arm down. If he moves, I'm liable to do more damage than help."

Roger turned to Elizabeth. "Also, dear, I need you to take his socks off."

"What the hell for?" she asked with a scowl.

"Well, unless you want your socks in his mouth, which I didn't imagine you did."

"Alright already." She cut him off as she stretched to look back and untied Daniel's shoes.

Roger returned his attention to the man lying on the ground. "Okay, before we start we're going to need to see the back of your shoulder."

"Why?" Daniel asked.

"To see how much proverbial shit we're in. If there's an exit wound, that's much easier to triage. If there's none, then we're in more trouble." He looked at Axel as he climbed off Daniel's immobile body. "Lift him gently onto his side and hold him there."

Axel nodded and seized both of Daniel's arms. He moved him to the side.

Daniel complained. "I can't believe this. A grown man is being treated like a damned baby."

Roger reached down and grasped the bottom of Daniel's shirt before lifting it over his friend's head. He leaned over to look at the back of Daniel's shoulder. "You're being treated like a patient because you got shot. I guess if you have the strength to complain, you should be fine. Your pallor isn't that pale considering." He paused for a few seconds as he inspected even closer. "Here we are. You do in fact have an exit wound of sorts. It looks more like it clipped the very top of your shoulder. We'll bandage that first. Then we'll patch up the front most part after."

"Joy to the world," Daniel scoffed.

Elizabeth tapped Roger on the shoulder. "Here," she said as she handed him her brother's socks. "No clue why you don't just use duct tape or something, but hey, if it works it works."

"That's a good point," Daniel remarked. "Use duct tape. I don't want socks in my mouth."

Roger shook his head. "This wasn't a kidnapping mission. We have no tape in the van. We have to make due with what we have here. It's either that, or someone else's clothes. Shirts, socks, and everything else would in theory work. I just didn't think you wanted someone else's sweat in your mouth."

"This is disgusting - but fine, I'll do it," Daniel grumbled.

"Now that that's settled, let's get started." He stuffed Daniel's socks into the mouth below him. "Now then, nurse, if you'd be so kind as to pass me the antiseptic."

"Right away, doctor," Elizabeth answered as she handed him a small brown cylinder with writing on it that sloshed as it was exchanged.

Roger looked at Axel. "Don't be shy, kid. Hold his arm good and tight. He's not going to like this. If I get punched, I'm blaming you. We're starting with the exit site, and then when that's wrapped up we'll lay him down on his back. Everyone got it?"

Axel grasped both of Daniel's arms and held them above his head. His knuckles turned white, causing a grunt of pain to escape the impromptu gag in Daniel's mouth. "Yes, Mr. Johnson."

"Call me Roger."

5

Muffled screaming erupted from Daniel's sock stuffed mouth as Roger removed his hands from the top of Daniel's shoulder. He leaned in and inspected the recently laid bandages.

"That's it for the top. Now for the stuff that's really going to hurt," he said as he pushed Daniel down onto his back. "Oh quiet, you big baby. It was just a routine cleaning. This next part is the one you should be worrying about. We have to do the same thing again but try and see if there's any shrapnel in the front."

Elizabeth tapped his shoulder as she spoke. "If there is? You're not qualified to remove that. He'd bleed out before you're done."

"Thanks for the vote of confidence, sweetie. In that case I'll clean it the best I can, and we'd have to get him out of here to a real doctor. We can't just leave it as it is though. It's likely to get infected." His voice fell to a ghost of a whisper. "I knew I should have looked this medical stuff up in my off time. I just had to play that mmo instead. It's just stupid and sloppy."

"What was that?" she asked.

"Nothing to concern your pretty face about," he answered as he climbed directly onto Daniel's chest. He looked down into his friend's confused eyes. "Don't worry, buddy. I just can't have you squirming all around is all." He looked over his shoulder. "That's your sign, dear. Stay on his legs. This is where he's likely to express displeasure, and I don't want a concussion."

Daniel's eyes narrowed and his teeth clenched around the wool inside his mouth as he bit down.

Elizabeth stood up before lowering herself onto her brother's lower legs. She placed her full weight down and let him know she was ready. "You know he'll have to go to a doctor anyway, don't you? This ain't exactly a sterile operating environment and all, doctor." She enunciated the doctor title in an exaggerated manner.

"No kidding. Still, it's better than bleeding out in the van before we can clean the rest of this shit up."

"Clean what else up?" Elizabeth pestered.

"Oh, you know, maybe the two bodies over yonder? That's probably important." Roger's voice dripped with sarcasm.

Elizabeth slapped Roger in the back loud enough to draw a wince from Axel across from him. "Wise ass," she admonished with a pout.

Roger rolled his eyes and nodded at the younger man. "Let's keep going." He leaned down and inspected the wound. "I can't see any debris lodged in there. That means it'll be the same as before. This time try not to kick up such a fuss, eh?" He held his right palm up over his right shoulder. "I need the antiseptic again."

She handed it to him with a small frown on her face. "Here," she snapped.

He accepted the container and undid the twist top. He angled the bottle over the wound and soon a quiet hissing noise made itself known alongside muffled groans that escalated into screams. Within twenty seconds Daniel's body went limp as a moan escaped his gag.

"Roger? Is he okay?" Elizabeth asked as she leaned forward. Her chest pushed against his back as she did.

Roger pressed two fingers against Daniel's neck. "He's fine. He just passed out temporarily from the pain."

"You're sure?"

"He hasn't bled nearly enough to be dead. He also still has a relatively strong pulse. He's just inadvertently being a drama king. Pay him no mind," Roger answered. He handed the brown cylinder over his shoulder. "I need the gauze," he said as his fingertips curled up in anticipation.

Elizabeth placed the antiseptic back into the small box, plucked out the bandage, and placed it in his hand. "That means we don't have to stay here, right?" she asked into his ear.

Roger's back straightened. "Oh, you want to just leave me high and dry when he wakes up? No dice, missy. Besides, it'll only be a few more minutes and we can start this cleanup. Just hold your horses. I need to finish dressing this, and I'm done."

"Fine," Elizabeth answered as she placed her weight back onto the legs underneath her. She crossed her arms and pressed her lips together waiting for her next command.

"There, I'm done now. See, that didn't take too long, huh? Now onto the real fun stuff. We have to clean this mess up. Axel, are you paying attention?"

The young man looked up. "Yes?"

"You're not to breathe a word of tonight to anyone else

ever. You understand me? It won't just be my ass on the chopping block if you do. It'll be both you and me, since the two golden children here won't be executed by daddy dearest. Are we clear?"

Axel gulped audibly with a sheen of sweat covering his face. "Not a word to anyone. I got it."

"Now if you two will excuse me, I have to go find something to dig with."

"Dig, sir?" Axel asked.

"Yeah. We've got two dead bodies only twenty feet away in a clearing just off a main road. You do understand the concept of cleaning up after yourself, right? If you don't, you're learning now." Without further words, Roger stood up and walked over to the van.

Elizabeth looked ahead of her directly at Axel. Her eyes narrowed and she leaned forward, causing her shoulder length hair to fall forward obscuring her eyes. She spoke in a tense, sharp tone. "Just to further elaborate, if you do say a word to Daddy, then you'll be the only one in the fire. That and you'll make an enemy of everyone here. You do not want that. If he asks you what happened tonight, then I hope you're creative - because I'll kill you if you blame Roger for these bodies. He's mine, and I will not allow you to get him killed. Got it?"

"Yes, ma'am."

"Good boy," Elizabeth said as her demeanor did a one eighty. Her mouth morphed into a smile, and she tucked her hair back behind her ears. She stood up and attempted to catch up with Roger, leaving Axel by himself with Daniel.

He looked down at his unconscious boss and whispered to himself. "First job and everything's gone sideways already. Fuck my life."

"She's right though," Daniel interrupted Axel's monologue. He looked down at his boss with his back straight. "You keep your mouth shut to the boss, or you'll answer to me and my sister." Daniel raised a fist to his mouth and cleared his throat. "Now help me up. We can't let them dig all by themselves, unless you want to hear all about it later."

Axel nodded and helped lift him up by his free arm.

Daniel turned to his right to face the man. "Get used to it, Axe. Jobs sometimes go shit side up. The times it doesn't are the ones you forget. You have to be ready for anything. Understand that and you'll be a head up on the typical grunt. Just stay calm, and things work out. Remember that, and you'll go a long way."

"I'll endeavor to remember that," he answered as they trudged toward the only man-made source of light nearby.

6

Roger shoved the end of the shovel into the ground amidst the loud music playing. He stomped down on top of it, causing it to go deeper into the earth. He placed his hands over his ears, turned to his left, and shouted toward the driver's seat of the vehicle they had come in. "Shut that up already!"

The sound of heavy metal music abated for a moment and then Daniel's voice came from the seat. "It makes it go faster though. Besides, I think you three are ahead of schedule. I think it's speeding you up. You're welcome."

Axel stood up and straightened his posture by placing a hand on his lower back and arching his back with a grunt. He looked over at the car for a moment, shaking his head without any words, then resumed digging on his knees with the plastic bucket in his hands.

Elizabeth spoke up across from him. "Don't tell me you're getting tired already."

Axel looked up from his kneeling position. He shoved a side of the bucket into the dirt and pulled it out with a groan. "No. I'm just not used to digging without a shovel."

"Yeah? Well get used to it, grunt. We only have one, and that's only because of the people we're burying." She turned toward her right and looked in front of her at Roger. "Speaking of which, why did they have a shovel on a camping trip?"

Without waiting for an answer, the same heavy metal music blared again. Roger slapped his forehead. He looked to his left and raised his hand to his throat. He motioned for him to cut it out.

Once the music had abated again, he answered her. "You never camped? You're supposed to dig your own latrine and fire pit. It teaches a kid responsibility I think."

Elizabeth shoved the knife she was holding into the dirt before talking back. "Latrine?"

"Just don't ask. You don't want the answer."

She flicked her knife over her shoulder flinging dirt behind her. "I'm more interested in how good of a father you'll be. Teaching responsibility is a big lesson that a lot of dads fail."

Daniel called out from the side. "Amen to that."

"Getting back to the activity at hand," he started and took a deep breath. "I'm almost done with my half of the hole." He looked at the other half. "Looks like you two are about half done. Look on the bright side, at least then you'll get the shovel."

Daniel waited no longer for their conversation and proceeded to deafen the rest of the group by playing music from the radio again.

———

Twenty minutes later...

Roger handed his shovel over to Axel and, without hesitation, made his way over to Daniel.

His eyes were closed, and his head leaned back. His head was bobbing back and forth with a smile spread across his face.

Roger reached inside the window past the man and twisted the knob, causing silence to sweep over the clearing.

Daniel's eyes snapped open. "Hey! What's the big idea?"

Roger withdrew his arm and looked down at the man. "I for one am sick and tired of listening to that noise. Not to mention, we're trying not to draw attention here."

"You think tons of people come here every night or something?"

"It doesn't matter if they do. Unless we want to be pinched by the police, we need to act like, yes, worst case scenarios are the default. That's how you stay out of prison. Besides, you have earphones." He reached down to the man's ears and pulled out two buds. "Use them."

Axel's voice interrupted their discussion as he talked with his digging partner. "I'm just wondering. How did you get the kid to stay in the car?"

Elizabeth giggled for a moment and looked up with a straight face. She raised a hand and rubbed her cheek, causing a large dirt smear to stick to her fair skinned face. "I just told him what would happen if he came out and interrupted us."

"I suppose you told him what those consequences would be then?"

"Yep." She stabbed the dirt in front of her. "That we'd have to kill him and then bury him out here."

Axel whistled. "Damn."

"You have to show kids who's boss."

Roger craned his neck to look back at the two working

and voiced his thoughts. "I think you may have scared the kid witless with that, Liz. You probably didn't need to put the fear of God in him."

"I wasn't trying to scare him. I was simply telling him what would happen."

"Sometimes you worry me," Roger said. He turned back to Daniel and pointed through the window. "Now no more music. Agreed? We probably already pissed off any nearby campers with the ruckus before. That was to cover the sound of gunshots, not to amuse you."

Daniel looked out the passenger window before mumbling something incoherent.

"Fine," Roger agreed as he turned around and went back to the two digging. He sat down a few feet away from Elizabeth in the dirt. He extended his feet in front of him and leaned back on his palms. "That is a good question though. What are we going to do with the kid? Anyone have any ideas?"

Elizabeth raised her left hand. "Yeah, just ice the kid. We take him back and this night only gets exponentially worse."

Axel spoke up next. "I'd recommend returning the kid personally. It may just be the one act that saves us from all-out war if they were with the Irish."

Roger turned toward the van. "What about you over there?"

Daniel turned to look out the window toward them. He lifted his left arm and placed it out the window. His fingertips tapped the side of the van. "Damned if we do, and damned if we don't. If we take him to Dad, then we'll never hear the end of it. If we return him, the same thing. And if we kill him, he may show us what it's like to kill without permission. In my opinion, we're screwed no matter what.

Roger angled his neck back to look at the star-studded

sky above. "Fantastic. So does anybody think it's a good idea to simply call the old man and ask?"

Elizabeth scoffed, drawing Roger's attention back to earth. "Look, handsome. That sounds great on paper, but it never works in practice."

"Really? Why not?"

"I'd guess the main reason is because Daddy hates deviations from the plan. If he finds out we royally botched the deal, killed two randoms, and abducted their kid, what exactly do you think would happen when we come crying to Daddy for help? It wouldn't be pretty. I guarantee it. Someone will get a dirt nap would be my guess."

Axel flicked the shovel behind him and sank the tool into the small hole before using the back of his muscular forearm to wipe the sweat from his brow. "I vote against that plan since I'd be the one killed." He looked at the other three beside him. "What? I'm just saying, I'm not the favorite of this group. I'm just hired muscle, right?"

Daniel slammed his open palm against the outside of the driver's side door which caused a loud clang. "Don't worry, Axe. I've never lost a man before, and I don't intend to start now." He looked to Roger. "We're not calling him, buddy. There are too many factors working against us for that to work."

Roger rose to his feet, walked to the yellow bucket beside Axel, and picked it up. He moved to the side of the hole so he could see everyone and extricated dirt alongside them as best he could. "Fine, but you never said what your plan was."

"That's because I don't have one, and I'm thinking." He snapped his fingers as his chestnut eyes focused in front of him. "I have a cunning plan as to how this will all work out."

"That's comforting to hear. Now what is it already?" Roger asked as he shoved the makeshift digging tool into the ground.

Daniel turned to his three compatriots with a toothy grin. "We'll use what we have to our advantage."

"Oh God, just say it already!" Elizabeth snapped. "I'm tired of the wait."

"You're just plain tired from digging. Deal with it."

"Brother, I have a knife in my hands. What is the damned plan?"

The brother and sister devolved into a petty argument as Axel placed his hand on one side of his mouth and spoke to Roger in a quiet voice. "Are they okay?"

"Yeah, they do this all the time. Get used to it. You just have to break it up before it goes too far," he answered. "Watch this."

"You've tried that line since you were thirteen, Sis. Do you really want to try this again? I'm up for the challenge anytime."

Roger inhaled deeply and coughed before speaking in a cool commanding tone. "Cool it. We're in deep shit already." He turned to the van. "Besides, you're injured. She has the advantage. So, hurry it up already."

Elizabeth smirked and laughed.

"That's debatable, but fine. My plan is to not tell father about this."

"Okay, and what do we do about the kid then?" Elizabeth asked. "We can't just pretend he doesn't exist. Either he goes away permanently, or what? We haven't established a better alternative yet have we?"

Roger spoke up. "We can't just kill him."

"Why not?"

"He's a kid, Liz," Roger spoke in a tense tone. He bit down and locked his jaw as he looked toward the other vehicle housing said child. "He's done nothing to deserve that except being born into a shitty family and being in the wrong place. It'd be like if you two were kidnapped at his age, and they decided to kill you. That wouldn't have been fair, would it?"

"Life's not fair, Rog," Elizabeth refuted while kneeling into the deep hole. "We don't get what we deserve. We get what comes to us. This kid got a crap deal, but it's him or us. Isn't it? Look, I'm all for keeping the kid alive so long as this doesn't bite us in our collective asses. Come up with a way for it to work, and I'll support it."

"Ok, how about we let the kid wander into the city and leave it up to the police and social services?"

Daniel clicked his tongue. "Nah, not a viable option. He's seen all of our faces now, thanks to a certain pair of people here." His voice became louder. "Which, by the way, was stupid as hell and forced us into this."

Roger looked down at the hole he was helping to dig as a blush crept into his cheeks. "I saw the kid sitting in the back-seat crying. I couldn't just leave him in there, could I?"

Elizabeth flicked some dirt onto Roger's shirt. "You could have. You didn't because of who you are, but I guarantee you certainly could have."

"Don't get too mushy over there." Daniel slammed his right palm against the steering wheel in front of him. "We're going in circles, and, seeing as I'm the leader, I guess it's my decision."

Elizabeth brought her knife out of the dirt and pointed it at her brother. "True, but I don't think Tanya would approve of offing the kid." She sang as she spoke. "We're best friends and tell each other everything. So remember that."

Daniel's face contorted into a grimace and a loud thumping noise was heard.

"Did you just-" Roger began.

"I'm fine!" Daniel snapped. His right arm snaked its way down to his leg and rubbed up and down. He kept his eyes stern and ahead as he did so.

"You're so stubborn. I don't see what she sees in you," Elizabeth continued. "I guess I shouldn't complain though, since it frees up the best man for me." She moved over to Roger's side as she said it.

Roger threw down the bucket, causing a loud clatter. "We're off topic now, but we're finally ready to put the bodies in. I think this is about six feet. Let's get this done first and then think on the way home. I don't want to be out here all bloody night."

Axel hefted the shovel over the top of the hole with a clatter. "Agreed. I'll go start moving them." He turned, climbed out of the grave, and walked toward the two bodies. He bent over at his waist, grabbed the man's arms, and started dragging him back toward the group.

"Guess that's my cue," Roger said as he climbed out of the hole with a grunt. Once he was out, he went toward the remaining dead woman. He squatted down and wrapped his hands around her wrists. He stood up and mirrored Axel's motions in dragging her back to the makeshift grave.

Not to be left out, Elizabeth reached up and dug her fingertips into the soil to drag herself up. She kicked the dirt in the side of the hole until her shoe dug into the soil, creating a foothold.

Her brother's voice reached her ears as she prepared her exit. "Having trouble there? Not enough upper body strength? Need some help?"

She growled to herself and put all her energy into climbing. She ascended the ledge with an incoherent yell and proceeded to roll a few feet once she was out.

Roger laid the dead woman's arms down. "What's with the noise? You okay, hon?" He walked over and extended a hand down toward her.

She slapped his hand away and sat up on her own. She glared over toward the car to see her brother with a cocky grin plastered on his face. "I'm fine. Let's get this over with so we can go home and sleep this night away."

Axel grunted as he approached. "This dude's heavier than he looks. Also, not to be a killjoy, but if we're going to lose the kid, shouldn't we dump him here too? Kind of a family burial thing?"

"We're not killing the kid," Roger said with a tone of finality. "Look, we can take him back to the apartment and figure out what to do with him there."

"Not to be a dick, buddy, but that's not going to help. If he escapes, they've got us on murder one, kidnapping a minor, and ownership of illegal firearms. That's just off the top of my head," Daniel spoke as the two other men lined up the dead bodies with the graves.

Roger inserted his foot into the woman's stomach and pushed forward. It caused her lifeless carcass to roll into the hole with a dull thud. A tiny puff of dust rushed upward.

Axel spoke up as he did the same. "We could keep him in a room without a window and a double locked door until we figure it out though." He turned to the group to see Daniel and Elizabeth looking at him with one eyebrow raised. "What? It would work. Not sure for how long, but I'd give up my room if need be."

"Fine," Daniel agreed. "We'll bring the kid back just until we figure out what we're doing with him. Now hurry up and fill those holes, would you?" Without waiting for an answer, he immediately switched the radio back on. The others present shook their heads.

The remaining three began the arduous task of throwing all the dirt back into the hole they'd just excavated.

7

Axel stuck his shovel into the soil before leaning toward Roger, cupping his hand around his mouth and whispering. "I gotta take a leak. I'll be right back." He jumped out of the hole and scurried into the surrounding forest without waiting for permission.

"Fantastic, real classy," Roger mumbled to himself as he wiped his brow with the back of his hand. He looked down at his handiwork to see dirt covered lumps in the ground. "Not even a fraction of the way done, and we're already taking breaks. I guess sleep is overrated, since we won't be getting much tonight."

"Where the hell did the new guy go?" Elizabeth's voice came from beside him directly into his ear. He instinctively leaned away and twisted his head to his right to see her on her knees immediately above him. He straightened out his posture and leaned into her ear and whispered. "He had to go."

"Go? Go where exactly?" She asked as she pursed her red lipstick clad lips together.

"You know, go."

"You're saying he's pissing right now?"

"I was trying to be a gentleman, but in so many words, yes."

She stood up, patted down her shins, and stretched. She leaned back and lifted her arms above her head. "Mm, I think I have to go too. Cover for me."

"Sure thing," he agreed as he returned his attention to the task at hand. "In the future we need to remember to carry digging implements, or at the very least my damned lighter along with some gasoline. It would've made this night a hell of a lot shorter." He could barely make out the sound of crunching grass behind him as he continued dumping dirt into the grave.

The rock and roll stopped with an abrupt pause. "Who are you?" Daniel's voice was audible amidst the latent ringing still in Roger's ears. He got onto his tiptoes to peek over the ledge of the hole.

He saw Daniel looking out the passenger's side window, but he could see no more from his position. *Oh fuck,* he thought to himself. He looked down to see the distinctive human silhouettes covered in dirt below him staring back at him.

He could hear a quiet, unfamiliar voice that he didn't recognize along with his friend's occasional remark.

"Yeah, we're just out here having a bit of a party. Sorry about the noise there. What? The holes over there? The other folks here are real survivalist nuts. You know, dig a hole and it keeps you warm since the winds aren't hitting you. I was just giving them a bit of music for their workout."

Roger rolled his eyes. *No one would be dumb enough to believe such a blatant lie, right? I guess a guy can pray.*

The voice became a bit louder, and he could make out some of it. It was obviously a man's voice, but not overly deep. "I think that usually is reserved for snowy areas, isn't it?"

Daniel laughed. "Not when you forget your tent. Am I right? Got to improvise sometimes, especially since it's such a nice night tonight. Nothing like sleeping out under the stars."

"Right. So why are you folks out here so late tonight?"

Roger ducked down and looked at his feet. *Oh Lord, tell me this guy isn't some park ranger or such shit.*

The unfamiliar voice came again. "So you came out here for a camping trip but forgot your tents?"

"Sounds pretty dumb when you say it out loud, doesn't it?"

"What happened to your shoulder, if you don't mind my asking?"

"Well that's a bit of a long-"

Roger interrupted the two men by climbing out of the hole he was in and raising his voice. "Who are you talking to up there?" He got to his feet and could see the stranger's face through the windows of the van.

The interloper was a man dressed in blue jeans and a long sleeved red shirt. He held a flash light in one hand, and a large knife could be seen sheathed at his hip. He wore a baseball hat turned backwards. "Oh, hello. Sorry about that racket from earlier," he said as he sidled over to the two men. He extended his thumb and pointed it toward Daniel. "This knucklehead has no concept of common courtesy. Sorry if his music woke you up."

"It's not a problem. This place usually doesn't have many folks. That's why I was curious about what that racket was."

Roger walked around the front and leaned against the van. "To answer your earlier question, this dingus here got behind me when I was digging. The result was a pretty nasty gash on his shoulder."

"Right." The man agreed and left it at that. An awkward silence overcame the small group until the sound of a twig snapping from in front of Roger caught their attention.

A loud, slurred, albeit feminine voice made itself known right after. "You find the retards yet, Howard? Some of us are trying to sleep. They need to learn some manners. Who sets fireworks off and plays music at this hour?" A small silhouette stumbled through the tree line behind the man.

"As you heard, Howard is my name. I'm sorry for this," Howard said as he brought his hand up to his face. He lowered his hand and leaned closer to the two men. "She's a bit sloshed, so please don't get upset with her. She's had a bit of a rough time the past few days. Let me go explain everything real quick."

Daniel waved his hand in a dismissive manner from side to side. "I know all about that. Don't worry." He leaned to the left to see around the man. He could see her approaching as fast as was possible for someone so utterly inebriated. Her head was hanging down and her steps were unsteady as she staggered forward.

Howard turned and jogged toward his companion. He spoke in a quiet tone so Daniel and Roger were unable to hear.

The woman looked over Howard's shoulder and asked in a loud voice. "What the hell are those holes for? They look like damned graves."

Roger could feel a trickle of sweat going down the side of his face as he forced a smile.

"That's not any of our business. These folks are just camping out under the stars. They already promised no more music, so how about we go sleep this off, hm?" Howard asked in a gentle manner.

She looked at Howard for a brief moment before stepping around him and walking up to Roger. She inspected him from head to toe before leaning forward and whispering in a husky voice. Her breath reeked of alcohol and caused Roger's nose to curl up. "You look nervous," she giggled. "Does my beauty get you all hot and bothered, handsome?"

Roger stepped back and intentionally kept his distance while keeping his eye on Howard. "You are striking, ma'am, but I'm already-"

"Don't worry about Howie over there," she interrupted, taking a step toward him. "We're not together anymore. We can go get to know each other if you want."

Howard came up behind the woman and placed a hand on her shoulder. "Christi, we should get back to camp and leave these nice people alone for the night. We've already interrupted them enough."

She puffed out her cheeks and stuck her tongue out at the jean clad man. "They were the ones who woke us up." She moved to Roger's side and leaned her head against his shoulder. "I think someone should take responsibility for that."

Roger looked through the windshield at Daniel, only to see him grinning at him. *Fat lot of good you are.*

Another feminine voice made itself known from behind Roger. This time Elizabeth's voice called out, causing him to wince involuntarily. *Shit,* he thought as he turned around toward the voice and the graves. This motion caused Christi to clutch his sides as they twirled in place.

"My, my, what's happening over here? Didn't expect to meet anyone else out here tonight," she said as she made her way over to the ever-growing group. She stopped a few feet from Roger's free side. "Darling, you appear quite popular tonight." She was smiling as she talked. "You haven't been cheating on me, have you?"

Christi took her head off Roger's arm, backed off a few feet, then stepped in front of Roger to come face to face with Elizabeth. She eyed her up and down before speaking. "Who the hell are you? His woman?"

"Christi, we really need to be going." Howard reached his hand out toward her with a soft voice.

"That's right," Elizabeth answered with a smug smirk. Her left hand fell to her belt line and patted.

"She's just a little drunk, dear. No harm, no foul. Right?" Roger asked as he wrapped his left arm around Elizabeth's shoulders.

"I may be drunk, but I guarantee I can rock your world better than Little Miss Stuffy can."

Roger looked down at his feet and only three words came from his mouth in the form of a whisper. "Oh fuck me."

This caught the attention of the two women. Elizabeth grasped something at her belt line, while Christi balled her fists.

Daniel coughed, causing all parties to look at him. "Sis, let it go. These nice folks were about to go to sleep, and we should too. Let's let it go," he said with a straight face and a stern voice. His eyes were locked onto hers as he spoke.

She narrowed her eyes and released her grip on the object at her side. "Fine," Elizabeth agreed, but not before she used a hand to reach around the front of Roger. She placed her hand on Christi's nearest shoulder and pushed.

The force was sufficient to cause her to lose her balance and begin staggering backwards. In her attempt to regain her balance, she turned and started heading right toward the holes nearby. She turned in a circle. Her arms at her side were windmilling as she desperately attempted to regain her balance. Eventually she tripped and fell backwards, directly into the grave.

Without delay, Howard sprinted over to the hole. "Christi!" he cried. "You alright down there?"

Roger sighed and, with his right hand, reached inside his coat and grasped one of his revolvers. He leveled a glare at Elizabeth before whispering loud enough for her and her brother to hear. "No choice. We have to drop them now. Turn on the damned music for a minute."

"Yes sir," Elizabeth answered as she reached down the front of her pants and retrieved her own revolver.

No sooner had the two of them brandished their weapons than a shrill high pitched scream pierced the night. Howard's voice was now frantic. "What's wrong? Are you hurt?" he asked as he lowered himself to the ground in preparation for jumping down.

"Let's do this quick," Roger said to Elizabeth before he walked toward the holes.

A loud thud, followed by Howard's voice again, came from the hole. "Hm? You landed on something you say? Get up and we'll see what it was." A pregnant pause followed. "What is that? It looks like a ..." He trailed off.

Roger cleared his throat, getting the attention of the newcomers. They looked up from the ground to see Roger and Elizabeth standing on either side of the hole with revolvers pointed at them.

Howard was the first to speak. "Oh please, no. We won't tell anyone!" he shouted. "Just let us go, and we'll forget tonight ever happened. Hell, she won't even remember it with how shitfaced she is."

Roger was the only one to respond. He pulled back the hammer with a click. "Sorry, Howard. I like you. Really, I do. I just can't take that chance. Goodbye."

Daniel took the cue and turned the radio on causing pulsing heavy metal music to play.

Without waiting for a response, Roger squeezed the trigger. A nickel sized hole appeared on Howard's head as his eyes glassed over and he crumpled down onto the soil. His carcass fell directly on top of Christi. Her arms shot up between his arms, her palms waved frantically.

"No, don't do this," she begged the group above her.

Elizabeth locked her eyes onto Christi's. "Not in the cards. Besides, he's mine," she restated before squeezing the trigger and ending the woman's desperate begging.

The music faded along with Christie's voice.

Loud stomping along with snapping twigs and rustling grass met their ears. They raised their weapons toward the tree line.

Axel jumped through and, upon surveying the scene, put his hands into the air. "Easy now. Why do you have your weapons out? Did something happen?"

Roger lowered his weapon before holstering it inside his jacket. "Yeah, two more complications, but we took care of them."

Elizabeth shoved her revolver down the front of her pants. "What the hell took you so long? I thought you'd gotten eaten by a wolf or something."

Roger interrupted the exchange with a quiet laugh. "He was probably taking a dump."

Axel looked away. "It took longer than I was expecting." He walked up toward the holes, looked down, and whistled. "Well, I guess it's time to finish this and get home."

"Agreed," Roger said. He turned toward the van Daniel sat in. "Get out here and help us."

"What? I'm injured."

"Yeah, and this was your fault, so this isn't a suggestion. Get your ass out here and start helping fill these in. I don't care if you can only kick piles of dirt in, any extra labor will help. We need to get out of here sharpish. You got me?"

"Yes, boss," Daniel replied as he exited the car. He slammed the door behind him and made his way over.

"Now after we fill in these holes, we need to make sure no one finds this, or we're screwed. It's more than likely since we're right on the beaten path. Who wants that job?"

Axel reached down onto the ground and picked up the abandoned shovel. He stood up and shoveled dirt down into the hole. "I'll do it, I guess. Should I just place sticks, rocks, grass, and whatever I can find to disguise it?"

"I guess so. We need something to keep wandering eyes from noticing the recently disturbed dirt. Are you three going to be fine while I go gather the necessary materials?"

Daniel got onto the ground near the large pile of dirt and looked at Roger. "I'm pretty sure we can handle filling in a hole."

"Just trying to cover all bases. I'll be back in a few minutes then," Roger said before he walked toward the tree line. His silhouette disappeared behind numerous bushes, leaving the group to themselves.

Daniel shoved his good hand into the pile of soil and tossed some into the makeshift grave. "I call first shower when we get back."

"Hey, you can't do that," Elizabeth whined. She flicked her knife toward her brother, causing a mist of dirt to hit him square in the face. "Haven't you ever heard of ladies first, you boorish oaf?"

Daniel raised his hand up and rubbed his eyes. He lowered his hand and blinked rapidly. "Haven't you ever heard of catering to the injured or sick, you insensitive nympho? Besides, you'd probably just take Roger in there with you."

"What business is that of yours? Besides, that way two of us get clean at once. It's a more efficient use of time and water."

"Some of us don't like listening to your escapades. Every time you two-"

Axel coughed, which drew their attention. He grunted as he hefted another shovel full into the hole. "I don't mean to interrupt whatever this is, but it would go faster if we all pitched in. That way we'd all get to shower earlier."

The two siblings looked at each other and down at their current project. Without further words they resumed their work.

After a few minutes Elizabeth spoke up as she continued shoveling. "This has been a fucked up night."

Daniel scoffed. "That's the understatement of the year."

"So, I'm guessing not all jobs go this way?" Axel asked.

"No, Axe. They don't generally go this poorly," Daniel answered his subordinate. "Normally, if things stray from the plan we withdraw before it gets any worse. Tonight that didn't quite go to plan, as you no doubt noticed. Call it a mix of bad luck and poor diplomacy I guess. Also, you're driving our interloper's vehicle. Dump it somewhere no one will notice. We'll follow and then drive you back to base."

"Yeah, you're not exactly ambassador material," Elizabeth chided. "Should be Rog who does the talking if you ask me."

Daniel turned toward his sister with narrowed eyes. "Maybe." He paused. "I'm the more experienced though, so that makes it my job according to Dad. Keeping everyone safe falls on me, including your boyfriend."

"Phenomenal job so far tonight," Elizabeth muttered.

8
———

Roger closed the door and reached down to the knob. He twisted the lock until he heard a click. He let out a large exhale, turned to his right, and walked down the narrow dark hallway toward a larger room with a faint glow coming from the lone television. As he approached, he could make out two figures sitting on a large couch directly in front of it. He glanced to the right of it to see that the solitary chair was open. He seized the opportunity and sat in it before speaking up. "Kid's in bed, if anyone cares."

"Great. Now when are we supposed to figure out what exactly to do with him?" Daniel asked as he looked to his right toward Roger.

Roger reached into his pocket, pulled out his phone, and swiped the screen until a faint light came from it. "Since it's five in the morning, we can always sleep on it and figure it out tomorrow I guess."

"Not to be a dick, but you were the one who insisted on sparing the munchkin."

"You say that like it's a bad thing."

"It very well may be if the boss hears about it before we

handle it," Daniel answered back immediately. "We're holding a random kid. You think he's just going to say 'Oh, you group of rascals, it's okay? No. He'll flip his shit, and probably make us deal with the fallout. I mean, we dropped over a dozen bodies tonight on what was supposed to be a simple exchange. Never mind the fact that we iced a couple, hell it could be four, civvies. That brings a load of heat when and if they're found."

Elizabeth stood up from her spot on the furthest end of the couch before speaking up. "I vote we get to bed and do whatever tomorrow. I'm beat after our little adventure tonight."

A loud creak interrupted the trio. They turned toward the noise down the hallway to see an open doorway and steam rolling out. Axel stepped out clad in only two towels wrapped around his bulky frame. He crossed the hallway and tried the door Roger had just locked. Once he found the knob was not moving, he stood there scratching his head.

Daniel raised his right hand to shield his eyes and looked away. "Dammit, man, get some clothes on. Nobody here wants to see that."

"I would, but someone locked my door while I was in there. You didn't already put the kid in there did you?"

Elizabeth walked over to the lone recliner, circled around, and stood behind Roger. "Who the hell doesn't take their clothes into the bathroom when they take a shower? Guess you're learning the hard way tonight, rook."

Daniel laughed at a raucous volume. "Just don't sleep anywhere near me." He raised his legs and placed them on the now vacant rest of the couch. "I got the couch as usual. Guess you're on the floor then."

Axel's shoulders slumped. "Do we at least have a sleeping bag?"

"Does this look like a fricking camp-out? No, we don't. We weren't supposed to have any guests, if you'll remember," Daniel said, staring directly at Roger.

Elizabeth spoke up in a loud tone. "It's your fault anyway. If you had listened to Rog and not got your ass shot, none of this would have happened."

"Piss off," Daniel lashed back. "How the hell was I supposed to know they wanted a full shipment? Everyone else wants a trial deal first."

"You were supposed to feel them out and set up a proper deal. It's your fault this all happened. You knew they were desperate for fire power. You were put in charge, and look what happened."

Roger raised a hand and placed it over Elizabeth's, which had fell over his shoulder. "Now, now, let's not fall to pieces. He did the best he could."

Daniel looked away and crossed his arms in front of him.

Elizabeth exhaled, looked toward Axel, and finally back at Roger. "Why don't you head to bed? I'll be there in a few minutes."

Roger leaned forward in the recliner before arching his back and extending his arms straight up in a large yawn. "Good idea. We'll sort this mess out tomorrow." He stood up and began his trek toward the hallway. He turned to his side and side stepped around Axel. "Good night, everyone," he said as he trudged down the hallway with his right hand up in farewell.

The sound of a door closing greeted the rest of the group. Elizabeth circled around the chair and took the now vacant seat. She leaned forward with a soft voice. "You guys know that kid is a world of trouble. Right?"

"Of course, but Captain Virtuous won't let us solve that problem," Daniel spat out.

"True, but I have an idea, and if it's done right, we'll avoid that pitfall."

"Oh, do go on," Daniel said as he sat up with a wince and leaned forward toward his sister, cradling his chin in his hand.

Elizabeth looked over at Axel before gesturing him over and speaking in a low whisper. "Okay, here's my idea."

Five hours later...

Roger groaned as the piercing noise of the alarm clock to his side did its job. He reached out with his right hand and slammed down onto the infernal device, causing it to cease its noise. He looked down to see a tuft of black hair clouding his field of vision. He could feel his bed mate's arm looped over his chest, along with her leg over top of his. He raised his left hand and trailed his fingers along the back of her head, whispering in a soft voice. "Liz, honey? Time to get up. I know it sucks, but we have work today."

She nuzzled into his chest and made a series of high-pitched whining noises. "Mm, tired. Just five more minutes. Please?"

He lowered his hand to her back and tapped with gentle care. "It's never just five minutes. We've got to deal with the kid today. Remember? We can't put it off."

She rolled to his left and extricated herself from him. She sat up, facing him, revealing her long shirt and short shorts. She rubbed her eyes with a large yawn as she arched her back. She fell backward and her long pale legs stayed vertical, giving Roger quite a show.

Roger got to his feet and made his way to the nearby dresser. He pulled out the drawer and rummaged through the contents. He grasped a red shirt and threw it over his head in a hurry. "I'm going to go check on the kid. He's probably hungry or something," he declared as he walked toward the lone door in the room.

"Okay," Elizabeth agreed. She stood up and walked toward the oval mirror hanging on the wall near the bed. She brushed her hair as she spoke. "I think we've got cereal in the kitchen. Kids like cereal, don't they?"

Roger reached for the doorknob leading out into the hall before turning back with a smile. "I think everyone likes cereal. It's a good thing we've got the sugary stuff."

"Yeah, who knew my brother's sweet tooth would do anything except give us all cavities?" she quipped with a giggle.

Roger opened the door with a creak and made his way into the hallway. He looked in the direction of the living room to see two feet propped up on the end of the sofa and a large figure laying perpendicular to the sofa on the floor. Loud snoring could be heard in the small apartment.

He turned the other direction toward the room he'd left the child inside. He walked over and knocked on the door. "You hungry?" There was no answer to his inquiry. He knocked harder and raised his voice a little. "You okay in there?" Still no reply came from the bedroom. "I'm coming in," he declared as he reached for the locks he himself had set earlier in the morning and twisted in the opposite direction.

Multiple clicks emanated in the quiet apartment, followed by a low prolonged creaking sound. He stepped into the small bedroom, looked at the lone bed, and found it empty. He looked left and right while calling out. "Kid? You here? I'm here to get you some food, so come on out." A closed door beside the bed caught his attention. He slowly made his way over and reached for the doorknob. "Kid, are you in the closet? Hiding isn't going to help you or me. I'm your friend here," he said as he twisted and pulled the door open. The musty smell of dust reached his nostrils as he swung the door open. He raised his hand to his nose to cover it. He saw numerous t-shirts and suits hanging from clothes hangers. He looked down and saw countless dress shoes, flip flops, and tennis shoes. He squatted down and leaned forward. He looked left and right but found no other occupants in the enclosed space.

"Oh God," Roger muttered as he stood up. He brought his right hand to his mouth. "He's gone," he whispered to himself. Without further pause he ran out of the bedroom and toward the main room containing the other men. "We've got a huge problem here!" he shouted.

"Be quiet." Daniel's sharp, deep voice came from in front of him. He rolled to his side with a grunt.

"To hell with that. You need to get up now."

A loud sigh came from the sofa, along with feet swinging to the side and Daniel's head rising. He raised his hand to his face and rubbed his bloodshot eyes. "What's the problem? It better be good, waking me up at this hour."

"Okay, first off it's 10 a.m. Get your lazy ass up. More importantly, the kid's not in the room. He's gone."

Daniel lowered his hand, revealing his eyes wide. "What?"

"Exactly what I said. He's not in there. Did you hear anything last night?"

Daniel looked down and toward his left at Axel's half

naked, towel clad sleeping form on the ground. "Get up, Axe. If I'm awake, you're damn well getting up too," he ordered as he used his left foot to kick the unconscious man below him.

A loud illegible noise followed. "I'm awake. What now?" Axel asked. He rolled onto his stomach and pushed himself up, eventually getting into a sitting position with his back to the sofa.

"You guys hear anything last night?" Roger asked the newly awakened men.

Daniel and Axel briefly looked at each other and back toward Roger. Daniel was the first to answer. "I didn't hear anything except your screaming earlier."

Axel shook his head. "No sir. I was out as soon as my head hit the pillow."

"How in the world did the kid even get out of the room? Where would he be? How are we going to find him?" Roger asked at a rapid pace.

"There are no windows in there, so it follows he must have gone out the door." Daniel's tone dripped with sarcasm.

"Don't you get it, man? We're fucked if he outs us. We've got to get out there and start looking for him."

The sound of a door closing and a feminine voice met their ears. Elizabeth strolled into the living area and stood beside Roger as she talked. "That's all well and good, but to what end? Grabbing a kid in broad daylight in a major metropolitan area isn't smart, hon. In our effort to avoid heat, we'd bring it crashing down on all of us."

"So, what? We just sit here and hope the kid doesn't talk to the police? That doesn't sound much better."

Elizabeth walked past Roger into the small half kitchen they all shared. She opened a nearby cabinet and pulled out a bowl. With her other hand she grabbed a box from on top of the refrigerator. "Not at all. Besides, I have a question. If Danny is right in his inappropriate, sarcastic reply and he went out the door, then why was it locked? It was locked when you went to check on him, right?"

"Yes, but couldn't the kid have locked it himself after he got out?" Roger asked.

"Possibly, but I wouldn't think a small child's first instinct would be to lock his former prison back."

"He would if he wanted the ruse of his leaving to last longer. A door wide open would be a big sign he was gone," Roger mused. "Still, he's either escaped or someone took him somewhere."

"No one knew we had the kid, did they? He had to have escaped. The kid's probably scared shitless after last night. I doubt he'd say a word," Elizabeth reasoned as she poured a bowl full of cereal and opened the refrigerator.

"Sure enough to bet all of our freedoms?" Roger fired right back.

A loud ringing from Daniel interrupted their discussion. He reached into his front pocket and tapped the screen before bringing it to his ear. "Yes?"

A thick Brooklyn accent answered him. "You all need to report back here immediately," it growled into his ear. "Get over here now!" The yelling caused him to wince and hold the phone a few inches away from his ear.

"Yes, sir. We're on our way." Nothing but a click awaited him. He hung up and placed the phone back into his pocket. He looked at the group in front of him with a sigh. "That was Dad, and he wanted us to get over there now. I mean right now. No time for eating. We've got to go right this second. He sounded pissed off."

"Oh, God. How much do you think he knows?" Roger asked.

"What we did last night with the Irish has no doubt hit the streets already. If we're lucky, it's just an admonishment - but I doubt it will be that tame," Daniel answered. "Regardless, we need to go now. No more questions. I don't want to set off the old man any more than necessary. Get your suits on, and get out to the van as soon as possible. Got it?"

The other three answered in unison, "Roger."

"What?"

Daniel shook his head. "Just go."

9

"We're clear on what we're saying when we get there, right?" Elizabeth asked the cramped cabin from the back seat.

"The Irish jumped us, and we did what we had to? Basically, we're telling the truth and omitting certain other facts?" Roger asked the woman sitting to his right.

"Precisely. No word on the kid. We'll fix that after this. For now, we have to focus on what's in front of us."

"The problem with putting it behind us, hon, is it could very well bite us in the ass later," Roger chimed to his girlfriend.

"We're all aware. For now, this is all we can do. I suggest we focus until we're done with this meeting. We don't know what Daddy knows yet."

"Oh, I know what he's going to say," Daniel declared from the front passenger seat as he faced forward. "He's going to chew my ass out because I was in charge of the Irish deal."

"I'd keep my head down if I were you," Roger advised.

"He's not going to want to hear any explanations if I know your dad. He'll see it as weakness."

"What he'll see it as," Elizabeth began, "is laziness. You didn't even ask them how many units they wanted beforehand, which led to our unfortunate altercation last night. Don't even mention bugging the place and showing up armed. And we couldn't even utilize it because you didn't leave a charge on Roger's laptop."

"Thanks for the obvious advice," Daniel muttered in an even voice. He turned to the driver's seat where Axel sat and poked his shoulder. "Keep your mouth shut unless he asks you a question."

Axel nodded but kept quiet as the conversation continued around him.

"Keep your hands away from your waistline too," Roger added. "The old man is paranoid, and his bodyguards won't hesitate to light you up if they think you're a threat."

"Don't hesitate to answer either if he does ask you a question," Daniel said. "Basically, keep your hands behind you, show respect, and you'll be fine."

"Now that the newbie's been briefed, we need to prepare for the worst," Elizabeth said.

"The worst?" Axel asked as he turned the wheel while the turn signal clicked.

"Yeah. We'll likely get busted down to collection or some other crap job. It could just be Danny though since he'll think it's his fault," Elizabeth explained with a hint of glee in her voice.

"I'll handle the old man," Daniel said. He lifted his leg and placed the heel of his foot against the glove compartment in front of him.

Roger inhaled deeply. "I don't know about the rest of you, but I'm getting ready to be dressed down."

"I like the sound of that," Elizabeth teased. "Seriously though, we're screwed."

Bernard's Compound...

The group lined up side to side in the spacious conference room. A large table sat in front of them. Windows lined the walls around them. Sunlight poured through the lavish, ruby red drapes. Bernard paced back and forth in front of them.

"Whose fuck up was this?" the old man asked in a commanding deep voice tinged with his Brooklyn accent. "You?" He stopped a mere foot in front of Roger and leaned in. The graying widow's peak accentuated the front of his forehead. He poked his chest with his index finger. He shook his head. "No, not your style."

"It was mine," Daniel said with a straight look on his face. He kept facing forward, never daring to look directly into his father's eyes.

Bernard looked to his left and stomped over the few feet between them. "That makes more sense. You mind explaining just why I got a phone call in the middle of the night saying that we were at war with the Irish? Imagine my shock. I explicitly told you to avoid this when you were begging me for the job," he sneered. "I knew I should have put Lenny on this. It was a dumb ass mistake to give the job to the kids. Do you morons know how this makes me look to the other organizations? At best, I'm ruthless. At worst, they won't work with us anymore since they'll be afraid of all dying at the meet. This will have far reaching consequences that you retards can't even comprehend."

Bernard reached into his back pocket and pulled out a handkerchief that he used to wipe his face. He breathed in deeply and exhaled. "So, what happened?"

"The McCranes wanted more hardware than we had at the meeting."

"What did I tell you, boy? Being an arms dealer isn't so much about the guns themselves. It's about being a good salesman. Please tell me you at least called him before you idiots ran over there. I explained the method thoroughly. Did you just not pay attention?"

"Daddy," Elizabeth interrupted. "Can we just-"

"No," Bernard said. "I want to hear just why this happened from his own mouth. Otherwise, he'll never learn a thing."

"In my mind I thought-"

"Your first mistake," Bernard quipped. "I didn't send you there to think. I sent you there to sell automatic rifles. Continue then why don't you."

"I thought that they'd want a trial run, so to speak, so they could get used to dealing with us and finding out what quality of gear we have, like any other crew."

"Mm," Bernard grunted. "Sensible. But again I ask, why did you not simply call them beforehand and find out how much they wanted? I gave you the number they gave us to contact them. Nothing is certain in this line of work, Son. No organization is just like the others. No matter how 'safe' the bet was, you should have checked. I know I hammered this into your skull before I gave you the job."

Daniel looked at the ground in front of him and remained silent.

"No excuses?" Bernard asked. "Fine, I'll tell you why. You're overly impetuous and don't think things through."

He paced past his son and stopped in front of Axel. "What do you have to say about this? Anything?"

Axel shook his head side to side. "No, sir."

"You pussy. Too scared to talk huh?" He glanced toward his children and nodded in their direction. "Or did they order your silence? Maybe they threatened you? Well, let me give you a piece of advice, young man." He leaned in close, causing the large man to lean backward. Bernard's voice was low and even as his eyes locked onto Axel's." Do not lie to me. I don't care who tells you to. If I ask you something, you damned well better answer to the best of your ability. Got me?"

Axel nodded.

"So? Anything to say?"

Axel looked at his three companions before returning his attention to the older man in front of him. "They did everything in their power to make this deal work, sir."

"Hmph," Bernard huffed. "Is that right? For all I know you're trying to cover for your crew." He turned his head to the side away from the group, his voice lowered to a barely audible volume. "Certainly not the worst trait in an employee I guess." He returned his gaze toward the muscular man and raised his voice loud enough to be heard. "I better not find anything contrary to what you're all telling me. If anything else happened, you'd best tell me now. If I find out any of you are hiding something, it won't be pretty."

Bernard continued pacing from side to side. "Anyone want to say anything else?"

The group remained silent under the intense scrutiny their boss was levying their way. Bernard stopped his movement once he was at the center of their line before raising his voice louder. "Fine, have it your way. You all know what's about to happen. I can't let you all stay on this, not after your screw up. It wouldn't be fair to the rest of the family. You're all getting reassigned."

"Daddy, how about we get a chance to redeem ourselves?" Elizabeth asked. She opened her eyes wide and her lips quivered as she stared at her father.

Bernard looked away from his daughter. "Sorry, dear. I can't be seen playing favorites. If anyone else had messed up this bad, heads would roll. As it is, you all are going to be busted down to collection runs. I can't see how you could screw that up. You understand me? You're in charge of the three blocks near you. Go and collect our protection money. We're going to need it since we're now at war."

"What if the Irish interfere? Do we have a green light to engage?" Daniel asked. He looked to his side to see Roger silently shaking his head side to side. "It's a legitimate question. If you want to hurt someone you go after their income. They'll come after us if they're smart."

"Standing orders are not to die." Bernard sighed. "That should be easy enough to remember, even for you. Just try not to start any more wars. Alright? If they come into our territory and piss on our shoes, take them out." Bernard turned and started walking toward the lone door, then stopped and said over his shoulder. "One more thing. I think you four could use a new leader. Liz, you're now in charge. Do not even think of arguing, Daniel. You had your shot, and now it's your sister's turn She's always been the cooler headed of the two of you. Now stay out of my sight. I need to start cleaning up this shit storm you all started."

With that Bernard continued toward the door and exited the room, leaving the four in silence.

"I vote we get our ex-leader some medical attention before we go," Roger said to his new leader on his left.

Elizabeth looked at him before nodding. "Agreed. If he's

lucky, he might even get to see his crush while we're here."
She leaned forward and looked past Roger at her brother
with a grin. "I bet Tanya would love to see you. She's here, so
why not pay her a visit before we go?"

Daniel walked forward, putting his back to the group.
"Humph," he grunted. "You did say I needed a real doctor. I
guess that makes sense." He walked in the direction Bernard
had taken moments before. He reached the door and turned
around. "Try to amuse yourselves while I'm getting patched
up."

"You're not the boss anymore, Bro," Elizabeth said to her
brother.

Daniel leveled a glare her way before turning back to the
door, opening it, and stepping through.

"You probably didn't need to rub his nose in it," Roger
added.

"He's a big boy. He'll get over it." She redirected her
attention back to her boyfriend at her side. "Speaking of big
boys, I think I know how we might amuse ourselves while
we wait."

"I'm not really sure this is the appropriate time or place."

A cough interrupted the two lovers. They looked to their
right to see Axel blushing and fidgeting in place.

"What? Did you want a show or something? Get out,"
Elizabeth ordered, her voice short and snappy.

"I'll uh, give you two some space then," Axel said.

"No, you don't need to-" Roger started.

"Yes. Leave already, and lock the door," Elizabeth
ordered.

Without further words, Axel left the same way the two
previous occupants had exited, leaving the two alone in the
boardroom.

"Well, that was rude," Roger remarked. "I know you're

not planning on doing this here? This is your father's business tab-"

He was cut off as he was pushed backwards onto the table. She jumped on top of him. "Consider it a promotion party then."

10

"Oh, this is pretty bad, Dan," the blonde woman inspecting his unwrapped shoulder said. "I mean, this is a pretty hacksaw job they did. Did you see a real doctor yet?"

"We were more than a little busy, Tanya. It wasn't our top priority last night."

Tanya leaned back and puffed out her cheeks as she looked at him without a word.

That pink lipstick really accentuates that adorable expression, Daniel thought. He shook his head. *Now's not the time.*

"Must have been a hell of a night if this wasn't your first thing to take care of. Then again, the talk around is that this new war is all your group's fault. Any truth to that?"

Daniel looked to the side, examining the small room they found themselves in. He saw three personal computers, all hooked up to a veritable wall of monitors that lined the wall to his left. "What else are they saying?"

"All manner of things. I've heard people say the boss should turn you and your partner over to the Irish to settle the beef. Others fancy themselves soldiers and want to wipe the McCranes out. I've noticed it mainly centers around if they like you or your sister."

"The old man could turn me over if he wants. It was my fault. No one's going to turn Roger or Liz over though. They'd have to climb over my dead body first." He threw his dress shirt onto the floor, leaving only the dressing on his upper body.

Tanya turned her back to Daniel. She walked to his right to the twin bed on the opposite side of the room as the electronics and opened the lowest drawer of the nearby nightstand. She rummaged around until a loud shuffling noise indicated she had found what she was looking for. She pulled out a small box with a picture of gauze bandages on it. "Judging by this wound, they won't have to climb too far." She walked over and shoved the box onto his lap before going back and sitting on the bed. "You probably should wrap that back up."

Daniel glanced down at the box in his lap before raising his gaze toward her. His eyebrows raised as he saw her pulling out her phone.

"You're obviously a big boy who doesn't need help, so go ahead," she said as her fingers danced on her phone's screen.

"Oh gee, thanks," Daniel uttered under his breath.

"Stop whining, you big baby. I'm calling the local saw bones right now."

"I hate that term," Daniel said as he used his good arm to reach inside the box and pull out a rolled up unit of white cloth.

Tanya brought her phone to her right ear and her left index finger to her lips. "I need to speak to Doctor Williams." She paused for a moment before speaking with more force. "No, this cannot wait. Tell him the Morris family has an emergency. Now!"

She got up and moved to the monitors on his left before sitting in the lone office chair. She covered the bottom of the phone with her left hand and rolled her eyes. "Why do receptionists always try and delay? It's like they think that's their jobs or something." Her eyes widened. "Yes, Doctor Williams? We need you to come over, like now." She looked over at Daniel before continuing. "No, Williams, this cannot wait. Well, not unless you want your wife to know your late night habits. Oh I'm sure she'll be glad to know her husband is neck deep in gambling debts to us. Hey, maybe she might have some money for us." She cradled the cell phone on her neck. Her hands typed at a furious pace. After a few moments, a detailed spreadsheet came up on the middle top monitor full of numbers, with the name 'Gerald Williams' on top. "From what I see here in your bank balance, you already could pay it back. Oh boy, that's not what you told us. I could tell my boss about that if you'd rather." She looked over at Daniel and gave a thumbs up. "Okay, good. Your cell phone is charged isn't it? Well, because I'm going to send you the location to go to. Great. Make sure to bring supplies for a gunshot wound. Oh no reason at all. Just do it," she ordered as she grasped the phone and ended the call.

Daniel sat wide eyed, staring at the woman. "You know you can be really frightening when you want to be."

"Good thing I don't want to be very often then, isn't it?"

"I think you need to stop hanging out with my sister. She's beginning to rub off on you."

"Aww," Tanya whined. "Why? Not girly enough for you?"

"Not at all, but sweet suits you better," he said before turning away with a radiant blush covering his face.

"Is that right, Romeo? Are you trying to use flattery to get me to redress that for you?" she asked pointing at his injured shoulder.

Daniel refused to meet her gaze and continued looking at the floor. He remained silent at her question.

"You're so rude sometimes, you know?" She sighed and made her way to his side. "Or is that just embarrassment? Is the big man shy?" she asked as she leaned forward, bringing her face close, her voice tinged with a hint of playfulness. She used her left hand's index finger to flick his forehead, causing a surprised grunt to come from Daniel. She swiped the box out of his hand. She reached into the box and pulled out a roll of cloth. "I guess you're just lucky I'm so 'sweet', as you worded it."

"You love teasing me, don't you?" Daniel asked as she circled around behind him.

She wrapped her arms around his arm and started the tedious process of covering his wounds. She giggled into his ear. "Teasing is part of the sweet act, right?" she whispered. "That's what you want, isn't it?"

"I want you to be yourself around me, nothing more," he instantly answered with his voice barely above a whisper.

The arms around his shoulder disappeared behind him with his admission. He started turning his head when he heard cloth shuffling. Immediately the arms reappeared, but this time they wrapped around his neck without the bandages. The smell of strawberries met his senses. "You can't be saying stuff that earnest all of a sudden," she said. "A girl can get anxious, you know?" she asked with her voice shy, almost mouse like.

He angled his head down with a smirk on his face. He raised his voice loud enough for her to hear. "Can I tell you something in confidence?"

The arms untangled themselves from him. A few moments later they reappeared and resumed their previous task of dressing the wound. She leaned forward, pressing her modest chest against his bare back. "You know you can. Is it that bad?"

"On a scale of one to ten, it's about an eleven."

"How very trite; but fine, what happened?"

"I mean it. You can't tell, talk to, or discuss this with anyone except our little group."

He felt a small amount of force push down on his uninjured shoulder. "I get it already, Dan. What happened?"

"It's a little worse than everyone's saying."

"Just a minute," she said. "There we are. You're ready to go," she announced as her palm patted down on the cloth on his shoulder. She removed her arms and moved back to the bed with the box held under her left arm. She sat down, placed the bandages on the floor beside her feet, and kicked her feet out in front of her. "Now go. I'm ready."

"Well, after the infamous meet we were on our way back to the safe-house. Well, I'm sitting in the back bleeding. Roger and Liz are freaking out. Then I hear that we're being followed."

She leaned forward. "Uh huh? What happened?"

"We figured it had to be the McCranes. So instead of getting into a shootout on the freeway, we made our way to the local national park."

Her eyebrows furrowed downward. "You're talking Harriman State Park? Isn't that a local camping spot?"

"Yeah, as it turns out it is. I know from personal experience now."

"Oh no," she said as her head fell into her hands. Her voice was muffled as she spoke into them. "Do I want to know what happened next?"

"I don't know if you do or not. You asked before, so I'll assume so. We drove down a small dirt path until we came to a clearing. We got out and headed into the woods to set up an ambush."

"You did that with that shoulder?" She asked as she pointed at the wound.

"I made Roger the defacto leader when we got in the car, and it was his idea. I agreed with it, and we set it up. Next, he took Liz, and the two of them got set up a good distance away. Meanwhile, the new guy kept me from bleeding out in the dirt. Next thing I know, I hear a hail of gunfire that ended as quick as it started. Minutes later we see the two of them coming back with a kid in tow."

"You didn't?" She gasped with both hands clasped over her mouth.

"No, we didn't. We took the kid back to the safe-house. We couldn't just leave him out there all alone with his parents dead."

She raised her head back up and shook it side to side. "Well at least that's something."

"I wasn't finished. While we were digging, two campers came upon us."

"In the middle of the night? Well, I guess gunfire might attract attention. How bad does this get?"

"It's just about over," Daniel answered. "Well, long story short, they're now permanent residents."

She cradled her head in her hands. "So, what about the kid? What in the world are you all planning? This is serious shit here, Dan. You all can't just be playing around."

Daniel looked away and scratched the back of his head. "He's, uh..." he trailed off. "He was gone from the apartment as of this morning."

Her eyes bugged out and her voice became shrill. "What? You're joking, right?"

Daniel raised his hands and motioned downward. "Cool it." He looked back to the door leading into the hallway for a moment before refocusing his attention on the woman across from him. "We're still working on a way out of this."

"Please tell me you told your dad about this."

"Are you nuts? Why would we? So we can be lined up outside and take a nice dirt nap? We both know that's the old man's solution to loose ends. We didn't want the kid dead, so we improvised the best we could."

Tanya got up from her bed and came closer without a word. She knelt down in front of him, took his right hand in hers, and brought it up to her mouth. She kissed his hand before standing up and moving to her office chair. She spun around once before she stopped and pounded away at the keyboard.

"It's not like I'll understand it, but what are you doing?"

"Helping save your stubborn ass. I'm going to help you all find the kid. I don't suppose you even looked at one of their identifications before you buried his parents? That would speed this up if I had a name to work with."

"I'm afraid not. We were too preoccupied with burying them and getting through the night in one piece."

Her hands stopped typing long enough for her to swivel and look at Daniel. "You at least got a hair color? Anything would help find this kid."

Daniel bent forward and scooped up the white dress shirt off the floor. He lifted it above his head and put it on. "Wish I had a different answer, but nope."

"You took the kid back to your safe-house, and you have no idea what he looked like?" Her voice lowered. "Were you passed out or something?" she sarcastically asked. "Well

84

what in the blue hell am I supposed to do with that? I can't find the kid with nothing to go on in a metropolis like this. I can't work miracles from nothing. I guess I'll ask your buddy. He probably paid a sliver of attention," she said before she reached into her pocket and tapped the screen with her two thumbs.

"He's probably off with his new leader getting it on. I doubt if he answers that text."

Tanya pumped her fist and tucked the phone back into her jeans pocket. "He's on his way. Wait a minute, new leader?"

"Yeah, the old man busted me down and put Liz as the new group leader. You know he can't stand Roger, and he damn sure wasn't going to give it to the newbie."

"Really? He hates that handsome stallion Roger?" she asked as she turned back to the wall of monitors. "He seems like a nice guy."

Daniel remained quiet as his left hand clenched into a fist.

"Oh relax. Jealousy doesn't suit you. Besides, if I went after him it'd strain me and Lizzie's relationship. It's not going to happen." She looked over with a wink. "It's kind of cute how jealous you can get from innocuous things though. Just don't make it a habit. It's not attractive.

11

"He had red hair, was about five years old, and was quiet? It doesn't seem like much, but if I run this through the police database, I should be able to narrow it down quite a bit," Tanya said. She extended her leg and pushed against the wall under the desk, causing her chair to lean back.

"You sure you want to be messing with the police network?" Roger asked.

"Some of us didn't skimp on our tech training in lieu of firearms. You'd know how to do this too if you'd stayed in our division instead of shacking up with that big lug over there," she said with her thumb pointing toward Daniel.

"Hey, someone has to be the tech in the field. Right?" Roger asked.

"It usually works better when your laptop's charged though," she said with a giggle.

Roger turned to his left and glared at Daniel. "I guess so," he said. He returned his attention to the monitors and tapped her shoulder with his left hand. His right hand pointed at the top middle monitor. "It looks like they're trying to run a trace. You need to get out right now."

Tanya waved her left hand to the side. "That's not a problem. They can try it all they want, but I'm covered. Even if they had been running that for the past hour, they wouldn't find my source. That's the beauty of bouncing your signal around the globe: virtual private networks, multiple layers of encryption, dynamic ip, and more than a couple proxies along with more protection that our other viewer wouldn't understand. So relax a little, will you?"

"Seriously? I didn't know you could encrypt your connection."

"Yep, you sure can. It just requires a little know how. It's not foolproof, but it'll stop most of the blowback."

Daniel spoke up. "I can't help but notice your use of the word 'most'."

"Well, they'll still know someone was in their network. They might even be able to narrow it down to the USA, but that's about as far as they'll get. I mean, local PD isn't exactly an alphabet organization devoted to information gathering. They're more than likely a bunch of folks who don't even know how to competently work a pc." A beep interrupted Tanya's explanation. "Looks like we need the administrator's password."

"I assume you have a plan for this?" Roger asked. He leaned forward against the back of Tanya's chair with his gaze transfixed on the monitors.

"Watch and learn, former student of mine," she said just before she typed at a furious pace. "All you need is a specific type of program, and you can get into almost anything online."

"Want to share with the rest of the class what kind that is?" Roger asked.

"I wrote this one myself. I'll give you a thumb drive with it before you leave. It's easy to work with if you know tech even a little. Just plug and play essentially. You just have to tell the program what text field to hook into and you're set."

All three stared at the monitor as a window came up. The password field showed various characters all cycling at an incredible pace. Tanya leaned back. "It's not always the fastest, but it'll get the job done eventually. It's fastest with short passwords, but it can work with any if you have the patience. It's better than the alternative if you want to remain undetected."

Daniel spoke up, causing the two at the computers to turn to him. "What alternative might that be?"

"I think she's talking about a bypass," Roger said.

"Yep, you can get in quick that way, but it's obvious as day someone's broken in. Not too secure that way either. You're lucky if you get away clean most of the time if someone's watching their security."

"Right," Daniel said. "I hope you're taking notes, buddy, because I can't understand a word of this."

"I'm learning as much as I can," Roger said as he returned his attention to the screens in front of him.

"You'd get more done if you didn't insist on playing that one online game," Tanya said. She leaned her head back and looked up at Roger. "How many hours have you wasted on that?"

Roger bit his bottom lip. "A guy has to have a hobby. Video games are a pretty mild one in my opinion." His right hand lowered and flicked the back of Tanya's head. "Besides, someone has been playing that longer than I have. If I recall correctly, you were the one who dragged me into it and got me addicted."

"My guild needed a healer for raids," she said with a smile before angling her head down.

"Whatever the hell that means," Daniel muttered.

"Oh, it looks like we have a hit," Tanya interrupted.

"That's him," Roger said. "That's the kid!" he said as he pointed at the monitor.

A sudden thunking followed by a creaking sound drew everyone's attention to the doorway. Elizabeth scanned the room left to right before entering and closing the door behind her. "What's everyone doing in here this late?" she asked.

Roger turned to her with a small smile. "We're looking to solve our little problem from this morning, Liz," Roger said.

Elizabeth came up behind Roger. Her hand reached out to his neck and pinched him.

"Ah God!" he exclaimed. His right hand reached up and covered the back of his neck. "What was that for?" Roger asked.

"What problem?"

Daniel chuckled. "No use playing dumb. She already knows."

"Yep, and you should thank your brother. Without him telling me, you all would have no clue where to start looking. The kid's name is Terry Cooper."

Elizabeth turned her head to her left and glared at her brother. "So much for keeping it in house. Why not just tell everyone?"

"You know I won't tell anyone else," Tanya said. Her eyes were focused on the screen in front of her. "Now if you're done blaming each other, I have a place you can go look. According to this, he goes to a local school about twenty minutes from here."

Roger looked down at Tanya. "You really think a kid would go to school after last night?"

Tanya shrugged as she brought her arms up behind her head. "Dunno, but it's more than you had to go on before."

"Wait a minute," Daniel interrupted. "Police database has that kind of info on the kid? I thought only people with records were in there? When the hell did a person's profile contain where they went to school?"

Tanya answered. "Don't you pay attention to congress at all? They passed that some two years ago. Some bullshit about gathering information increases security nonsense. Every person in every city is now in police databases. Makes it real convenient for those of us with the know how to access it."

Elizabeth let loose an affirmative grunt. "They just want to know where us peons are, from the moment we're old enough to get into school. It doesn't help anyone."

Roger stood up and arched his back. He patted Elizabeth's upper back. "Except us this time."

"Yeah, it helps criminals more than the officials who made it. Ain't that the way the law always works now?" Elizabeth asked with a large grin.

"You'd think they're made out of corrupt politicians or something," Tanya added with a quiet giggle.

A knock interrupted the jovial atmosphere. A deep voice came. "There's a doctor here claiming he's here to see Miss Tanya."

Tanya called out, "Let him in." She turned the swivel chair around. "Alright now you two," she pointed at Roger and Elizabeth, "time for you to make yourselves scarce for a little while. We've got to patch up this guy over here now. You'd just get in the way."

"Of course," Roger said. "I can tell when I'm not wanted." He grabbed Elizabeth's hand and tugged. "We don't want to get in their way, dear."

"It won't be too romantic with a doctor in the room, but sure." She guided Roger's hand to her hips and walked side by side with Roger toward the door. "Have fun you two lovebirds," she said as they left the room with a loud slam.

Hours later...

"I heard you all had an eventful night yesterday." The woman set down a cup on the nearby table. "It's the talk of the family."

Elizabeth leaned forward and snatched the cup's handle before waving her other hand in a dismissive manner. "Let them talk, Ana. It's not like it really matters. How're you and Michelle doing? Judging by that getup, I can guess. What is that - a French maid's outfit?"

Ana looked left and right before leaning in. "This? Yeah. When it's our turn to clean up he makes us wear it." She reached up and pointed at the white head piece. "This itches like a son of a bitch. You know how it is. All that old pig trusts us girls to do is cook, clean, and whatever other mundane thing he needs done. I got lucky. I'm just on maid duty tonight, cleaning up after the boys. Michelle's stuck on kitchen detail, probably doing dishes or cleaning the floor as we speak. You're lucky you're his daughter. If he's not ordering us to do something, he's pinching our asses or some such crap."

Elizabeth's eyes softened. She brought the cup up and took a sip. "I'm sorry. I've been trying to get Daddy to transfer you to our group, but he won't budge. After last night I'll be lucky to stay where I'm at."

"I know you're doing everything you can for us, and we girls appreciate it." She straightened up and looked to her right toward the main room. "Rumor has it the boss isn't too thrilled with your little boy toy over there. Heard he got tore up earlier."

Elizabeth followed her gaze to see Roger surrounded by men talking and laughing. "First, he's not a boy toy; and second, we all got it bad earlier. The worst part is it wasn't even his fault."

"When does that ever matter with your father?" she said with a thin smile. "You're actually serious about him? Color me surprised. I never thought I'd see the day you'd be this taken with a guy."

"You better believe it, sister." Her voice grew soft. "He's a good man. There's not too many around here, but you can trust him as much as you trust me."

Ana sat down on the couch next to Elizabeth. "I'll remember that. Say, I heard a rumor that you're the leader of your group now. It's not all bad."

Elizabeth brought a hand to her mouth to stifle a giggle. "Yeah, it's the whole one bright patch of last night. If I play my cards right it might propel me upward, and that can only benefit us girls."

Ana lowered her hands and smoothed out her skirt. "I wish you all the best. The sooner you get to choose your crew, the sooner we're out of this hell."

"Hey, you over there!" a male voice called out. "Get your tight ass to work."

The two women looked over their shoulders to see Bernard stomping down the stairs. "Get me a coffee, will you?" He approached the men resting. "It'll be a long night, won't it boys?"

A round of "Yes sir" came from the group of men as Bernard passed them.

Ana immediately stood up and bowed. "Right away, sir," she said before running off in the direction of the kitchen.

Elizabeth stared at Roger until he caught her gaze. She raised her right hand up and motioned him over. He said one last thing to the group he was in before standing up and making his way over.

"What's up? Everything okay with your friend?" he asked as he sat down close to her.

"You saw her, did you?"

"Well, she was near you. Kind of hard to miss really."

She leaned over and rested her head on his shoulder. "You are too damned corny. You know that?"

"I say and do what comes naturally. You know that as well as I do."

The two sat there with contented smiles on their faces for a moment, until a frown graced Roger's features. "Not to spoil this moment, but the boys over there let me know the general consensus around here."

"I'm guessing it's not good then."

"It's about fifty-fifty. They'll stand behind us on the Irish. The real controversial topic was you, dear."

She leaned her head up. "Me? Do tell."

Roger looked away and licked his lips.

"God, just say it already."

"They don't approve of you being promoted is all. The guys know your brother and his reputation. He's something of a legend around here after all. I guess they're worried you'll be too soft."

Elizabeth straightened up and turned around on the couch to see the group sneaking glances at them. She raised her right hand and presented them with a single finger. She turned around with a huff. "God, it's like high school all over again."

"Yeah, except everyone's packing heat now." Daniel's voice came from behind them.

The two followed the voice to see Daniel and Tanya approaching. "You two have a fun rest while I was getting cut up?" he asked as they sat down across from them on the opposite couch. "Doc said it was mostly superficial. I should be good to go - might be a little pain though. I'll be fine."

"Just talking office politics is all," Roger said. "Are we finally ready to head out and get to work?"

"Yep, and we've got a new addition as well." He gestured behind him with his thumb toward Tanya.

"Turns out the boss doesn't trust you too much after last night, Mr. Johnson," Tanya said with a smirk.

"Welcome to the team," Roger said. He extended his right hand across the table. She took it and shook his hand. "Guess that means I'll be focusing more on being boots on the ground?"

Elizabeth elbowed his side. "You don't wear boots though."

Roger looked at his girlfriend with a straight face. "Really?"

Tanya burst into giggles. "Oh, this is going to be so much fun. I hardly ever get to go out."

Daniel stood up with a groan. "Let's get going then. We've got a lot of work to do and little time to do it."

Elizabeth raised up and moved in front of her brother. She spoke with authority. "Brother, that's not your decision anymore you know," Elizabeth said with the right side of her mouth angling up into a grin. The two locked eyes and stared each other down.

Hushed whispers could be heard from the nearby group.

"Guys," Roger started, "you may want to take this pissing contest outside, unless we want more rumors floating around."

"Humph," Daniel grunted. "It's fine. She's the boss now, buddy. Her word is law."

Elizabeth moved to the side. "Good to hear. Let's go."

Roger stood up and tapped Elizabeth's shoulder. "What was the point of that?"

"Have to give them a show."

12

"Do you two want to tell me what that was all about before we left?" Roger spoke up in the dark cabin.

"Politics," Daniel answered without looking back from the front seat.

"What? That's all the explanation I'm getting?"

"Think about it, man. If I gave up my command without a whimper, the boys would have a field day. If I made a huge deal and refused, I'd be considered a whiny bitch who doesn't follow orders."

"Whereas, if he mentions it and gives a mean face but ultimately gives in, he saves pride without looking weak. You really need to learn office politics. Besides, it also reinforced his sister's public resolve. I mean, she stood up to Grave Digger Morris and kind of won," Tanya spoke up from beside him. The pale light from her laptop illuminated her face as she spoke.

"Right," Roger agreed. He looked to his other side toward Elizabeth. "So now that we're on the move again, what's the plan, boss?"

"We're going to find that kid. Isn't that obvious?" Elizabeth asked. She had her head propped on her right hand staring out the window into the dark cityscape.

"Yeah, we'll keep him quiet is all," Daniel said.

"Oh, so what? We just roll up on the kid, kidnap him, and cut out his tongue? No fuss?"

Daniel brought a hand up and tapped his chin. "That is a good idea." He paused for a moment before responding. "Well, I mean, I guess we could talk to him first and see what he plans on doing."

"Jesus Christ, you're a savage."

"Hey, I said talk to him first didn't I?"

"Take a right on the next street," Tanya ordered.

Axel flicked a lever down, causing a constant clicking sound. "Got it," he said as the vehicle slowed.

"I feel like I'm out of the loop here. What's going on now?" Roger asked.

"Don't worry. I've got a plan," Tanya said. "I just booked a room at the motel near the school the kid goes to. If we're lucky, we'll see him. I only booked it for two, so our leader gets to decide who will go I guess." She leaned forward and reached across Roger's lap before tapping Elizabeth's arm.

Elizabeth's eyes widened as she jumped. "Oh, sorry. I was just thinking. What am I deciding again?"

"Some leader," Daniel scoffed from the front.

"Ignore that idiot," Tanya said. "He's just tired and hurting. He needs to man up already. You need to decide who will keep a lookout for the kid in the room I booked."

Daniel turned toward the back seat and glared.

Elizabeth looked around the car for a full minute before speaking. "Alright, I got it. You'll be going." Her left hand wandered over and grabbed Roger's knee. "You'll be going with Axel. You think you two can handle it?"

"Of course. You can count on us," Roger answered with a grin.

"Yes, ma'am. If the kid goes near it, we'll get him," Axel agreed, never taking his eyes off the road.

Elizabeth laughed out loud. "Good. That's what I like to hear, boys. Now if you do find him, I want you two to bring him back to me. You got it? Good. The rest of us will get a head start on our new job. It's about time for collections after all."

The two men replied in unison. "Understood."

Inside the motel room overlooking the school...

"I'll take first watch. Get some rest," Roger said. He grabbed the blinds and moved them to the side. He grabbed a chair from the nearby table, dragged it over to the window, and sat down.

Axel loosened his blue tie and removed his suit jacket, tossing it on the foot of the bed beside his partner's before sitting down "To be fair, sir, I doubt the kid's going to be going there at one in the morning."

"You're probably right, but you're overlooking one important thing, newbie," Roger said. He extended his left dress pant clad leg and pushed against the wall underneath the window. He leaned back as he spoke. "You want to be the one to tell the boss we weren't looking the whole time? That's a fast track to pissing her off, man. Trust me, you don't want that."

"Can I speak candidly, sir?" Axel asked. He laid down on the lone bed and looked over to the window.

"One thing you'll learn, I'm a lot more easygoing than the twins. Go for it."

"The past couple of days have been a right proper mess, haven't they?"

Roger's head angled back as he laughed. "You won't get any arguments from me. It all started with the deal going bad; and here we are looking for a loose end, while our betters are out collecting without us. I just hope the inevitable retaliation doesn't happen while we're sitting here."

"You think they'll strike back soon?"

"I would if I were them. Wait a minute. Come over here for a second." Roger raised his hand and used his index finger to beckon his partner over. "See that?" He pointed out the window toward a parked van near the school. "That is a load of trouble, my boy."

"Who is that?" Axel asked as he made his way over to the window. He leaned forward and squinted his eyes. "It's too dark. How do you know they're trouble?"

Roger stood up from the seat, causing the chair to tumble over backwards. His hands snaked their way up and pulled out his two revolvers from their shoulder holsters. "Well, I've got to say it's probably because I can see them loading machine pistols in the front seat. Get your phone out and call the group now," he ordered.

"That's some good eyesight you have there." Axel reached into his pants pocket and pulled out a cell phone. He tapped a button and brought it to his ear. "We've got company here. We need backup now."

"What?" Daniel's voice asked. "Who are they?"

Axel reached behind him with his free hand, grabbed his pistol, and readied it at his side. The two men stood on either side of the window. "We don't know. It could just be gang bangers?"

Roger looked over at the man with an exasperated look and remained silent. Two clicks resounded in the otherwise quiet apartment, signaling the hammers were cocked and ready.

"Okay, just trying to be optimistic here."

"You need to work on your definition of optimism." Roger leaned forward and peeked out the window. "Shit, here they come. What the hell are they doing here?"

"Okay, kid, we're on our way. Do what Roger says and you may live to see another sunrise," Daniel said before a sudden click ended the conversation. Axel put the phone back into his pocket before turning to Roger. "They're on their way."

The sound of an engine became more prominent. Light poured into the window, causing both men to shield their eyes.

"They're going to try to blind us with their brights. I don't suppose we have a plan?" Roger asked. "You are the one with military experience after all." He looked beside him to see Axel standing still, staring at the carpet beneath them.

Roger stomped hard. "Come on, man! Stay with me here. I can't have you going into la la land."

Axel awoke from his stupor with a jump. "Yeah, I'm here." He peeked through the window as the rumble of the engine cut out. "Sounds like they're about ready to start. I recommend we get behind the beds for cover. It'd be better than this flimsy wall. Right?"

"Fuck if I know. Probably," Roger said. He broke into a run, leaped onto, and slid over the bed before turning around, raising his arms, and pointing his revolvers toward the door. "Well, come on then, Mr. Tactician. Don't get your ass shot off."

Axel followed suit and got near the opposite end of the bed. As soon as the maneuver was finished, a deafening hail of gunfire erupted. Splintered wood blasted out from the cheap motel door, along with tiny shards of glass raining down.

"Get down!" Roger yelled. He curled up and covered his ears.

Axel lowered himself down to the floor and laid on his stomach.

The sounds of automatic gunfire ceased ten seconds into the assault. Faint clicking sounds met their ears.

"They're reloading, kid. Now's the time. Aim for the door, or what's left of it." Roger got into a kneeling position and placed his elbows onto the bed. His revolvers pointed at the entrance, his hands steady.

Multiple voices could be heard outside the mangled door. A shaky voice asked, "Did we get them?"

A different, steadier voice answered. "I don't know. We should go make sure, right?"

"You first. I ain't going in there."

The steady voice fired back. "You wuss. Fine, let's go. They're probably already dead anyway, and we can't stay here all night. The cops are probably already on the way."

"Get ready, Axel buddy," Roger whispered to his side. "Here they come. Ready up."

A thunderous boom shattered the relative silence of the bullet ridden room. A leg protruded through the door-frame. A tall figure stepped through with a rifle at the ready.

A series of deafening shots rang out. The figure fell backwards and landed on his back, unmoving.

"Jesus Christ!" An obviously Irish voice called out. "You bastards!"

"Ya fucking mick pricks. Come in here, and we'll take care of the rest of you," Roger called out.

A confident, altogether different voice replied. "Hold steady, lads. It's obvious these plonkers are about as thick as two short planks." A few assorted laughs could be heard from outside.

"What's that mean?" Axel whispered to Roger.

Roger gave him a sideways glance and shook his head. He nodded toward the door. "I'll watch the window. You cover the doorway," he whispered.

"You lads seriously screwed it last night. Do you know that? I even heard your crew had yourselves a change in leadership. Old Grave Digger is no longer in charge I hear. Rumor is it's the darling little sister. That's so progressive. It's all over the street. I hear your new leader's no show pony, but she'd do for a ride around the house."

"Better looking than the sheep you shagged last night, Micky."

"Ah now, that's just a dirty stereotype. Typical Americans. No class at all I tell ya."

Roger spotted a shadowy silhouette on the right side of the illuminated, punctured window. He inhaled and squeezed the trigger in his right hand. The glass splintered further with the sudden blast. The shadow outside disappeared below with an audible thud.

"They got Michael!"

"You fuckers got my nephew! I swear I'll kill the whole lot of you!" The same voice called out, this time more shaken. "Come on boys, let's sort them out."

"Go time," Roger muttered

The distant howl of sirens was becoming louder now.

"Shit!" the voice called out. "Alright boys, we've got to get out of here now." A lone finger emerged from the left side of the door frame. "This isn't over yet."

A shot came from Roger's right. The digit disappeared as a shrill yell replaced it. "Mother of Christ! As God is my witness, I'll end all of you. Mark my words."

A chorus of footsteps met their ears, along with numerous slams. The sound of an engine roared to life. A high pitched squealing came, along with the smell of burning rubber that quickly faded.

Roger got to his feet. He remained low to the ground as he moved around the bed, grabbing the two jackets as he went toward the doorway. He kept his weapons at the ready as he checked outside. He exhaled and holstered his weapons before donning his formal suit jacket. He gave a tug at his apparel, securing it in place. He looked back into the room. "Come on, buddy. We've got to get out of here. Now!" He handed over Axel's jacket. "Make sure to cover your face from the traffic cameras the same as we did when we entered."

Axel nodded and moved to follow Roger. He reached behind him and placed the gun down his belt line. Once their weapons were no longer in view, they hopped over the dead body and growing pool of blood beneath it in front of the doorway. They walked out into the dim parking lot and down the concrete side-walk with a hand to their face, obscuring their identity from the lone camera. Roger looked to his side. "To answer your earlier question my friend, I don't speak much Irish slang, but I'm pretty sure they called us idiots."

"What about the jab at our new leader?"

Roger's face darkened. His upper lip raised, baring his

teeth. He replied in a low, dangerous growl. "Use your imagination. It wasn't flattering."

A ringing interrupted their conversation. "That's me," Roger said. The previous anger had disappeared from his voice. He pulled out his phone and answered it. "Yes?"

Daniel's voice came. "You're still breathing I hear. That's good. We're nearly there. Are you guys okay over there?"

Roger looked over at Axel. "You hit?"

Axel shook his head.

"We're whole. Can't say the same for the Irish hit squad they sent. One of them is in deep shit now, because of our newest addition I'm proud to say."

"Can't wait to hear that story. We're on our way to pick you up now."

"Using my phone signal, huh? I forgot you had another techie there. Good. It makes things simpler. We'll see you in a little bit," he said as he hung up.

"What did I do, sir?" Axel asked.

Roger smiled. His right hand reached out and gave a playful swat to Axel's shoulder. He brought his middle finger out for a moment. "Maybe you didn't notice, but when we exited the room that finger was still on the ground. The cops are going to love that DNA evidence. We're in the clear since we left none. Only thing they got on us was the expended cartridges. Since we make our own ammo, it's pointless. They never saw our faces, and the fake names Tanya used should keep us out of it."

An all too familiar black van turned onto the street in front of them.

Roger raised his arm and beckoned them over. "Looks like our ride's here."

13

"How many pot lickers were there?" Daniel asked. He reached forward and twisted a dial. Cold air blew into the cabin.

"We couldn't see how many," Roger said. "They never got a step in the door, and by the time we got outside they had dragged their fallen away except for one body. There had to be at least four or five, if I had to guess. What do you think, Axel?"

"We know there were at least three. There was someone named Michael that we blew away, someone's nephew, that leader guy, and some scared recruit wasn't it? So, if they managed to drag them away, I'd guess around six or seven."

"That sounds about right," Roger agreed. He turned to his left to look at Elizabeth. Her eyebrow was twitching, and her mouth was contorted into a nasty snarl.

"Those fucking clovers are in for it now," she growled.

Tanya interrupted with a loud click of her keyboard. "Not to interrupt this scholarly debate of racial slurs, but I have the answer here. All I had to do was look at the traffic cameras. It looks like there were five of them. It's blurry, but

I can make out a little. There was the getaway driver, but he stayed in the van the whole time. I never got a good look at his mug. I did however get a picture of the four shock troops here, and it's not good news, guys. If you heard right and Michael was there, then the one who had his finger blown off was probably Murtagh. They're a notorious uncle and nephew team that always get the job done with maximum casualties. I never thought we'd be mixed up with the infamous O'Connels."

"Is that name supposed to mean something to me?" Elizabeth asked.

"It should Lizzy, yes," Tanya answered. "They are real heavy hitters in the Irish underground. If they're involved, then their boss sanctioned the hit. He only sends Murtagh and Michael when someone absolutely needs to die. Also, if you add that to the fact that you killed Murtagh's nephew, we've made a hell of an enemy tonight."

Roger craned his neck to his left to look at Tanya. "There is good news though. The DNA left over should keep Murtagh busy, shouldn't it? I mean, he's going to have to get out of the states. He can't chance that evidence going to a lab and having them start a manhunt. He'd move to the top of law enforcement's radar, wouldn't he?" Roger asked.

"That will take a few weeks, my friend. DNA testing is usually quite slow, unlike in those television shows," Tanya said. "In that time, he can easily make another attempt before getting himself smuggled out of the country."

"Let him try," Daniel said. "Next time I'll be there myself, and we'll see how far he gets."

"Before you go off on a rampage, we need to report this to Father," Elizabeth said.

Daniel turned around in his seat to look at his sister. "Which will do what exactly? He'll just send an extra squad to accompany us. It'll also paint you as a coward of a leader who can't take care of business."

"Danny, tone it down." Tanya glared toward the front passenger seat.

Daniel rolled his eyes and turned to face forward again.

"It's okay," Elizabeth said. She reached across Roger's lap and laid a gentle hand on Tanya's forearm. "He may be wording it like an ass, but I'm pretty sure he's trying to look out for me." She withdrew her arm and wrapped it around Roger's nearby arm. "He's right though. We've got to answer back, or I look weak. This is our turf after all."

"We won't have that," Roger said. "So, anyone know any Irish businesses nearby?"

Tanya sighed. "Please tell me we're not going to do what I think we are?"

Daniel looked to his left over his shoulder. "You're damned right we are, sweetheart. Everyone loaded?"

Roger reached into his coat, removed a lone revolver, and flicked open the cylinder, dumping the spent casings onto the cabin floor. "Give me a minute. I'm empty." He dug his hand into his pants pocket and pulled out several cartridges before loading them one by one, then repeated the process with the other revolver. "I'm done and ready to rock."

The sound of metal shuffling accompanied Daniel's voice. "Good man. Now where are we going?"

———

Thirty minutes later...

"You all know this is a terrible idea, right?" Tanya asked the quiet cabin. "I mean, what's this going to accomplish except a lot of senseless death? What's hitting one of their front companies going to accomplish? I mean, we're in hell's kitchen. This has historically always been the Irish's turf. They're not going to take this lightly."

Daniel cocked his handgun. "I bet not, but I don't take it lightly when they try to kill my friends. They're going to learn that today the hard way. Get it?"

Elizabeth reached down the front of her pants, removed her revolver, and checked the cylinder. "What we're doing is sending a message. They hit us, we hit back harder. It's the way of things in the concrete jungle. If not, we look weak."

"If we don't, they'll keep hitting us," Roger said. "Why wouldn't they if there's no retaliation? Think of it as a preemptive defense."

"Whatever you all have to tell yourselves to sleep at night," Tanya said in a quiet voice. She typed before she shook her head. "Alright, fine. So, let's go over the plan one last time. There is no room for errors here if this surveillance feed is to be believed." She flipped the laptop so the screen faced the rest of the occupants. "Okay, so this is the main reason we're going in there." She reached above the screen and pointed to the top right video playing. "As you can see, this is where all their money is counted. It's heavily guarded, even in the middle of the night."

"Wonder how much is in there," Axel said. He snapped out of his reverie and looked to his comrades to see them staring at him with narrowed eyes. Axel redirected his attention to the screen and refused to speak further.

Tanya cleared her throat. "Anyway, it's on the second floor. From what I can see, there are two men counting the money in there, along with two overseers that function as guards." She lowered her arm and pointed to the window below it. "First we have to get there, and, if this is right, we have multiple men patrolling the downstairs hallways. So, this is likely to get down and dirty before it's all said and done."

"You know just what to say to get a man revved up," Daniel said with a smirk.

"Ignoring the inappropriately timed insinuation, you should probably split into two groups. One group will go in the back, and the other through the side entrance. The team that goes in the back has the enviable job of taking care of the guards, since the side entrance goes into a closed off room that leads into the middle of the floor. So who's going where?" she asked.

"I'm going in the back," Daniel said with a raised right hand. He pointed to Roger. "You're with me. We'll take care of it."

"What makes you think I'm sending him in with you?" Elizabeth asked.

"I'd say because we have the most experience in room to room combat. You want to send the new guy in?"

"To be fair, Axel is a crack shot from what I saw," Roger interrupted.

Daniel reached out and backhanded Roger's knee before continuing. "Anyway, come on Liz, do the smart play. Think of it this way. You send us in, and you get the glory of getting the big payday."

"Yeah, but what exactly is the upside for us?" Roger asked. He looked beside him to see Elizabeth with a fist to her chin. She was looking down at the floor.

"You do make a good point." She turned to her left, wrapped her arms around Roger's forearm, and leaned close. She brought her lips up to his ears and whispered. "What do you think?"

Roger's back straightened up. He looked left and right to

find everyone staring at him. He exhaled and shook his head. "Yeah. I can do it."

Elizabeth released him and pumped her fist. "Yay! I guess that's the plan."

"Saddle up, boys and girls. It's about to go down," Daniel said.

14

Daniel and Roger stood with their backs to the freezing bricks with the door between them. They stood with their weapons drawn as they breathed out clouds. Roger turned toward his friend. "Why the hell did you volunteer me for this?"

"I didn't want the inexperienced among us to get themselves killed. They may be able to aim, but there's a huge difference from accurate shooting and being good in a firefight."

"Oh, so you just volunteer my ass to get shot at? Did I ever mention what a great friend you are?"

"Your girlfriend wanted you to do it too, didn't she? Besides, you didn't want her getting shot at did you?"

"She never said that." Roger leaned his neck back until it rested on the bricks. He stared at the stars above. "Wait, did she?" He lowered his gaze back to the man beside him. His arm shot out and backhanded Daniel across the chest. "You jackass, don't make this about her."

Tanya's voice came into their ears. "Yeah, he's a dick, but let's focus guys. As soon as you open that door be prepared for anything. There's no camera in that hallway, so I'm blind. For all I know, they're right on the other side."

"Got it," Daniel said with a finger in his ear. He removed it and moved in front of the door. "Ready?" he asked.

"Ready as I'll ever be. Go for it," Roger said with his weapon at the ready.

Daniel leaned back, lifted his right leg, and propelled it forward with a loud crack. The door remained blocking their way, however. Daniel's hands balled into fists, and a solitary tear rolled down his cheek.

Roger rolled his eyes and reached for the door knob. He twisted and heard a click. His left hand gestured for Daniel to go first. "Helps to see if it's unlocked first so you don't screw your leg up, Mr. Door Kicker," he whispered.

Feminine muffled laughter met their ears.

"Don't you say a word," Daniel muttered. He reached forward and laid his left palm on the now open door. "Let's go," he said as he pushed it open with a high-pitched creak. His right hand had his 9mm pointed forward and to the right. "You cover the left," he said.

"Understood," Roger said. He angled both his revolvers to comply.

Daniel was the first to speak once they were through the door. "No one's here. Let's get moving." He inched forward using both arms to steady his weapon.

Roger followed behind and covered his friend's blind spots as they moved forward into the taupe colored hallways. Their footsteps clacked on the tiles beneath them. "I don't see anyone so far," he said with his voice barely above a whisper.

"Good. Keep going forward and, according to these floor plans, you should reach the side entrance so you can let Lizzy and the new guy in."

"Nope," Daniel interrupted. "We're going for the guards first."

"That's not the plan, Danny," Tanya's firm voice reminded.

"Plans evolve, sweetheart. I'm not leaving a wandering patrol that'll bite us in our asses later." He stopped in his tracks and raised his right fist. "Hold on. Did you hear that?"

"I hear voices," Roger said. "Where are they coming from?"

Daniel pointed to a solid, wooden door on their right. "I'm pretty sure they're in there. You take the right side," he said as he ducked down and moved to the left side of the door.

Roger got into position and whispered. "Can you see if there are guards in a room labeled 'break room'?"

Tanya's voice buzzed to life. "I think so. Why? Oh, you two are not going to do what I think you are, are you? They're not a threat!" she yelled.

"Yep," Daniel answered. "Ready, buddy?"

Roger's thumbs reached up and pulled back the two hammers with a click. "I am now. Let's do this."

Daniel reached for the doorknob with a wince. His other hand reached up to his injury before nodding to his partner. He turned the knob and pushed the door open. He ducked back behind cover as Roger moved in front of the door and fired into the cramped room as fast as he could manage. Horrifying screams echoed throughout the hallway, along with the cacophony of gunshots, until it ended abruptly. An eerie silence filled the void once the last shot was fired. A river of blood flowed out of the doorway.

Roger ducked back behind cover as his weapons clicked. He began the arduous process of reloading by hand as Daniel peaked around the corner. "They're finished."

"Oh, dear sweet Lord. There's blood all over the place," Tanya's voice quivered. "Was that really necessary? I mean, couldn't you have just locked the door or something?"

"Enough already," Daniel snapped. "We'll discuss this afterwards. For now, we need to focus." His voice grew softer. "Alright?"

Tanya huffed. "Fine. You should be clear now, at least until you all get upstairs, so go open the side door for Liz and Axel. They're waiting on you as we speak."

Roger flicked the second revolver shut. "I'm ready. Do you need me to lead? That shoulder of yours looks to be slowing you down."

"My shoulder is fine. Focus on your own business."

"Fine then, Mr. Snippy. Let's go."

The two men walked side by side with their weapons at the ready. Daniel turned to Roger and gave a playful punch to his shoulder with the butt of his 9mm. "You know what would happen if anyone else said that to me."

"Yeah, but what are you going to do? Kill your best friend? Liz would kill you, and we both know it."

Daniel guffawed. "She'd try no doubt, but she'd fail."

"You never know with that pothole in your shoulder. She might have a shot."

"How in the hell are you two joking around right now?" Tanya asked into their ears. "You just slaughtered a room full of unsuspecting people!" She sighed. "Take a left, and it's the first door on your right."

They came up on the turn. Roger placed his back to the corner and peeked around. He turned to his right and whispered. "What the hell? There's another one here. He's visibly armed, looks to be a semi-automatic, and he's coming this way."

"Let me handle this one," Daniel said. He pulled back

the slide of his pistol and got into a ready position, facing ahead. He strafed to his right and fired as soon as he cleared the corner. A loud thump followed four shots.

"Guys," Tanya's voice reached their ears. "You've got trouble coming. They heard your little commotion downstairs and are on their way. Do you see the stairs down that hallway on your right past the door you're looking for? They're coming down it, so get ready."

"When it rains..." Roger started. He flicked the hammers back.

"It fucking pours," Daniel finished with a feral grin.

The distant sound of footsteps was becoming louder. Roger knelt and brought both weapons to bare around the corner. He spoke as he faced forward. "Bet you wish you had that shotgun now."

"We make due with what we have."

"Well, I wish you had it."

———

In the side room a few minutes earlier...

"You got what we talked about the other morning done, right?" Elizabeth asked with her back to the wall. She lifted her right leg and placed her foot against the wall.

"It's taken care of," Axel said. He folded his arms in front of him, looking across the small room at her.

"Good, because Roger will not find out." She stepped forward toward the large man, reached up, grabbed his tie, and leaned in. She whispered in a low feral voice. "If he does, you'll wish you were the kid instead. Do you understand me?"

Axel gulped and backed up against the opposite wall. "Yes, ma'am."

Elizabeth backed off but kept her eyes locked with his. "Good. I'm going to give you a bit of career advice. Secrets are sacrosanct in this line of work. You keep them, or you don't last. It also helps to kiss up to the right people. That one's up to you to figure out."

A barrage of loud cracks interrupted them. Elizabeth cupped a hand around her ear and pressed it against the door. "Sounds like the party's started." She bit her bottom lip and shifted her weight back and forth.

"I'm sure they'll be fine," Axel said.

She leveled a glare at him and opened her mouth when the ruckus died down to a deafening silence. "Sounds like it's over already. They should be here soon. Remember what I told you."

Axel brought his right hand up to his face and moved his index finger across his mouth.

"Lizzie, we have a bit of a problem on our hands." Tanya's voice rang in her ears. "The boys' little battle caught the attention of the guys upstairs. They can't get to you yet."

"Son of a bitch," Elizabeth cursed. "How close are they?"

"Right out in the hallway, but that's where the Irish are coming down in a minute. You two need to sit tight until they open the door. If you bust out there now, you'll be in the crossfire."

Elizabeth clapped her hands in front of her. "Alright, time for the next lesson on when to improvise a plan."

"You have an idea?" Axel asked.

Elizabeth scoffed. "Of course. Now what I need you to do is kick the door open."

"No disrespect, but that doesn't seem all that wise."

"Do it," Elizabeth commanded in a no-nonsense voice.

"Shit," Axel muttered under his breath as he moved in front of the door. He raised his right leg and launched it forward. A shattering boom accompanied the door swinging open. He immediately took position next to the door with his pistol in his hands. "What now?"

Elizabeth raised a finger to her ear. "Hey, which direction are the Irish coming from? Tanya?"

"I think they should be coming from your left. The boys are on your right. I wouldn't go near that doorway though. It's about to pop off out there."

Elizabeth examined the storage closet they were in. She snapped her fingers and moved to pick up a nearby abandoned mug. "Catch," she said with an underhanded throw. She reached up to her ear. "Tell the boys to hold their horses. We're going to give them a little distraction." Her eyebrows raised. "What are you waiting on? Get to the door and throw that as far down the hallway as you can."

"I got it," he said. He moved to the door and knelt with his back to it. He looked to his right and saw Roger and Daniel both locked and loaded, aiming his way. He transferred the cup to his left hand and hurled it around the corner to the left. The loud sound of glass breaking stopped the approaching sound of footsteps.

An unfamiliar but distinctive Irish voice could be heard. "What was that? Sounded like glass. They're on the right, boys." The footsteps resumed until he could hear them directly behind him.

Axel looked up to see Roger tilting his head toward the room holding Elizabeth. He nodded and inched back into the room. He sighed once he was safely inside the room. He turned to Elizabeth to see her with crossed arms and a scowl on her face. "What are you doing? Get out there."

"They told me to go back in here tho-" He was interrupted as a booming hail of gunfire erupted. The door he was just behind sprouted holes. Piercing screams met their ears.

"Where the fuck are they? Ah, I'm hit! Get ba-" the voice went silent.

An unsettling silence came down but was soon replaced by the telltale clicking of reloading.

"You can come out now," Roger's voice called out.

Elizabeth pointed out the door. "You first."

Axel poked his head out the door. He looked down the hallway to see four bodies in various positions on the floor and an ever-spreading pool of red beneath them. He felt a hand on his back that pushed him forward, causing him to stumble into the middle of the hallway.

"It's about time you got here," Elizabeth said as she walked toward the two men. "What took you two so long anyway?"

"We got hung up. Sorry about that," Daniel said. He pulled the slide back and glared at Axel. "What the hell was that? You two were supposed to stay in there. You think this is a game, just jumping into the middle of a soon to be kill zone?"

Roger's right hand reached up and tapped Daniel's shoulder.

Daniel shrugged off the contact and marched up to Axel. He jabbed a finger into his chest and leaned in close. "You trying to get yourself killed, kid? If so, good job. That's how you do it. Follow the plan next time, chucklehead." He stepped around him but pushed forward with his good shoulder, causing Axel to take a step back.

Axel looked down at his shoes until he saw another pair in front of him. He looked up to see Roger shaking his head. He patted him on the shoulder. "That just means he likes you. Think of it this way, he doesn't want you dead. Now let's go. I don't want yelled at for being late."

"Hurry the hell up, people. We're on a time limit here," Daniel said from further down the hall.

"Too late."

15

"Let's grab as much as we can and get out of here. The cops are no doubt on their way by now," Daniel said with an armful of filled bags. "I've got all I can carry. I'll head back to the van. I expect you all to be right behind me." He pushed past everyone and disappeared out the door.

Roger grabbed another bag and piled it on the three already cradled in his arms. "Come on. He's right. We made a lot of noise." His eyes lingered on the back of Elizabeth.

She stood at the table with a bag in either hand, staring into the wooden grain.

Roger turned to his side and bumped her with his hip. "Come on, boss. We need to go unless we want to get pinched." He saw Axel to his left with a veritable mountain of bags in his arms as he made his way to the door.

"Hey, if you can carry all those and see where you're going that's great, man. If not, you may want to drop a couple."

"Don't worry, I've got it," Axel replied. His head poked around the side as he moved forward.

Elizabeth let loose a loud exhale as she turned around.

She marched over to the man and grabbed a few bags. "Know your limits, big guy. Now let's scoot. We're already pushing it as it is."

The small group made their way out of the building. They were descending the stairs when Roger spoke up. "I never got a chance to ask, but what happened earlier when me and Axel here got visited at that motel? Everything go okay?"

Elizabeth continued facing forward with an even expression. "It was a normal collection run. Well, as normal as it can be with my brother at the front. You know how it goes with him. A little blackmail, graft, and threats of violence solves almost every problem in that department. We did have to cut it a little short, but we got the money. Don't fret. We won't have to worry about Daddy."

"Good. That's one less thing we have to worry about at least." They reached the bottom of the staircase and could now see the still open exit. "Hey, how do you guys feel about a movie night tonight?"

"Oh God, seriously? You've been hanging out with my brother too much I'm telling you."

"Movie night?" Axel asked.

"It's a bit of a habit for those two. After a successful job they've started unwinding by watching a movie at the safe house." She turned to Roger. "I thought you two would have grown out of that by now."

"Nope. You never outgrow a cozy night in with popcorn and a good movie."

"Hmph," Elizabeth grunted with a small smile. "Boys will be boys I guess."

"Damned straight." Daniel's voice entered their ears.

"You can hear us?"

"Tanya showed me how this stuff works. You guys do

know she can hear everything we've been saying, right? She's a pro at this tech stuff."

Elizabeth's face paled. "She what?"

Tanya's subdued voice came into her ear. "I heard everything, Liz. We need to talk later."

The group exited the building to see Daniel standing next to their vehicle, holding the back door open. His right hand beckoned them closer before he circled around the front of the van, opened the front passenger door, and climbed in.

Daniel spoke from the front seat as they approached the van. "Just toss that stuff in the back and let's get going. Some do gooder has to have called the cops by now with all that noise we made."

"Unnecessary noise I might add," Tanya added in a flat tone. A bag landed on her foot, causing her leg to jump up. "Oh, come on, at least don't hit me with them," she whined.

A muffled snicker came from the front seat. "Relax. It's over now, and we're on our way home."

"I'm not going to be relaxing any time soon. You guys ignited the war the other night, and now we've stoked the flames. Who knows how many teams they'll send after us with all the bodies dropped tonight? That's not even mentioning your little witness problem that's still unsolved. Are you guys even thinking about that?"

Roger brought a hand up to his forehead. "Oh yeah, with all the excitement I kind of forgot. Should we even have the movie night? I mean, we really need to find that kid."

Daniel kept his face forward as Axel entered the driver's seat and slammed the door shut. The hum of the engine made itself known as the vehicle pulled out onto the street. "The last time we went looking for the kid, you two ended up dodging bullets and meeting the infamous

Irish Reaper. I'd rather not have a repeat of that. If we're going to look, we're going together." He turned around and brought his elbow up to the top of the seat. "What do you think, boss? It's your call," he asked, looking directly at his sister.

Elizabeth locked eyes with her brother. "He's right. It's too risky to go looking piecemeal like that."

"Riskier than leaving a witness wandering the streets who's seen our faces?" Roger asked. "I don't know if I agree there."

"She's the boss, bro. Better get used to it," Daniel said as he reached forward and slapped Roger's leg.

"That's true," Roger said. He turned his neck to look at Elizabeth. "You're sure? I don't mind going and looking again if it'll keep the lot of us out of the clink."

"Yes, Lizzie, are you sure?" Tanya asked as she glared at the other woman. "You sure you know what you're doing?"

Roger looked left to Tanya with raised brows and back to his right at Elizabeth. "Uh, everything okay here, ladies?"

Tanya's frown turned into a smile when Roger looked over. "Oh yes, for the time being. I just have a few questions for your boss."

Elizabeth leaned her head against the window. "We'll talk later. For now, we need a little rest after the past few days. Movie night actually sounds pretty nice right now."

Daniel clapped his hands. "Hot damn, I know just the flick too. It's got tons of action, a little intrigue, and a nice little romance subplot."

"I sincerely hope you're not talking about the kind that's tacked on. Way too many movies nowadays have a happily ever after ending with two people who just met that day or some crap. Real connection takes longer than that suspension bridge effect nonsense," Roger said from the backseat.

"Suspension bridge nonsense? No, you're thinking of that movie on the Golden Gate Bridge."

"Not quite. That's a physical bridge. The suspension bridge effect is..." Roger trailed off. "Oh, never mind."

"Whatever," Daniel replied.

Roger leaned forward and flicked Axel's shoulder. "Hey, you alright? You've been awfully quiet lately."

Axel's back straightened. "I'm okay. There's just been a lot to process in the last couple of days. You know how it is."

"Yeah?" Daniel asked. "You better get used to it, kid."

"I mean, to be fair, we're not normally in this many fire-fights," Roger added. "We wouldn't have survived this long if we were. Unfortunately, with this new turf war, it'll get worse before it gets better. So, he's right. You'd better get used to it. If you lose focus it might not be just you that catches a bullet."

"Don't scare the recruit, guys," Tanya said.

Daniel laughed. "He'd better be scared. These Irish will kill all of..." he started until he turned around and saw Tanya's illuminated face glaring at him. "Never mind that."

Roger turned to his left. "You've got to teach me how you do that."

"Do what?"

"Shut him up like that."

"It's a lady's secret. You could never pull it off, Rog," Tanya said in a whimsical singing voice.

"Damn. Women are scary," Roger said with a grin.

"You're telling me," Daniel agreed from the front.

Back at the safe house.

Tanya stood in the kitchen and placed a bag into the microwave before pressing a few buttons. A whirring noise filled the small room. She turned to the living room and called out. "Okay, the popcorn's on." She turned and grabbed Elizabeth's elbow. "Liz, we need to talk in private."

"Yeah, sure. Just let me go get the boys some-"

Tanya's tone allowed no counter argument. "Now, Liz. The boys can get their own refreshments."

"Alright already. Geez." She walked arm in arm with Tanya into the living room. "Us girls are going to have a little girl talk. Feel free to start."

"Girl talk huh?" Daniel asked with an elbow into Roger's side. "Don't take too long now. We'll watch the previews to give you two some extra time."

Tanya led Elizabeth down the hallway and opened a nearby door.

"Why are we going into my room?"

"We need privacy for this, for your sake."

Tanya entered first and stayed by the door inside. She waited for Elizabeth to enter and closed the door behind her. Her arms fell to her hips and her voice fell to a shushed whisper. "I heard your little clandestine conversation with the new guy earlier. You know the one I'm talking about. The one about the kid?"

"You just spied on us?"

"I was monitoring the situation from a tactical standpoint, that's all." Tanya scowled. "Hey, don't try and turn this on me. What were you two talking about? Something about how he'd wish he was the kid if he didn't keep your lies. Feel like sharing yet?"

Elizabeth's mouth warped into a smirk. She stepped closer and brought her voice down to an even tone. "You need to drop this, okay?"

"What's the matter? Afraid I'll tell your boyfriend? I might suggest, girl to girl, that lying never works out well."

Elizabeth brought her right index finger up and poked it into Tanya's shoulder. "You listen to me. Stay out of my business. I'm doing all of us a favor with this."

Tanya brought a hand up to her mouth. Her muffled voice came out. "What the hell did you do?"

"I kept us out of prison is what I did. Now, let's go. The boys will start getting curious if we stay in here."

"Let them. It sounds like Roger needs to know a little bit of what his girl is doing."

Elizabeth grabbed Tanya by both her shoulders and squeezed. "That would be a grave mistake. You understand?"

"Good God, you're not saying what I think you are? I'm your best friend for Christ's sake."

Elizabeth's hand relaxed and rubbed Tanya's shoulders. "That's right, and as my best friend we need to stick together." She moved beside her and wrapped an arm around her shoulder. She moved them toward the door. "Now we're going to go have a fun night and forget all about this, okay? Do we understand each other?"

Tanya reached up and removed her hand. "Just tell me where the kid is so I can fix your screw up. If you're lucky, Rog may not leave you by the time I'm done. I'm trying to do you a favor here, Liz."

Elizabeth exhaled. "Fine. I'll show you where the kid is tomorrow. Okay? Just don't breathe a word of this."

"Good. Then it's a deal. Also, in the future you really may want to simply take a vote. I know you've got executive power now, but we're all on the hook when you do things like this. Okay? We just want to know what we're getting into is all."

"I understand. I'm just still getting used to this being in charge thing. I'll learn as I go." Elizabeth reached forward and opened the door. "Now, let's not keep our guys waiting."

Tanya moved forward into the hallway. She turned and leaned forward with a whisper. "Alright, I'm holding you to this. We're going tomorrow then?"

Elizabeth whispered as she passed her friend. "Of course." Her voice became loud enough to hear over the television. "Ooh, dibs on the buttered popcorn."

Daniel's voice called out. "Too late. It's already claimed."

Elizabeth moved closer to the couch. She leaned forward and placed her chest on Roger's head. "Damn it. Hey, honey, you've got enough for me, don't you?"

Roger raised a bowl above the back of the couch. "Yes, dear."

16

"Where exactly are we going, guys?" Tanya asked from the backseat of the van. She looked to her side out the window. Uncountable numbers of trees passed by as they drove along the sparse highway. "I mean, we're way out of the city."

Elizabeth peaked her head around the seat and looked back at her. "We're taking you to where the kid is, exactly as I said I would." Her hand reached out to the driver's seat and landed on Axel's shoulder. "How much longer until we're there?"

"Not too much longer, ma'am. We're maybe a couple of minutes out."

"Good, and slow down. We don't want to be pulled over for speeding."

Tanya stared out the window. A green, rectangular sign broke her out of her reverie. "Harriman State Park? Wait a minute now."

"Calm down. It's not what you're thinking," Elizabeth said, now facing the front of the van.

"Calm down?" Tanya asked in a shrill voice. "Isn't this

where you guys left a little mass murder the other night? No, I don't think I will. Look. I know you want to keep this quiet, but this isn't the way you want to do this, Liz. Your brother will kill you if he finds out. You know that, right?"

Elizabeth raised her left hand up. "I told you it's not what you're thinking. You're not getting eighty sixed out here. Just calm your tits."

"Then what are we doing out here?"

Axel interrupted their argument along with a turn of the wheel. "Excuse me, but we're here," he said as he pushed his foot down on the brake pedal, causing the van to slow down to an eventual stop. He opened his door and stepped out along with Elizabeth, leaving Tanya alone in the vehicle.

"Shit. Well, I'm already in it. I may as well finish it," she said as she opened the door and stepped out into the forest. She saw the other two walking ahead of her. She jogged and caught up with the pair. "May I ask what we're looking for at least?" Tanya asked. She looked between the two beside her. "Seriously? Not even a hint as to what we're doing out here?"

"Shh." Elizabeth raised a finger to her lips and with her other hand pointed ahead. "We're almost there."

Tanya raised a hand and cupped her ear. "I hear a child laughing. What are we doing? Crashing a family camping trip? I know we need a vacation and all, but this is ridiculous."

Elizabeth raised a hand and placed it over Tanya's mouth. Her other hand pointed downward. She crouched down, along with Axel, behind the nearby bushes. Tanya followed suit as the voices became louder from in front of them.

Elizabeth pointed ahead toward a small campground.

Tanya peeked over the bushes and saw two tents and a fire pit. "I don't see anyone."

"Give it a minute," Elizabeth whispered.

Tanya continued watching until she heard a zipping noise. One of the tents opened, revealing an older man and woman with graying hair.

The other tent opened after that, and a short child bounced out, followed by a subdued child whose gaze never left the ground.

"Son of a bitch," Tanya gasped. "That's the kid."

"Exactly," Elizabeth whispered with a smile. She placed her hand on Tanya's shoulder. "I told you he's fine didn't I?"

"No, actually you didn't in so many words. Who are they?"

"Axel did a little digging back at HQ and found out the kid had grandparents. His parents are officially missing, but he's not talking."

"I'm shocked you're trusting the kid to remain quiet."

"Well, I'm a regular saint, aren't I?"

"I wouldn't go that far," Tanya said with a grin. "Still, is this going to be alright?"

"We need to head back. We'll talk on the way, alright?"

"If you say so."

Elizabeth ascended into a hunched posture. "Axel, could you be a dear and give us girls a little privacy?" Elizabeth asked.

"Sure thing. I need to nail down a few things with the grandparents anyway. I'll call someone for a ride back," he said. He stayed behind a nearby tree as the girls crept back the way they had come.

Axel reached into his pocket and pulled out his trusty side arm. "What the hell am I doing with my life? Those aren't even his grandparents." His right hand reached up to his ear and pushed the button on the device. "You in position?"

A male voice responded. "Roger that. Just don't miss. After that, we'll clean all this up."

"Let's do this," Axel ordered. He reached into his back pocket, pulled out a long cylindrical attachment, and twisted it onto the end of his firearm. He waited until he heard the motor of the van, then waited for it to leave. He pivoted around the tree and raised his right arm...

Back at the safe house

"What do you think the girls are doing so early in the morning?" Roger asked. He placed the bowl in his hand onto the kitchen table and sat down.

"You're asking me? Shit, dude, who knows what women are thinking most of the time?"

"I wouldn't let Tanya hear you say that."

Daniel closed the refrigerator, poured milk over his own cereal, and sat down across from Roger. "Like I'm going to take relationship advice from a guy pussy whipped by my sister."

"Hey now, I'm not-"

"Yeah, you are," Daniel interrupted. "You know what Dad taught me about women?"

"I'm sure this will be good."

"No man will ever understand a woman, Son. The only ones who do are other women, and they hate each other. So don't even try."

"I'm pretty sure your dad got that from someone else."

Daniel shoveled a spoonful of cereal into his mouth and spoke with his mouth full. "He's not wrong though."

The clinking of spoons filled the room until Roger

placed his spoon on the table beside the bowl. "It's just weird. I mean, isn't Tanya a bit of a technophile? It's not like her to go out and about."

"She's out with Liz. I don't know. They're probably out shopping or something."

"I'm pretty sure that's considered sexist."

Daniel pushed away from the table. His chair screeched across the tiled floor. "You really need to man up. You've been spending too much time under her thumb to be saying bull like that. You know what you need?"

"I'm sure you're about to tell me."

"We need to have a guy's night out soon. Get some testosterone back in you."

Roger's eyes glazed over for a moment before snapping open. He shook his head. "That usually means a trip to the bookie's and a strip club, among other things. You know how much shit I got into the last time Liz found out?"

Daniel snapped his fingers. "My point exactly. You're sitting here worried and afraid about what she'll think. You need to do what you want, man. Show some dominance. Who knows? She may love that too. If not, well at least you'll be living life like a man should."

Roger stood up, brought his bowl to the nearby sink, and placed it inside. He turned to Daniel. His eyes shifted to the side. "Can we score some herb before we go?"

Daniel grinned. "You do love that stuff, don't you? Didn't Liz hate you smoking that, and that's why you gave it up?"

Roger's eyes met Daniel's. "Yeah, but I love it, and I want some."

Daniel got up and slapped Roger's shoulder. "My man, that's what I'm talking about. Hell, let's go now while they're out." He reached into his pockets and fished out a set of keys. "I'll drive. You still have your old dealer's address, right?"

Roger pursed his lips. His eyes danced left and right before settling on his friend. "Ah, what the hell? With everything that's happened lately, I could use some. Let's go."

The two exited the kitchen and made their way to the door. Daniel opened it and held it open behind him. "We'll make a man out of you yet. Seriously though, I don't know the guy's address."

Roger closed the door behind them and locked it. He turned around to see Daniel leaning on the guard rails overlooking the populated parking lot. "Yeah, don't worry about that. I know the way there like the back of my hand."

Daniel took the lead. He led the pair to a flight of stairs leading down. "All I ask is you don't let it overtake you, and you keep your head straight when we're on the job. Deal?"

"Dude, it's not like it's opiates or hardcore psychedelics."

Daniel stepped down onto the black asphalt. He waved his hand to the side. "It's all the same to me. Just keep your head on straight. Okay?"

"That's quite possibly one of the dumbest things I've ever heard you say. You should really read some studies before making up your mind on things."

Daniel opened the driver's door of his car. "You really want to be badmouthing your partner in crime that's helping you score against your girl's wishes? I'm the guy who'll be holding this secret from her you know."

Roger followed suit and entered the passenger side. He leaned his chair back with a wide smile. "I guess not." He looked to his left as the engine roared to life. "I need to talk to you about something serious."

"Way to ruin the mood." Daniel's foot stepped on the gas. "What's up?"

"Not to be a nag, but we really need to settle this kid business."

"You're referring to the leftover witness I assume?"

Roger lifted his right leg and placed his foot on the glove compartment. "It just feels like a guillotine is placed above all of our necks right now, and no one's really trying to deal with it. We need to, you know."

Daniel gave him a sideways glance before returning his focus to the road. "I may have lied earlier."

Roger's sarcastic voice came back. "Oh fantastic. About what exactly?"

"I know where the girls went."

"Well by all means, tell me the truth."

Daniel reached up and scratched his stubble covered chin. "Liz took Tanya to the kid."

Roger's voice gained a few octaves. "Wait a minute now. What? Nobody has told me jack. Where's the kid?"

"Calm down and let me explain."

"Is this about me not wanting the kid dead?"

"He's alive, as Tanya will tell you. We found the kid's grandparents, okay? He's staying with them. The kid's gone mute since that night."

"What happens when the kid finds his voice again? Oh, turn left here."

Daniel turned the wheel to the left. "He won't speak. Some of our boys explained how it wouldn't be in his best interest if he loves the rest of his family."

Roger ran a hand through his hair. "Jesus Christ. You're just willing to trust that?"

"Nope, that's why his lines are tapped. Even if he does flip, he'll never get to testify."

"Oh, I guess that makes sense." Roger's voice hardened. "Still, next time you better tell me beforehand. You got me?"

"I got it."

"I'm serious."

"Right. Oh, this guy lives in a pink house?"

"Yeah. I'm sure you'll remember that."

Daniel turned into the driveway and pulled up alongside the snow-white sports car already parked. "I'll never forget that."

"Yeah, I'm not surprised." Once the car came to a stop, Roger opened the door. He bent down and looked at Daniel. "Just let me do the talking, alright?" He closed the door without waiting for a reply and made his way to the front door.

"Got it," Daniel said to the empty car. He stepped out of the vehicle and caught up with his friend who was busy ringing the doorbell. He stopped a few feet behind him and crossed his arms. "Think he's home?"

"I'd be shocked if he isn't. I mean, he never left home unless he was resupplying." He turned and pointed at the sports car. "Well, that and his car's here." Roger reached out and pushed the button again. He tapped his feet. "He's probably in the shower or something."

Daniel grunted and moved to their right toward the row of windows. He peeked inside. "I don't think he's in the shower."

"What makes you say that?"

"I see him lying on the floor in the living room, and he doesn't look to be moving."

"Shit," Roger cursed. He reached for his revolver. "You want to surround and breach?"

"I'll take the back. Go on ten," Daniel said. He reached for his own 9mm and jogged around the house.

"Eight, nine, ten," Roger chanted under his breath. He reached for the knob and twisted. He pulled and flung the door open. He raised his revolver in front of him as he inched his way into the house. He snapped his focus left and then right with his finger over the trigger. "Front room clear!" he called out.

The loud crack of glass breaking from deeper in the house interrupted his search. A few moments later, as Roger was moving forward, Daniel's voice echoed through the residence. "We're clear back here."

"What the hell was that racket?"

"My entrance."

Roger scanned the room until his eyes wandered onto the floor and saw the body. It lay there with headphones on and a contented smile on his face.

Daniel entered the room. "I'll check upstairs." His eyes followed Roger's to the body. "Is he dead?"

Roger moved over and nudged the body with his foot. An unintelligible shout erupted from his mouth. Joseph sat up with wild, wide eyes. He looked up to Roger and then to Daniel's frame. He reached up and ripped the headphones off his head. "Jesus Christ! Just don't kill me, man."

"What?" Roger asked. He followed the man's eyes down to his revolver. He holstered his weapon. "Look, Joe, we thought you were dead, and the murderer was still in here."

"Man, hell no. I'd just finished a bowl and felt like relaxing. Wait a minute. I know you, don't I?"

"I should hope so. I was one of your biggest customers a while back."

"Roger Johnson, is that you?" he asked. He made his way to his feet. "I thought you died months ago. You came over weekly and then poof, after your last visit you stopped coming."

"I'm not dead yet, but I went through some crap. You know how it goes."

"I know I nearly lost a car payment when you disappeared. That's what I remember." He raised a hand to his chin and pointed at Roger. "Yeah, and I remember some crazy chick who didn't like me the last time you showed up. She was your girlfriend, wasn't she?"

"Yeah, you could say that."

Daniel stifled a snicker with his free hand. "He's still with that 'crazy chick' you know."

The color of Joseph's face turned white. "You're joking? She threatened to-" He paused and cleared his throat. "It's probably better to not say."

"Afraid not. He's still with my sister. She doesn't know about this meeting. I'd suggest not telling her if she asks."

Joseph walked to the nearby couch and sat down. "That was your sister? I'll keep that in mind." He turned to Roger. "I presume this isn't just a social call? What can I get you today? I got H, E, acid, poppers, mushrooms, nose candy, and of course good old cannabis. What's your pleasure today?"

A click came from Daniel. Joseph turned to stare down the barrel of his 9mm. "He's not here for heroin."

Joseph raised his hands up. "Damn, man. It was just a question. Your boy here used to love it. That's the only reason I asked."

"Precisely, and it was a bitch weening him off it. We're not playing that game again."

"Cool it," Roger said with an outstretched hand. He reached around to his back pocket and pulled out his wallet. "I'm here for some herb is all today, buddy."

Joseph got to his feet, keeping his gaze on Daniel all the while. "Right on. Your friend here could use some. Just chill here, okay? Any preference?"

"Yeah I need an indica. It's been one of those weeks."

"Gotcha. Be back in a sec, fellas."

Joseph disappeared down the hallway to Roger's right. The sound of a door opening met their ears. Roger looked to Daniel. "What happened to 'let me do the talking'? Don't you trust me?"

Daniel holstered his pistol and shrugged. "Just looking out for you is all."

"It's nice to know you trust me so much," Roger fired back with biting sarcasm.

"It's not that. That junk turns anyone who uses it into a different person."

Joseph's voice called out. "How much you want, bro?"

Roger rolled his eyes at Daniel before answering. "A half an ounce will do me fine."

"He's been back there a while, hasn't he?" Daniel asked.

"He's probably weighing it and bagging it. It takes a minute."

"How well do you know this guy?"

"I've known him since high school. Why?"

Daniel's hand fell to the top of his 9mm. "Has he ever been associated with any crews?"

"Well he's a street pharmacologist, so I'd assume he kicks a vig up to someone."

"He could have graduated."

"You're always so paranoid."

Daniel's eyes stayed locked on the corridor Joseph had gone down. "It's why we're still alive."

The sound of a door slamming along with footsteps came from the hallway. Joseph came into view. He was holding a bag full of green nuggets. "Sorry about that, guys. As a reunion bonus, I hooked you up with a little extra. The price is the same as it always was. One hundred and fifty for a half O."

Roger opened his wallet.

Joseph continued with a wide smile. "However, since I'm a swell guy, it'll be one hundred and twenty for today only."

Roger slapped the bills into Joseph's outstretched palm with a grin. "I appreciate that."

Joseph handed over the bag and sat down on the end of the nearby sofa. "I don't suppose you want to stay and try it out? You've even got yourself a designated driver here." Joseph jabbed a thumb in Daniel's direction.

Roger sat down on the couch beside Joseph. He looked to his right toward Daniel. "We don't have anything better to do. Right?"

A low growl came from Daniel's throat. "I suppose not." He took a seat between Roger and Joseph.

Roger leaned forward and looked at his host. "I don't suppose you've either got papers or a piece I can use do you?"

"As if you need to ask. Which do you prefer, my man?"

"I always liked a nice glass piece, if that's alright?"

"My best spoon is on the table to your right. Knock yourself out. You can use the magazine to break it apart if you want."

Roger set to work breaking apart one of the top nugs in the bag.

As he did, Daniel spoke up. "So, Joseph, how's the hustling going?"

"You know how it goes. There's always someone who wants a slice from us honest vendors."

"Uh huh, and were any of them Irish?"

Joseph's eyes wandered to the ceiling. "Come to think of it, yeah there was one group. They called themselves the McConnels or something like that. I heard they got into a beef with someone recently."

Daniel's eyes narrowed. "You mean the McCranes?"

"Yeah, that's it."

Roger brought the small pipe up to his lips and placed his thumb over the hole. The sound of moving air filled the room. He removed his thumb and coughed out a large cloud of smoke. "You know anything about them?"

"All I know about those crazy bastards is they threatened my clientele if I didn't play ball."

Daniel's right hand fell to his waist line. His right eye twitched as he spoke. "What do you mean, 'play ball'?"

Joseph avoided eye contact and remained silent. "They said they'd kill my mother, guys."

Daniel stood up and pulled out his pistol. He leveled it at Joseph. "What did you do?"

"I had to do it, or they would have gone after my family."

Daniel stomped toward the man and smacked him with the butt of his weapon. "Tell me now, or I'll do what my sister always wanted to."

Joseph curled into a fetal position on the couch. "Alright already. They told me to call if I saw any of the Morris family."

"You gave us up, you low-life piece of shit?" Daniel asked with a snarl.

Roger placed the spoon back on the table. He stood up and brought a hand up to Daniel's arm with a smile. "This won't solve anything. There's only one play here, if we want everyone breathing by the end of this."

"Who says I do?"

"Just give me two minutes." He turned to Joseph. "I assume they're on their way?"

"Yeah," he sputtered out in a whiny voice between wheezes.

"Here's what's going to happen. I'm going to go and take all your product, and you're going to tell them we robbed you. If you're lucky they'll believe you, and you'll live to see another day."

"If they don't?" Joseph asked with a sniffle.

"Then you're no better off than if we left the decision to my friend here," he said with a slap on Daniel's back.

"How am I supposed to pay the bills or even resupply without my merchandise, man?"

Daniel growled. "You should have thought of that before calling those psychos on us."

"He's right," Roger added. "At this point it's either your drugs or your life? Which is more important?"

"You guys suck. You know that?"

Roger headed down the hallway that Joseph had disappeared down earlier. "We get that a lot."

Joseph stood up, but was kicked back onto the sofa.

"Hold it right there," Daniel ordered.

"Do you know how much that all is worth? Tens of thousands. And you're both just going to take it all? Hell, I won't be lying when I tell them you screwed me."

Daniel's eyes narrowed. "If I know my friend, he'll probably get it back to you in a few days. He's a do-gooder like that."

"Really?"

"Sadly, yes."

Roger came into view after a slam. He was holding a large, black trash bag. "Got it. Now we're all good on the plan, right? I'll bring these back in a couple of days after we're sure it's clear. You play the victim and go on about how you hate us."

"I think I can handle that," Joseph said through gritted teeth.

Roger strode past him with a wide smile on his face. He opened the front door and took a single step outside. He turned to the two men. "Let's go already. I'd rather avoid another run in with the Reaper."

Daniel backstepped toward Roger. He kept his pistol trained on Joseph the entire time. "Stay out of trouble now and do be discrete for all of our sakes. If you tell them what happened, you're the next body in the ground."

"You think they'll kill me?"

"If they don't, I will," Daniel said with a straight face. He moved past the opened door and closed it, leaving the man alone.

Daniel holstered his weapon, turned, and walked back to his car. He saw Roger close the back door and circle around the back toward the passenger side.

Daniel made his way back to the driver's seat. He looked to his right to see Roger plop down next to him. He struck the steering wheel with his palm. "You know, when I started today I never thought I'd be transporting tens of thousands of dollars' worth of drugs."

Roger chuckled with his reddened eyes narrowed. "Life comes at you fast."

"I don't mean to 'harsh your mellow' or whatever, but have you given any thought as to how this is going to go down?"

"How do you mean?"

Daniel turned the key in the ignition. "I mean, do you plan on hiding that bag somewhere in particular? I doubt the girls will want it around the safe house once they find out what's inside."

"I didn't really think of that."

"Somehow that doesn't surprise me," Daniel scoffed. "The way I see it, we have a few choices. We need to figure it out before we return. Either we keep it in the apartment or find another place to keep it." He pushed his foot down on the pedal, moving the van forward. "If you want my opinion, I'd suggest keeping it somewhere else. If Liz finds that H, we're both going to be in deep shit, bro."

Roger snickered. "We could just send it up the line and give it to the family to sell?"

"That could work, but what about the guy you just promised to give it back to?"

"Oh, yeah. I forgot about that."

Daniel rolled his eyes. "Somehow, I feel like I've made a big mistake today and can't quite put my finger on why."

"Do what now?"

Daniel sighed as he pushed on the brakes. "Oh, never mind. It's not like you'll remember longer than ten seconds right now anyway. I'll fix this."

"What's your plan then?" Roger asked.

"I've got just the thing. It'll take care of the Irish, help your friend, and keep our asses out of the fire in one go. There's just one problem. I don't know how we'll get it there by ourselves. We'll need the girls' help on this one."

"You're talking about planting it in one of their fronts and calling the cops?" Roger asked with his eyebrows raised. "That would work, unless they have someone on the force that can warn them."

"It's either that, or we dump these drugs and piss off your dealer. Which one is better?"

"I guess we're going out tonight with the girls."

17

Daniel and Roger walked into the apartment. Roger carried the large bag in his hands. The sound of applause and feminine cheers erupted from down the hallway in the main room. Daniel nodded in the direction of Axel's nearby room and opened it as he passed.

Roger ducked into the opened door and tossed the bag into the corner before moving back into the hallway. Daniel approached the couch from behind. "You girls are enjoying your game show I see."

"I am more than she is," Tanya spoke with a gleaming smile.

"Who the hell thinks an average car like that is worth fifty thousand anyway? An idiot is who."

"It was fifty-one thousand, thank you very much," Tanya said with a smug expression.

"Yeah sure, whatever," Elizabeth offered in an even voice. She turned around to face the two men. "You two were out for a while. Have fun?"

"You could say that," Daniel answered. "Liz, can I talk to you in private?"

Elizabeth elbowed Tanya's side and stood up. She moved beside her brother as she caught sight of Roger entering the room. "I suppose so. I guess you and Rog have some catching up to do anyway."

Roger circled around the couch and sat down in the now vacant spot Elizabeth had occupied. "Yeah, I heard an interesting story earlier. I hear you can explain it a bit better."

"If it's what I'm thinking, sure," Tanya beamed.

"We'll leave you two to it then." Daniel tilted his head back down the hallway he'd come from. "Let's go." He took off with his sister in tow before disappearing into the very room Roger had ducked into earlier.

Roger turned to Tanya. "So, is it true the kid is alright?"

"I wouldn't say alright, but he's still breathing if that's what you mean. I mean, he's gone mute. The poor kid had his parents stolen away." She turned to see Roger staring down at the ground, gritting his teeth. "Oh my God, I'm sorry."

"No, you're right. It was my mistake that got them killed. I deserve it."

A piercing set of screams from Elizabeth caused them both to turn around. "You two did what? Oh this better not be what I think it is!"

Roger's face fell into his hands.

"You want to explain?" Tanya asked.

He raised his head and stared unflinchingly at the television. "I have a feeling it'll all come to light in a few minutes anyway. Let a man enjoy his last television show in peace."

"That bad huh? You must have really screwed up if you won't tell me."

"Define 'screwed up'."

"That's what I'm asking, wise guy. What did you do this time?"

"I'm not getting any peace, am I?" Roger asked.

"Not even a little. You've got me curious now."

Roger brought a palm up to his forehead and leaned back. A door slamming caused him to break his reverie. "You'll know inside of a minute." He slapped his cheeks before spinning around. He came face to face with Elizabeth, hunched over to be on his eye level. Her narrowed eyes stared back into his. He raised an index finger. "I guess you heard our plan then?"

"Your plan for what exactly?" Tanya asked.

Elizabeth stood up straight and crossed her arms in front of her. "Their plan for dealing with the Irish. Which, I might add, is my job to come up with, not yours," she explained looking deep into Roger's hazelnut eyes.

"That doesn't sound too bad, Liz. I mean great leaders take ideas from their subordinates."

"Oh, just wait. You haven't heard the best part. Do you want to tell her, or should I?"

"Fine," Roger started. "The plan was to hide a bunch of narcotics in one of their front businesses."

"Then call it in ourselves?" Tanya asked. She scratched her nose. "That would certainly put their minds on something besides retribution."

"Well, they already started this plan without my go ahead," Elizabeth snapped. "As of today, we're officially sitting on tens of thousands of dollars' worth of drugs."

The sound of a door opening, along with Daniel's voice, interrupted them. "That's only for now, Sis. It'll be gone by tonight."

Elizabeth pivoted in place to face her brother. Her hands fell to her hips. "You're assuming I okay your little plan in the first place?"

"That's right," Daniel said. He made his way around his

sister and sat between Roger and Tanya. "Of course, the alternative is you waste this opportunity. Dumping the drugs is just as risky as planting them, so I'm not really seeing that appeal."

"We could just flush them," Tanya added. All available eyes moved to her. "Never mind. He's right though, if you wanted to drop them off somewhere. Wait, where did you two even get that amount of drugs?"

Elizabeth faced the group, placed her hands on Roger's shoulders, and leaned into him. "There's only one person here who has connections like that. I wonder who that could have been." She leaned down by his right ear and whispered loud enough for everyone to hear. "Hmm? Is there something you want to tell me?"

"To be fair, drug dealers are an important asset to have," Roger said. "I mean, not as much as a good money launderer, but you'd be surprised what they can help you do."

"Oh, I agree," Elizabeth said in a jovial tone with a squeeze of her right hand. "My question is, who did you rob for that? We don't have enough enemies as it is? You two jokers need to pile on?"

"Okay now, it's not what you're thinking," Roger said. "We did it for his own good."

"Really? Pray tell, how was robbing a low-level dealer for his own good exactly?"

Daniel interrupted. "You weren't there."

"That's right. I wasn't." Elizabeth raised her hands and placed them on the sides of Roger's head. "So I ask again, dear, how was it in his best interest to rob him?"

"If we hadn't, the McCranes would have made short work of him," Roger admitted.

"What the hell do they have to do with this exactly?" Elizabeth asked.

"It turned out they owned his street. When he left the room he called them, so as to stay in business," Daniel interrupted.

Tanya snapped her fingers. "So robbing him keeps him in their good graces via a common enemy. That's smart if you care about this guy. I mean, you probably cheesed him off, but he's still alive. Right?"

"To the best of my knowledge, yes." Roger said.

Elizabeth's fingernails dug into Roger's shoulder causing a wince. "Okay, let's say that makes sense. There's just one thing I'm not exactly clear on yet."

"Here we go," Daniel said under his breath.

"Why did you two go over to a dealer's residence in the first place? It's not like we shake down drug dealers in McCrane's turf daily."

Roger glanced over at Daniel and felt Elizabeth's hands lift off his shoulders and fall onto either side of his head. She reoriented his neck back to the television. He heard her annoyed voice above him.

"Don't look at him. I'm asking you."

"Lay off, Liz," Daniel said.

Elizabeth lifted her hands off Roger and moved to the side of her brother. Her hands fell to her side and clenched into fists. "I don't get the luxury of relaxing on stuff like this. You should know that as well as I do. I mean, it's your fault we're in this mess."

Daniel stood up and went toe to toe with his sister. "Mine?"

"Yeah, yours. If you hadn't pissed off the Irish, we wouldn't have any of this. Would we?"

"Guys, can we not do this right now?" Roger asked. "This isn't the time for-"

He was interrupted mid sentence by both Daniel and

Elizabeth turning to him. "Be quiet!"

"Okay then." Roger looked down at his lap and twiddled his thumbs.

Elizabeth poked an index finger into her brother's chest. "I don't know how you ever got to be boss of our little group. Every deal you ever headed either resulted in a firefight or cold-blooded murder, usually by your own hand."

Daniel spoke through gritted teeth. "What are you trying to say?"

"The only reason you're where you are is Daddy."

"That's rich coming from his favorite little girl. You never wondered why you weren't put on cleaning detail? It wasn't because of your tactical and diplomatic prowess I'll tell you."

The two continued lobbing insults back and forth as Roger leaned over and tapped Tanya's shoulder, causing her to turn to him. "Yes?"

He whispered. "We need to stop them, or we'll have a brawl on our hands in a couple of minutes. If we can separate them for a little while, it'll all blow over. I'll take Daniel?

"Aww," She whined with pursed lips. "Are you trying to avoid your girlfriend right now?"

"I know how to calm him down; her, not so much when she gets like this."

A smirk appeared at the corner of Tanya's mouth. "Yeah, but I like live entertainment. A little sibling rivalry never hurt anyone."

"Tell me you're not serious. What happens when they come to blows? Someone in a neighboring apartment calls the cops, and we have a trash bag full of narcotics. Hmm? What happens then?"

Tanya gazed forward until her eyes got wide. She jumped off the couch and moved behind Elizabeth. She placed a hand on her shoulder as Elizabeth raised a lone fist. "Now let's not go overboard here, children."

Roger got up and maneuvered to be beside Daniel. He whispered loud enough for his friend to hear. "Let it go, dude. We don't want attention, and a fist fight will get plenty of it if someone beside our apartment calls it in," he said.

Daniel scoffed with an arrogant smile. "Your boyfriend is right. This serves no one," he declared. He moved back to the couch and plopped down.

"Let's just take a few minutes to cool off, okay?" Tanya asked. She patted Elizabeth's shoulder.

A loud growling escaped her throat. "Fine," she snapped. "I can't be around you right now," she said with a glare at her older brother as she immediately took off down the hallway. She opened her and Roger's door before slamming it shut behind her.

Roger made the only comment offered. "I guess that means we're not planting that crap tonight then?"

Not a sound besides the television permeated the dim room. The remaining occupants took a place on the sofa. Tanya leaned over the side of the couch and hefted her trusty laptop up onto her lap before opening it.

A series of rapid clicks came from her fingertips until she spoke up in her meek voice. "Why the hell was she so wound up about this? Do either of you two know?"

Roger leaned forward and looked to his left at her. "Yeah."

"You want to elaborate on that a little?"

"Not really," Roger said in a bored tone.

"She's worried," Daniel said. "She's under the proverbial gun here, and she gets news her crew hit a dealer?"

"That's it?"

"No," Roger added.

"Well, you can't leave it there."

Roger leaned his neck back onto the sofa and closed his eyes. "I can, and I will."

"Okay, ignoring your little secret, then why were you two even there anyway? You never answered."

"We didn't?" Daniel asked.

"No, you didn't."

"There must be a reason for that."

Tanya returned her attention to the screen in front of her with a loud scoff. "What is it with men and secrets anyway?"

"Like you've never had a secret?" Daniel said without pause.

"Not when it comes to friends."

"Oh, you mean like that time you stole Elizabeth's boyfriend in high school, and then it came out at prom? That was a hoot. Do you remember the riot that broke out after you two came to blows? It was monstrous. I mean, you should have seen those two go at it, buddy," Daniel said with a chuckle as he elbowed Roger in the side.

Roger's head pivoted to his right. "She did what now?" Roger asked.

Tanya pointed at Daniel without looking away. "That is not the same thing, and you know it."

"It sounds similar," Roger said.

"It's not at all. God, what is wrong with you two?"

"We're not the ones with the problem here. We simply brought back a plan that would take care of the Irish and save a friend," Daniel said.

"Yeah, if by brought back you mean jumped over her head and did it without her knowing," Tanya said.

Roger grasped the remote control to his left. "The point is that this will benefit us all if we do it right."

"If we don't? What happens then?"

Daniel spoke up. "If not, then at least we kept an old friend of Roger's alive and kicking. Is that good enough for you?"

"It sounds like you guys are the crappiest saviors ever. I mean that for everybody involved. The guy gets robbed, your sister gets the blame from the higher ups, and he probably hates our organization now. I sincerely hope it was worth it."

"I'm not going to apologize for helping a friend in need," Roger added with a somber look on his face and a jaded tone to his voice.

"How nice of you," Tanya said with a biting sarcastic edge in her voice. "The bottom line here is that you guys took it upon yourselves to 'save' him and ended up ruining the man's livelihood. Never mind the fact that it was unsanctioned to even go near that neighborhood in the first place."

"Drop it," Daniel said with an edge to his voice.

"Fine," Tanya said in a huff. She stood up, carrying the laptop under her arm, and made for one of the unoccupied rooms down the hallway. "I have to go do my dailies anyway."

Another slamming door reverberated throughout the apartment leaving the two men alone.

Roger handed the remote control to Daniel. "I'm starting to wonder why I ever take any of your advice."

"Did you have fun today?"

"I did until we got back."

Daniel shuffled over to the opposite side of the couch. He raised his hand and pressed a button on the control, changing the channels. "Which means they're the ones with the problem. You do what you want, man. That's life. They'll accept it eventually, or they won't. If they do, great. If they don't, then do you really want to cater to them if they won't accept you? Either way, never apologize for doing what you think is right."

Roger paused before answering. "You got that from a Saturday morning cartoon special, didn't you? No, don't deny it. I think I saw that one last weekend."

"Doesn't make it any less true."

"True that," Roger said.

The two sat there for a few minutes facing the television until Roger continued the conversation. "Where's Axel anyway? I haven't seen him all day."

"That you'd have to ask your girlfriend. He went with her today, so I don't know."

"Ah shit."

"I wouldn't do that right now if I were you."

Elizabeth's booming voice interrupted the two. "Rog, get in here!"

Roger exhaled and his face fell into his hands. "It doesn't look like I have much of a choice, do I?"

"Sure you do," Daniel answered with a shit eating grin. "I'd recommend going though, judging by her voice."

Roger stood up and circled around the sofa before turning back. "What happened to doing what I want?"

"Eh, sometimes there are limits. It's called being a man and facing the music."

Roger turned his back and walked while whispering under his breath. "That's the first thing I agree with him on today, and I hate the advice."

He reached his shared room and, with a final look back at his friend, opened the door and slipped inside.

He saw Elizabeth sitting on the side of their shared full sized bed. She wore a large over-sized shirt and kicked her short covered legs out toward him. She brought an index finger up and motioned him over. She patted the spot beside her.

Roger, without pause, moved to sit beside her.

As soon as he neared her, she reached out and grasped his wrist. She pulled him down into a sitting position, her vice like grip never wavering all the while. "You do understand why I am so upset right now?"

"I have a pretty good idea." He brought his free hand over to his captive one only to have it slapped away by her other hand."

She shook her hand. "Do you remember when you first joined?"

Roger looked down at the floor with a somber expression. "How could I forget that excruciating experience? It's not every day you go through a soul crushing opiate withdrawal."

"Imagine my surprise to see piles of that shit in Axel's room."

Roger turned to her and stared deep into her cerulean eyes. "You know I would do anything to save you if you were in trouble. Right?"

Elizabeth's eyes widened and she leaned back a bit. "What the hell are you going on about?" she asked. She looked away as a faint red invaded her cheeks.

"That doesn't just go for you, honey. It goes for your brother, the new guy, and anyone I care about."

"Stop this mushy crap already."

"That dealer's my friend. I'm not going to apologize for doing what it takes to keep him breathing for at least another day."

Elizabeth faced him, any traces of her previous crimson hue all but gone. "So why were you visiting him then? Don't you even start thinking I forgot. It was a pretty good distraction you and my brother gave me though."

"You know what? Fine, I'll tell you. First I want you to look into my eyes and tell me what you see."

"What's the point of this?" she asked as she stared into his brown eyes. Her brows furrowed. "Your eyes seem a little red. Have you got pinkeye or something?"

Roger's stoic front shifted into a wide grin. "No, dear. You want to know why we went there? Honestly, I just wanted a little bud. That's it. Do you think I dragged our asses over there to fan the flames of the war?" He tilted his head. "You know me better than that. Now your brother, I can see why you might think that," he added with a small chuckle.

Elizabeth released his hands and turned around until her back was to him. She rummaged through the night table's drawers beside the bed. "You know how I feel about that shit. It never leads anywhere good for you."

"Yes," he answered in a firm voice. "I also know that I am my own man and make my own decisions."

Without saying anything, Elizabeth stood up and turned around to face him. Her hand dashed out and clutched his again. Her other hand shot forward and flicked her wrist. A low clicking echoed in the small room.

Roger looked down to find his wrist inside a pair of handcuffs. He looked up to see a feral grin on Elizabeth's face. He heard another click and felt the cold metal on his other wrist. "What the hell are you doing?"

"Since you took the liberty of doing what you wanted today, I figured I'd take your lead."

Roger cringed as he attempted to move his hands away, only to find them locked into place. "These are not just a gag gift are they?"

"That's right."

"What if I said I wasn't comfortable with this?"

"Did I get a choice when you got stoned today?"

Roger rolled his eyes. "I don't think that's exactly on the same level as this. No, I'm pretty sure this is worse."

"Proportional responses never work," Elizabeth started before pausing and leaning in close to his ear. She whispered in a breathy voice. "You have to raise the stakes so they know you're serious." She leaned back and eyed him up and down. "You're just lucky I didn't spring for the leg cuffs."

"Just release my hands. This has gone far enough."

"I don't think you realize the situation you're in, honey. I'm the one in control here, as you and my brother seem to have forgotten," she said in a sugary sweet tone. She placed her hands on his shoulders, pushed him onto his back, and climbed on top of him. She leaned in close to his face. Her breath tickled his nose as she spoke in a mere whisper. "Tonight, you are mine and you will do what I say. Is that understood?"

"If I don't?"

She placed a hand on the side of his face. "It's so cute that you think you have a choice," she cooed. "If you insist on being stubborn, I have numerous tools to persuade you."

"Tools?" he asked.

"Want me to show you?" she asked in a growl.

Roger glanced to his right at the open drawer to see a red candle sticking out. He turned back to the buxom woman on top of him. "I'll be good."

"Yes, you will."

A knock came from the door, causing Elizabeth to look to the side. She looked back at the man below her with a devilish grin. "Now as for my first order..." she started.

Back in the Main Room.

"It's gotten awfully quiet," Daniel said. He surfed through different channels until a door behind him opened. He turned around to see the door to the apartment opening, revealing Axel's large form. "Where the hell have you been, man? It's the dead of night. Did it take that long or something?"

Axel trudged forward until he came to his door. His hand reached out until Daniel's voice stopped him.

"I wouldn't go in there if I were you," Daniel warned.

Axel's hand froze halfway to the knob and he silently nodded. He continued down the hallway. He stopped by Roger and Elizabeth's door and knocked once before continuing toward the sofa. He took a spot on the other end of the couch. "It's finally done," he muttered.

"Good man," Daniel said.

The two fell into silence until Axel spoke up. "Who's in my room now?"

"Our resident techie is in there 'doing her dailies', whatever the hell that means."

"I see."

"Don't sweat it. She's just having a little hissy fit."

Axel placed his right leg over his left and leaned back with an exhale. "What did I miss?"

"The ladies are miffed at me and Rog for what we did today."

"It sounds like there's a good story there," Axel remarked with a grin.

"It wasn't quite as eventful as yours. We just kind of, you

know..." he trailed off, "took everything a dealer had and brought it back here."

"A drug dealer?"

"That's right."

"Was there a reason?"

"Would you believe me if I told you it was to save his life?"

Axel burst into a fit of laughs. "That's a good one." He stopped when he saw Daniel staring at him with a straight face. "You're actually serious?"

"Yes."

"I can't imagine your sister liked an unsanctioned job like that on her watch."

"That's putting it mildly." Daniel's left leg kicked forward. "We even came up with a way to use the poison in our little war with the Irish. I think the only reason there's any peace right now is because she liked that idea." He chuckled to himself. "Leave it to my sister to change her mind when she thinks she can take all the credit."

"Am I sleeping out here again?"

"You're sure as shit not sleeping in your room with Tanya," Daniel said with an edge to his voice.

"I got it, sir. I won't get any ideas."

"Don't call me sir," Daniel ordered. He crossed his arms and looked away before adding in a quiet voice, "It's not like we're together anyway. I'm not her keeper."

"Alright then," Axel said. The two fell into silence as the television droned on in front of them.

"How do you feel about another job tonight?" Daniel asked.

Axel turned and regarded the man with bloodshot eyes. "You're serious?"

"Well, with all the estrogen flowing around these parts,

someone needs to get the job done. Since Rog is busy, how about I go with you?"

"He's busy?"

Daniel grimaced. "Just please don't ask. If I had to guess with those two, they're probably being 'intimate' right now. You get me?"

"Right after an argument?"

"You don't know my sister, do you? From the stories Rog tells me, she has quite the appetite. It's even worse after a fight. She likes to show dominance or something." He paused. "God, I wish he'd stop telling me shit like that."

Axel rubbed his bloodshot eyes. "You'll have to drive. I can barely keep my eyes open."

"Make a cup of instant coffee then, because I need you fully awake for this."

Axel stood up and made his way to the kitchen. "This is an exhausting lifestyle, isn't it?"

"You don't have any idea, kid."

The sound of a door opening, along with light footsteps, caused both men to turn toward the noise. They saw Tanya walking toward them with a smug smile plastered on her face. "You boys going somewhere I hear?"

"How the hell do you know that?" Daniel asked.

"A little bird told me."

"You bugged this place, didn't you?"

"Yeah, I did. It was big boss Bernard's orders. I did it when you and Roger were out today."

Daniel released a large breath. "Okay, fine. You can come along. We could use the backup, with the other members indisposed."

"I think you're forgetting something, Danny."

"What's that?"

"You don't learn, do you? You need to let your sister know before you just go off half-cocked."

Daniel snickered. "Go off half-cocked. That's funny."

"For God's sake, grow up. Now you are going to go ask her, aren't you?"

Daniel pointed back at the couple's room. "Feel free. But I wouldn't go in there right now, unless you want a free show."

"What? Oh good gracious!" She exclaimed. "They're doing that?"

"I don't know. If you want to go find out, be my guest. It's not on my to do list tonight. Mine's filled with, you know, doing some work for the family and ending this new war."

"That's an awfully nice rationalization you've got there," Tanya said in a snarky voice.

"You going to go ask for permission from the boss lady or not? She'll probably not be amused if you go in there right now. I'm warning you," Daniel cautioned.

Tanya turned and gazed at the door for a full minute before turning back to the two men. Her head fell as she gazed at the floor. She spoke in a quiet, almost dulcet, tone. "Fine, I'm going."

"Sweet. Let's rock."

Tanya's neck craned back. "Oh, Lord. What have I just done?" Tanya asked the ceiling.

18

"Okay, boys, can we at least this time not turn this into a massacre?" Tanya asked from the backseat. "Dropping more bodies is kind of counter intuitive, isn't it?"

"For the last time, it was them or us," Daniel said.

"I don't think firing on a group of men who didn't even know of you constitutes as self-defense."

Daniel remained quiet. He pulled the 9mm out of his belt line and ejected the magazine. He held it up to the window before nodding to himself and inserting it back into the firearm. He pulled back the hammer with a reverberating click. He turned to see Tanya glaring daggers at him. "What? This is just in case of the worst-case scenario."

"Yeah, sure. Just try not to need it. Now according to their surveillance cameras, there are only three men inside. They're all on the upper level, so this will not need violence." She glanced up and looked at Daniel before returning her focus to the screen. "Just get in the door, find the nearest room, and dump it there. It'll be easy, so long as you two don't go looking for trouble. Is that understood?"

"Yeah, boss. It's clear," Daniel sarcastically said without turning around.

"I mean it. Just get in and get out. Now you're going to be entering via the back door. It may or may not be locked, so you may have to improvise."

"You can't tell?" Daniel asked.

"It's an analogue lock. I can't unlock it from here, if that's what you're asking. Find a way in and get right back out."

Daniel placed the pistol down the front of his pants. His right hand reached out and grasped the door handle. "You heard the lady. Let's get this over with, Axe."

Axel grunted in acknowledgement and opened the driver's side door. He stepped outside, along with Daniel. He circled around the van and opened the back doors. He grunted as he leaned forward and grasped the black bag. He closed the doors and moved to catch up with Daniel.

The two men ducked into the nearby alley. "The door should be right around the corner," Daniel said. "You have any idea how to open a locked door, if it is?"

"I don't know how to pick a lock, so my guess would be to shoot the lock?"

A loud, sudden burst of white noise, followed by Tanya's voice, interrupted. "That won't work."

"It won't?" Axel asked.

"No. All that will do is shatter the lock. It would actually probably jam it shut if anything."

"I don't know," Daniel interrupted as they turned the corner. "It works in the movies."

"Yeah," Tanya's sarcastic voice said, "because Hollywood never lies or churches up its stunts. Don't you even think of trying it, Danny."

"Yeah, yeah, I got it," Daniel said in a bored tone. His voice brightened up. "Well there it is. Time for the moment of truth I guess." His right hand reached out, grabbed hold of the knob, and twisted, only for it to refuse to budge. "Shit, it's locked," he uttered. He pointed his pistol just above the handle, only to cringe and raise his other hand to his ear.

"God dammit. I said not to!" Tanya roared into his ears.

Daniel rolled his eyes and holstered his weapon. "Alright already. I got it." He surveyed the alleyway around him. His left hand reached out and nudged Axel's shoulder. He pointed further down. "See that window? That gives me an idea, but you're not going to like it."

"You're going to break it, aren't you?" Tanya's deadpan voice asked.

"You're the one who said to find a way in without shooting the door."

"That's going to get their attention. You know that?"

While the two were going back and forth, Axel moved to the window in question. He set down the bag at his feet and reached up. He slid his fingers underneath the frame and pushed upward. A sliding shuffle was heard, along with the window opening. "Guys? It's open."

"See?" Daniel asked. "Axel knows what's up."

"Just go already," Tanya's exasperated voice ordered. "I want to get back in time for the raid tonight."

"It's midnight. Your group plays that late?" Axel asked.

"If you must know, newbie, it's a Pacific time guild. Now why don't you focus on your job?"

Daniel walked up to Axel and reached down to grab the bag. He hefted the bag and tossed it inside. "Is that good enough, boss?"

"Shut the window, you ninny," Tanya's voice said into his ear. "I'll make the call. You two are ready to get out, aren't you?"

"Hold up just a second," Daniel said. "This could be an opportunity."

"Oh no," Tanya said with a whining moan.

"Yeah, we could probably get a little intel inside. You said there were only three in there, right? Think about it. If we find where these micks are storing their merchandise, we can take that up the food chain and get back into the good graces of the brass."

"That was not the job, Danny. Did you not learn from earlier tonight? Get your ass back in this van right now."

"You know as well as I do that plans change.

"You're right, sometimes they do change. Normally it's because the boss says to. You remember who that is now, don't you?"

"Scared of my sister? No need. She'll take credit by the time it's all said and done."

"You hope so anyway. Otherwise, the previous argument will be nothing compared to this one. And may I remind you, she outranks you now."

"Come on, Axe. Let's go." Daniel jumped and grabbed the bottom of the window frame. His feet scratched and kicked against the wall, with a grunt escaping as he struggled his way upwards and into the building.

Tanya's voice came to life in Axel's ear piece. "Do not even think of following him in there."

"I can't just leave him alone in there," Axel vowed. He followed suit and climbed up.

"Why me?" Tanya asked. "Do you two even have a clue where this mythical intel would be?"

Daniel stood up and dusted off his front. "That's why we have you, isn't it?"

"Of course that's what you'd say."

Axel tumbled into the building with a thump.

"Well?"

"Give me a minute. I'm looking now." A brief pause later her voice came back. "Oh, fantastic. According to this, the main office is upstairs."

Daniel extended a hand to the downed Axel and helped him to his feet. "I guess we're going upstairs then."

"Just hold on now. We don't even know if these guys are strapped."

Daniel unholstered his weapon from his belt line. "We do know that we are though."

Axel's arm reached behind him and produced his own handgun.

"Just follow my instructions then. If you do, I think you can get in and out without them even knowing you were there."

"There, now there's the team player we need. You're in charge. Where are we going then?"

"This is such a bad idea," Tanya whispered. The sound of keys clacking and periodic clicking filled the otherwise silent moment. "Alright. I was wrong before. There's one guy downstairs. When you exit that room you need to hang a right. Now be careful. The new guy in there patrols that hallway, so go on my signal. Do try not to kill him, alright?"

"Is he in there now?" Axel asked.

"I don't know. There's no camera in that hallway. I only know because an adjacent hallway showed he moves that way from time to time."

"Well then do you see him in that camera?"

"Not right now."

Daniel readied the 9mm in his right hand. "Then we have to assume he's in there now." He used his left hand to signal behind him. "Stay behind me, kid." He hunched over and reached out with his left hand. He twisted and pushed the knob to reveal a tiled hallway. The sound of footsteps could be heard echoing in the distance. Axel took up position on the other side of the door.

The sound of clacking footsteps came closer until they heard a male voice. "What the devil? Was this always open? Screw it, they don't pay me enough." The footsteps started again to the right.

Daniel craned his neck and whispered. "Cover me. I'll take care of him." He immediately slinked his way out the door.

He poked his head out and looked left to see an empty hallway and then right. A large, heavy-set man had his back turned to him. His right hand had a mini flashlight connected to a thin piece of wire twirling around his index finger. A faint whistling sound accompanied the movement. A collection of vending machines was at the end of the hallway.

Daniel turned the corner and stalked the guard until the man stopped at the end. He reached into his pockets and began the process of feeding the machine. Daniel timed his footsteps with the loud rumbling of the machine. He came within arm's reach of the man and stood up from his hunched posture.

Daniel raised his right hand and bashed the back of the man's head with the butt of his firearm. "Ha," he laughed. "I haven't had the opportunity to pistol whip someone in ages."

A disgusted groan met his ear. "Oh God, don't remind me of that mess."

Daniel turned around to see Axel peeking around the corner of the door he had exited. His mouth opened, and his head tilted back in a yawn.

Daniel raised his left hand and gestured him over. He

tapped his left foot as his left eye twitched. Daniel spoke in a low, dangerous tone as Axel came closer. "What happened to cover me?"

"I thought he'd hear me if I tried to do that."

"You're lucky you don't have hair, or I'd grab it right now and show you how disappointed I am."

"Excuse me?"

"No, I won't. This isn't a game, Axe. The next time someone says to cover them, you'd better do so." He strode up to him and came face to face. "You understand me?"

A burst of static precluded Tanya's voice asking. "You boys about ready to go upstairs yet? You can't sit there all night. As much fun as listening to you discipline the new guy is, you need to get moving."

"I got it already." Daniel pursed his lips before a wide grin graced his features. "You're going first this time."

"Danny is that really wise?"

Daniel looked right into Axel's eyes as he answered. "He needs to realize that if he won't cover the point man, he gets to be him."

Tanya's wavering voice said, "Okay then."

"Don't worry. I'll actually be watching your back," Daniel said with a smug grin. "Pay attention."

"I'm not sure how he's supposed to do that when he'll have his back to you, but okay then."

"I, he'll have to..." Daniel sputtered. "That's not what's important here."

"Fine, I get it," Axel said in a quiet voice. "Upstairs we go then."

Another burst of static interrupted the two men, followed by Tanya's voice. "I'm afraid this will have to wait, boys. We just received orders to get back to headquarters as soon as possible."

"Fuck that, we're already here," Daniel said. "There's no sense in giving up now."

"Axel, if you know what's good for you, you'll listen to me. The crown prince of crime there may be able to get away with it, but not you or me."

"Hold your ground, Axe. You're staying right here until we're done. We'll be heroes by the night's end if you follow me, kid."

Tanya's voice immediately said. "You're liable to be in a shallow grave by tomorrow if you do as he says. You do not ignore the big man if you want to last long, Axel. Seriously, listen to me for your own good."

Axel wiped his forehead with his arm and shook his head. He exhaled a long breath, then pushed past Daniel, causing him to stumble back.

"You get back here right now," Daniel said with steel in his voice.

Tanya's amused voice entered his ear. "Sorry, Danny boy, but I'd follow him if I were you."

"What's that supposed to mean?"

"I may have just called the police, like the original plan called for. They'll be here in about seven minutes, if the local department doesn't slack off. This is for your own good you know."

Daniel punched one hand into his other palm. He followed Axel back to the first room they climbed in "If you say so," he muttered with clear contempt in his voice.

"You know how plans change," Tanya said.

He followed the large man back the way they had come. "Did they at least say why this is so important?" he asked as he lifted a leg to climb out the window.

"It was an encrypted mass mailing over the dark net. It wasn't chatty, considering everyone in the organization gets those. It simply said, and I'm quoting here, 'This is an emergency. Get back to main hq now. This is priority one.' If I had to guess, something big went down."

"Amazing deduction you made there," Daniel muttered in a sarcastic voice. He hopped down to the pavement and closed the window behind him.

"You'd best cool it, mister," Tanya said.

Daniel neglected to respond except for a series of grumblings and grunts. He reached the van and entered the passenger side. He sat down and leaned his chair all the way back. He placed his hands behind his head and closed his eyes. "Alert Rog and his beau, would you? We don't want them getting shit because they were 'too busy'."

"Oh good gracious," Tanya started. "I completely forgot. I'll call them now." She typed with renewed enthusiasm.

"You're not going to use the phone?" Daniel asked. He rolled his neck to his right as the engine roared to life. The van lurched forward down the street.

"That's so last decade. In this new millennium we have programs online that achieve the same thing." She paused for a moment with furrowed brows. "That's weird. His laptop doesn't have the program open. Let me just use a little remote access magic and I can..." She trailed off. Her eyes widened as a brilliant blush adorned her cheeks. She barely squeaked out. "Never mind. Use your phone and call Elizabeth yourself."

"What the hell just happened? Besides that, how do you know my sister would be the one to answer?"

Tanya shook her head left and right. She slapped her cheeks with both palms before looking at Daniel. "When I accessed his laptop, I naturally gained access to everything on it."

Daniel arched his back as his left hand dug into his back pocket. He fished out his cell phone. "Yeah? So what?"

"So every laptop nowadays has a built in web camera."

Daniel burst into uproarious laughter. He slapped his knee with his free hand and then brought it up to wipe away the tears now forming. "You get an eyeful, did you? I guess technology isn't always all it's cracked up to be."

"You two are to never tell them about this. You get me? If you do, I swear I will make your lives miserable."

"It would be such an hilarious conversation starter though," Daniel said as he punched numbers into his phone.

"Danny, I'm warning you. Do not push this further."

Quiet chuckling from the driver's seat interrupted the argument in its tracks. "You guys crack me up sometimes."

"Yeah whatever, chuckles. Just keep driving." Daniel brought up the phone to his ear. "I wonder if her phone is even on. It's been four rings already."

"She was busy."

"Yes. You established that already."

Daniel sighed and flicked the flip phone closed. "She's not answering." His left hand pointed forward. "We're swinging back around to pick them up, Axe."

"I got it," the still smiling man said.

Daniel angled to face the back. "Looks like we'll be a little late getting to the meeting."

Tanya put her hands to her face. "This is going to be great fun to explain why we were so late."

"Oh, you don't want to tell my father that his daughter was too busy getting plowed by the guy he doesn't like? You sure about that? It'll be a riot."

Tanya shook her head. "Poor Roger. This is not going to go well for him."

"Hey now, nothing will happen. Don't be stupid."

"How would you possibly know that?"

Daniel turned around in his seat and cracked his knuckles. "I wouldn't let it."

"Great plan you have there. You're going to punch out your father in the middle of a meeting? Oh Lord help me. Tell me you're not serious."

"You know me pretty well. Do you think I'm serious?"

"Oh shit."

19

A door slammed open revealing Bernard. "You sent the notice didn't you, boy?" Bernard asked the young man sitting by the nearby desktop in front of them. He looked over his shoulder at his boss as he approached. He turned back toward the monitor as Bernard approached.

"Y-Yes sir. I did." He stuttered out.

He leaned over the man and squinted his eyes. He rested a hand on his shoulder. "Send another, and would you make sure they know how urgent it is?"

"Right away, sir." The young man pushed his glasses further up his nose before he typed at a feverish pace.

Bernard laid a hand on the man's shoulder as he spoke. "Good man. That will be all." He turned around and made for the door. He stopped in the doorway and spoke a final line before exiting completely. "Keep this up, Paul, and you have a bright future here."

Paul's posture straightened up as he typed. "Thank you, sir."

Bernard closed the door and walked down the lavish hallway. He looked to his right and saw numerous works of art as he passed by. He muttered to himself. "Where are Daniel and Elizabeth? If those Irish bastards got a hold of them, I swear to God himself I'll kill them all."

He turned the corner to see a large set of double doors with two visibly armed men on either side. They nodded as he approached. "Almost everyone is here, boss."

"Who's missing? As if I have to guess."

"We're afraid no one's seen Mr. Morris or Ms. Morris so far."

"If they show up, show them in. Is that understood?"

Both men brought their right hand up to their chest in a salute. "Of course, sir."

Bernard nodded. The two men each reached over, grabbed a knob, and pulled the doors open. He stepped forward to see the large table almost filled on both sides, with only two vacant seats near his own. He stepped forward and pulled out the chair at the head of the table before taking a seat with a grunt.

"As we all know, we're officially at war. The Irish came after a few of us, but we fended them off. They're desperate now. You know how I know? They called in their Irish Reaper."

A man to Bernard's right with slicked back, greasy hair and a toothpick in the corner of his mouth spoke up. "Boss, it's worse than that. We think they got Lenny too. No one's seen him the last few days."

"Edward, are you sure about that? They went after Lenny too?" Bernard asked. He shook his head and closed his eyes in a moment of silence. His eyes snapped open in a steely gaze, and he spoke in an authoritative tone. "Alright, gentlemen. As you all know, we do not shirk from a fight." Men on both sides of the table nodded as he spoke. "We end it with overpowering force."

Men on both sides slapped the table, along with a chorus of "Damn right we do."

Bernard raised his hands, causing the ruckus to die down. "Boys, we're going to end all of this tonight. Those Irish are going to wish they'd never heard of the Morris family."

A knock behind him, along with a creaking sound, interrupted the meeting. Bernard angled himself around to look behind his chair. The same two guards, along with Daniel and Elizabeth, greeted him. He waved his hand to the side in a dismissive manner. "Thanks, boys. You may leave us now."

The two men bowed their heads before closing the door once again.

Bernard stood up and moved to his children. "How kind of you to grace us with your presence tonight."

Daniel jabbed a thumb to his right. "You know how heavy a sleeper Liz is."

Bernard pointed at Daniel and eventually poked him in the chest. "Be quiet, boy. This is no time for your wise-cracking ways."

Elizabeth's gaze fell to her own shoes, and a quiet voice escaped her mouth. "Sorry, Daddy."

A smattering of "Aw" came from behind Bernard.

Bernard sighed, and his scowl faded. He motioned behind him. "Just sit down already."

Daniel circled around to his father's right, only to be interrupted.

"You're not my right hand anymore, Son. That's your sister's seat now. You're over there." Bernard pointed to the seat to his left as he sat down.

Daniel leveled a silent glare at his father but gave a grudging nod and moved to his new seating.

"Now as I was saying before we were interrupted, we're ending this tonight."

A different man sporting a bushy mustache and a full beard sitting to Daniel's left spoke up. "We agree, boss, but what's the plan?"

"That's a good question, Bruce. A frontal assault is no good with these pricks, so we'll have to improvise. "

Elizabeth raised her hand off the table.

"Yes, dear?"

"I already had one of their biggest front companies hit and taken for everything we could carry. Along with that, I have a plan in motion that will cause them to start scrambling even harder."

Daniel looked at his sister and grit his teeth but remained silent.

"You did that without approval?" Bernard asked. "Very well, what is it exactly?"

Elizabeth leaned forward and brought her elbows on top of the table. She rested her chin on her hands. "As of an hour ago, the McCranes are the proud owner of about a truckload of assorted narcotics and psychedelics. Also, unfortunately, their second biggest front company got raided right afterward." She turned to her right with a smile. "It's a real shame when that happens, eh fellas?"

Uproarious laughter and cheers erupted from around the table.

A rare smile crept onto Bernard's face. "What can I say? You did good. But next time bring it up the ladder first."

"Yes, Daddy."

Bernard looked to his left. "What's wrong with you, boy? You're sitting there like a bull. Didn't you just hear your sister? You all struck quite a blow tonight. Be proud of it."

"Nothing's wrong."

"Putting aside the stick stuck up my son's ass, does anyone else have anything to say before we proceed?"

Eddy raised his hand, causing Bernard to nod in his direction. Eddy looked to his left at Elizabeth and then at Daniel. "With all due respect, your children's squad wasn't the only one attacked recently. They came after me and my crew earlier tonight with a death squad. One of my boys is down in the morgue now, and I want some payback."

Bernard nodded with solemn reverence. "I like your spirit, Edward. I just may send you and your group with the team I already had in mind." He looked to his left. "That includes you, boy. You're going."

Daniel perked up and looked to his father.

"I thought that that would get you out of your little funk. You and your sister's squad are taking point on this. We have it on good intel where their fabled hitman is staying. Not surprisingly, he's at their base of operations. We'll get you the specs on their building as soon as possible so you can plan. I'm not saying this will be easy, but the pride of the Morris family rests on this."

"We'll get it done," Elizabeth vowed.

"Good. Don't let me down. I'll let you and Edward discuss what personnel or equipment you'll need for this. Don't skimp out, and get it done the right way. Take whatever you need."

Elizabeth nodded and looked to her right at Eddy.

He took the toothpick out of his mouth and smiled. "You got it. With Gravedigger with us, it's as good as done."

A small, almost indecipherable, smile appeared on Daniel's face.

Bernard scraped his seat backwards along the hardwood floor and stood up. He placed his palms on the table and leaned forward. "Then that's it, gentlemen. By tomorrow we'll be done with this mess." He chuckled. "Now get your lazy asses back to work. You hear?" He turned around and left the room.

Everyone at the table followed suit and stood up. Most of them filed out the door behind Bernard.

Eddy and Bruce remained behind and approached the siblings.

Eddy stuck the tooth pick back in the corner of his mouth. "It's good to be working with you again, Daniel." He extended a hand.

Daniel mirrored the gesture and shared a firm hand-shake. "Eddy, the last time I remember running into you, we were having to carry your punctured carcass out after getting shot. Am I going to have to cover for your worthless ass again?" He asked with a straight face. A few moments passed before an unrestrained fit of laughter overtook them.

The two men extricated their hands and backed up a step. Eddy removed his toothpick and flicked it to the side. "It'll be nice working with a professional again."

"You boys done?" Elizabeth asked. She turned to Bruce. "When these two get started, they're almost as bad as him and Roger."

Bruce reached a hand up and scratched his bearded chin. "Is that young man still with you? From what I hear, he screwed up royally not too long ago and got us all into this shit. I would have thought you'd have dumped him already. That is, if the rumors are true." The corners of his mouth lifted.

Elizabeth took a step toward the man. "What did you hear exactly?"

Bruce matched her body language and stepped up to go toe to toe. His head tilted back as he spoke. The grin from before was still on display. "Rumor around the grapevine is he's in the doghouse. I'd have imagined you'd have dumped him."

Elizabeth bared her teeth, a twitch to her right eye."

Daniel laid a hand on her shoulder. "Forget about it, Sis. We need to start planning this operation if it's tonight. We have a lot of groundwork to lay if we don't want a colossal screw up," Daniel said.

"It is surprising we're going so soon," Bruce offered as he stepped back. "Normally, we have at least a week to get ready for something like this."

"It's like we're in a big hurry for some reason. It's not like Daddy to rush like this," Elizabeth said.

Eddy ran a hand through his gelled-back hair. "Don't worry, princess. Your dad knows what he's doing." He pulled up his left sleeve revealing a watch and brought it up to eye level. "Time's wasting away, and it's not our job to question the boss man - only to get the job done, boys and girl." His head swiveled between the siblings and Bruce. "In that vein, how about we start deciding who we're going to need for this little shindig?"

"Agreed," Elizabeth added. "We have a tech specialist that should be a great help."

"Is your little boy toy coming along with us?" Bruce chuckled.

"I've just about had it. I'd show him a little more respect, Bruce," Daniel warned in an even voice.

Eddy slapped the back of Bruce's head. "Stop being a dick," Eddy said. "He's saved my ass twice. Show him some fucking respect. You get me?"

"Yes, sir."

"Good." Eddy used his thumb to point at Bruce. "My second in command here doesn't know when to shut his mouth sometimes. My apologies."

"It's all good, brother," Daniel said. "So, we have a tech specialist and two operatives in me and Rog. Who are you bringing to this little party?"

"I've got the best sniper this side of the Mississippi River. His name's Jared. The kid's an ex-marine scout sniper. He's a little eccentric, but he'll hit whatever we tell him to aim at. It should be a good ambush for this little trap. I've also got a group of guys with automatic weapons who are pissed off."

"You can never have too many of those," Daniel said.

A quiet knock interrupted the planning, followed shortly by the creaking of the door opening.

Roger entered the room, holding a small pile of papers in his right hand. "I've got the specs you all need." He placed the papers on the table. "If you'll excuse me." He turned to exit the room.

"It's been a long time since I've seen you," Bruce said.

Roger stopped in his tracks and turned around. "I'm sorry, what?"

Bruce looked to Eddy to see him staring at him. He faced Roger again. "We've been talking about you is all."

Roger approached the group with an amiable smile. "Nothing bad I trust?"

Bruce passed a sideways glance at Elizabeth. "Not at all."

Eddy offered a firm handshake. "It's nice to see you again. I'll have to pay you back for all those times you've saved my life."

"Don't even worry about that. It's all in the past."

Daniel cleared his throat. "As much fun as this is, we need to collect everyone that's going on this little mission and have a meeting. You know, to make sure everyone knows what their job is."

"Then let's gather everybody and figure this out," Eddy

said. He made for the door with everyone filing in behind him.

An hour later...

"Is everyone here?" Daniel asked. He looked around the cramped room filled with chairs and men staring at him. Smoke floated up from the crowd. An occasional cough could be heard. He walked up to a large projector between the aisles of seats and flicked a switch. He grabbed the handheld device sitting on top and carried it with him. The image of floor plans appeared on the screen behind him. "As you all probably know by now, tonight we're going on a raid of sorts. The McCranes have fortified their estate out in the countryside, so we're going to have to get creative if we don't want a bloodbath on both sides." He turned behind him and nodded to Eddy.

Eddy walked up to the image and pointed at various points as he spoke. "This means a full-blown siege is out of the question. They have patrols on paths around the outside of the house that would see us before we even got anywhere close to the structure. Which is why we're going to send in a small three-man team to take them out. If anyone gets wise and comes investigating, that's where our sharpshooter extraordinaire comes in." He pointed to a young man in the front row who was raising his hand. "Yes Jared?"

"How are they going to know where the patrols are exactly?"

"Thanks to the wonders of technology, satellites, and a shortage of tree cover, that should be a relative non-issue for our specialist way in the back there." He pointed to Tanya sitting in the back of the room with her laptop open. "This should also give you a clear shot. If this happens, everyone else stationed here," he pointed to a point on the map on the north side, "will move in from the other side of the estate. You have far more tree cover on this side so take advantage of it. Your jobs then are to simply be a distraction for the team to get inside and complete the job. So be careful, and don't get your asses shot off. This is the worst-case scenario. Best case is the three-man team gets it all done without alerting anyone. Any questions?"

Jared raised his hand. "Where am I setting up for this?"

Daniel pointed toward the bottom of the diagram. "This right here is their driveway. It's long, straight and pretty much a perfect kill zone. It's up to you where to set up, but I'd suggest somewhere that can take advantage of this. We'll be sticking near there to ambush the guards. It has the perfect cover for our ambush with what few trees there are." He locked eyes with the young man. "Of course, if you're not confident you can hit from that distance, we can always change it."

Jared brought a thumb into his mouth and ripped away a piece of hanging fingernail before spitting it out. "I don't miss."

"Now that that's settled, let's keep going. Our main target is this man." He pressed a button on the device in his hand causing the image to change into a photograph. It showed a red headed man with numerous scars scattered over his face and a shorter man to his side. Both were holding rifles slung over their shoulder. The shorter man had a black X over his face. "You may have heard of this man. His name is Murtaugh O'Connel. You may know him better by his alias, 'The Irish Reaper'."

A few assorted gasps echoed in the small room.

Eddy stepped forward with a shout. "Don't start that now. He's a man the same as any of us. He's also injured right now due to one of our new recruits I'm proud to say. His middle finger was blown off as he was flipping the kid off," he said with a smile.

Sporadic chuckling erupted throughout the crowd before Eddy continued. "However, make no mistake; he is still extremely dangerous. We don't think he'll be deployed if our distraction is. If he is, then our three-man team will flank them and turn the tide in our favor. One way or the other, gentlemen, there's going to be a lot of dead Irish by the end of the night. If you're wondering who the shorter one is, it's his nephew. Michael was not as popular as his uncle Murtaugh, but just as deadly. Thankfully in the same shootout he was fatally wounded, so he won't be a problem."

Daniel stepped up past Eddy. "He's out for blood tonight. He's just one man though, and I'll be leading this operation personally along with my team. Anyone have a problem with that?"

Not a single word was spoken, or hand raised at that question.

"Alright, gentlemen. We leave here at ten tonight. Get some sleep. Make sure you draw night vision scopes from the armory before we go. It won't do for you to be firing blind and showing a muzzle flash unnecessarily. You may also want to take a few grenades. It's going to get down and dirty, gentlemen. Make damned sure you're strapped to the nines before we go. We'll be set up by eleven. By one in the morning this will be all over. Do not be late, or you'll answer to me. Dismissed."

As if on cue, most men stood up and exited the room.

This left only a handful who made their way up to the front of the room.

"Grenades? Well, I guess that makes it official," Roger said as he sauntered forward with his hands in his pants pockets. "I just have one question about this."

"What's that?" Eddy asked.

"I wonder why our objective is to simply take out a single hitman. Why not obliterate the entire organization if we're going this far?"

Daniel's brows raised. "I never expected you to ask that. You are right though, why not?"

"No, I'm not suggesting that we-"

"No, it's a good question, brother," Daniel interrupted. "While we're there, why not rid ourselves of this in one go?"

"Those are not our orders is why, Brother. I'm sure Daddy has his reasons," Elizabeth chimed in. She slid past Roger and stopped beside him. "Maybe he wants to relaunch a business relationship after all this is done? It would be rather difficult to do so if we wiped them all out. Hell, it could be as simple as not wanting everyone else to fear doing business with us if we kill them all."

"If we get a chance to take out their top brass, do we go for it or not?" Daniel asked.

"I'd suggest we ask your father that before we go," Roger said.

"That'll be hard to do, considering he left an hour ago right after the meeting," Tanya interrupted from now the second row of chairs. "I think we're on our own here."

"I guess it's up to us then," Daniel said.

"Oh Lord," Tanya sighed.

20

———

"What time is it?" Daniel asked with his back to a tree and his pistol in his right hand pointing down at the ground.

"According to my phone it's five 'til midnight," Roger answered while looking down at the phone in his left hand. His right hand held one of his trusty revolvers.

"Five more minutes until the party starts," Eddy said from his squatting position behind a nearby bush. He raised a finger to his ear and a beep could be heard. "Jared are you in position and ready?"

"Roger that. I can see anyone and everything moving down the driveway."

"Everyone else in position?" Eddy asked.

Bruce's voice answered. "Ten-four, sir. We're waiting on your signal."

"The patrols are on their way, Danny. You three best get ready to do whatever you're going to do. They're coming from your left in the direction of the compound. There're only two of them in this group."

"Sir!" Jared's voice said. "If you'd like, I can take them out now without fuss. They're walking straight at me."

"Hold your fire. Multiple sniper shots will only alert them to our presence."

"Understood."

Daniel's left hand reached down to his belt line and, with the sound of sliding metal, unsheathed his hunting knife. "I think that's our cue, gentlemen." He moved his knife to his right and swapped his gun to his left.

Eddy followed suit and unsheathed his own blade. He held the blade up and let the moonlight glimmer. "I've got the second one. Rog, can you get them to turn around?"

"Fine by me," Roger whispered. "I hate knives." He got down on all fours and felt around the dirt. He clenched his hand and got back into a sitting position. "Ready?" he mouthed.

The two men nodded. Roger flicked his arm, causing a small rock to go flying onto the far side of the gravel driveway. The incoming footsteps slowed as they approached. "Did you hear that? Sounds like it came from over there," one voice spoke.

"It's just a rabbit or some shit I bet. Still, I guess we'd better check it out," a different deeper voice said.

Roger pointed at the two men and tilted his head toward the voices.

The two men emerged from their cover and stalked toward the now visible guards. Daniel approached the one on the right, and Eddy flanked them on their left.

The two guards stopped side by side. "I guess it was nothing."

Eddy and Daniel's right hands were at their sides as they closed within a few yards. As they entered melee range, their left hands reached up and closed around their necks. Their right hands swung back and shot forward in a flash. Muffled screams from the guard on the left escaped Eddy's hand.

Daniel's guard went rigid as the knife entered the back of his neck. The sound of wet gurgling escaped his victim's mouth as he jerked around. His hands reached up and grasped at Daniel's in a futile display. It stopped for a moment as Daniel grunted, and his knife slid to the side with a sickening snap. His victim went motionless as soon as the knife slid to the side with a pop. He promptly collapsed into Daniel's arms and soon to the ground below.

"For fuck's sake, go to sleep you bog trotter," Eddy growled. His right hand kept moving back and forth into the man's lower back. The sound of ripping cloth and wet thunks could be heard with each thrust of the blade.

"If you'll allow me," Daniel said with a grin. He moved forward and brought his own blade up to the man's neck, slicing in a horizontal motion. Spurts of blood shot out of his neck and onto Daniel's wincing face. Within ten seconds the man had lost all fight and fell to the ground.

Eddy squatted down, grabbed his man's legs, and dragged him off to the tree cover he'd just abandoned. "How the hell did you do that so fast?"

Daniel grabbed the arm of his victim and followed Eddy. "I don't know. I aimed for his spine through his neck and tried to sever on the first stab. It's tougher than it looks though."

"You're supposed to go for the spine? I was always taught the kidneys were the ticket."

"Ah, it is fatal, but not nearly so quick as removing the brain from the equation. You just have to be sure your blade is sharp enough. Those damned discs in the neck don't mess around and can get you stuck if you're not careful."

They backed up through the bushes and dumped the bodies beside Roger's hiding place.

Roger stood up immediately. "I guess that's my cue to get ready." He raised a finger to his ear. "Tanya are there any more patrols nearby?"

"I'm seeing another two groups on the north side, so I'd say you have around ten minutes or so to get inside."

"Alright, I'll take point then," Roger said to the two men nearby. "I can't let you two have all the fun, can I? Not after these bastards tried to take me out." He jogged off ahead of the two men. He ran along the driveway on his right with only a limited tree line and the cover of darkness to obscure him. He could hear the crumpling of grass behind him as they moved closer to the estate.

When they got within one hundred yards of the mansion, a loud piercing crack stopped the group cold in their tracks. Roger whispered, "Oh God, please tell me that isn't what I think it is." It wasn't the end of the noise though, as suddenly a whole symphony of gun shots sounded off.

Daniel activated his microphone with a finger to his ear. "What the hell's going on out there? We said not to engage!"

A loud alarm bell echoed through the night along with the cascade of firearms. "Goddamn," Daniel started. "Where's that coming from?"

"Judging by all the lights, I think the first came from behind you and now the majority are coming from the north side. It looks like someone jumped the gun, quite literally here. As if that's not enough, I'm seeing a big crowd of heavily armed men pouring out the back of the compound and taking up what limited defensive positions there are out in the backyard."

"Are there any headed south toward us?" Daniel asked.

"Not that I can see, but it's a royal mess out there," Tanya said. "Keep your heads down. For all intents and purposes, you're in a war zone out there now."

"Great," Roger muttered. He turned back to the two men behind him. "I guess that means we got our distraction, so let's not waste it, eh fellas?"

"Right," Eddy agreed. He raised a finger to his ear. "Jarod? What the hell was that about? I told you to hold your fire."

No answer ever came.

"Jerry, you answer me right now."

"Come on, guys. This opportunity won't last forever. We have to go now," Roger said as he moved perpendicular to the road toward the structure, amid the constant noises pervading the air.

Daniel and Eddy fell in behind Roger. The group reached the house and placed their backs to the bricks. A short stairwell leading to the door was to his right. Roger looked to his right at the two men. "Are we going in the front door then?"

"It'd be where I'd go if I was Murtaugh," Daniel said. "Either that, or he's out back with the rest of them."

Eddy kicked off the wall and jogged up the stairs beside them to the door. "We'd best get started then." He reached down to the knob with his left hand, his other poised ready to fire through the entryway. He pulled the handle, angling his pistol into the building all the while. The door opened with nary a squeak. He peered inside and waved Daniel and Roger over. As they moved to catch up, Eddy went inside by himself.

"Hey, hold up, bro," Daniel called out. "We have to stick together." He and Roger skipped up the stairs to see Eddy holding his pistol at his side behind a large marble pillar on the left. He waved his free hand to the side, signaling to the two men to stay out.

Daniel quickly craned his neck to scan the room. He looked up to the second floor past a lavish stairwell. Numerous men were kneeling with rifles pointing down at them. They were inserting another magazine into their rifles. His eyes widened. Without pause, he reached out with his right hand and pushed Roger with all his might.

Roger crashed against the concrete handrail and ended up pinned behind the now open door with a grunt.

Daniel dove to the opposite side just in time to hear numerous hisses of air. He got into a sitting position, then pivoted around the door and fired a few shots blindly up into the air. His head leaned away from the door as he screamed. "We've got a rat, boys! Someone sold us out to these Paddies."

"If I catch him, I'll rip his spine out," Eddy shouted from inside. "Ah shit, I'm pinned down in here."

"Keep your head down. I've got a surprise for them," Daniel said.

"You're not going to..." Roger's question died on his lips as he peered around the door and saw Daniel fish a grenade out of his pockets. He huddled into the corner, covered his ears, and called out, "Danger close in there. Get down!"

Daniel pulled the pin and, without delay, angled himself to toss it around the door. He hurled it underhanded with a grunt. Without waiting, he tucked himself away in his corner and covered his ears.

A few seconds later a thunderous explosion shook the ground, accompanied by a symphony of screams. Directly after the screams, a crumbling noise along with creaking could be heard.

"What's that noise?" Roger asked. "I can hear something over the ringing in my ears."

"Take that, you muckers!" Eddy's voice cried out. No sooner had he yelled these words than a new deafening noise replaced it. "Son of a whore! The whole upstairs balcony is coming down in here. Make way out there."

Immediately after Eddy cried out, the sound of frantic stomps approached the front door. Eddy sprinted past the door and descended the five stairs before kneeling behind the concrete in front of Roger.

"I don't guess anyone can see inside?" Roger asked. When no answer came, he shook his head with a sigh. "Fine, I'll look then." He poked his head around the door and wrinkled his nose. He ducked back behind his makeshift cover with a sudden sneeze. "I can't see jack in there. There's too much dust obscuring the view. I guess that's the price of using a high explosive device. I'm just glad everyone's whole."

"Thank you, brother," Eddy said. "I thought I had made my last mistake there for a minute."

A crackle of noise in their ears caused them to cringe, and then Tanya's voice came. "This is nice and all fellas, but I have a positive ID on our target. He's upstairs firing out a window toward our forces on the north side. You have got to get in there now. We're being pushed back and are beginning to take casualties out there. I also am seeing a disturbing instrument on the roof. I'm not sure what that monstrosity is, but I think they're loading something into-" Tanya's voice became drowned out by a massive explosion. A slight rumble below them caused the glass above them to shatter. "Oh shit. That's a fricking piece of artillery up there! Move your asses now and take him out before all our men are blown away!"

A panicked voice screamed into the radio. "They have explosives they're raining down on us! For God's sake, tell me you're almost done. We're getting slaughtered out here! We need backup for Christ's sake! I repeat, we need-" Another thunderous sound rattled the earth, and the voice was cut off.

The ground shook. Roger held his chest as he spoke. "Jesus! My insides hurt even from here from that explosion. I cannot believe I'm saying this, but we need to hurry up and get in there. Eddy, could you lay down a hail of fire where you saw them before? I don't want to go in there with my ass hanging in the wind."

"I've got it," Eddy vowed. He exchanged his current magazine with a fresh one with the sound of shuffling metal and a click. "Just stay low. They were up top."

"Understood." Roger inhaled a deep breath and exhaled through his mouth. He pushed the door to his left allowing him to escape the hidey-hole he'd used as cover. He crouched down and pointed at Eddy.

Eddy angled his pistol up and unloaded a veritable stream of bullets.

Roger seized the opportunity and moved from his hunched down position. His right hand waved back and forth in front of his face. He squinted his eyes as he looked for any sliver of cover in the now obliterated foyer. He slid behind the still standing handrail. He called out. "The stairs are still intact, along with the door at the top. Come in, but be careful. I'll watch your backs. Keep going straight and up the stairs." He brandished his six shooter and peeked out behind the negligible cover.

Daniel went first and followed Roger into the building. He covered his mouth and could barely make out Roger's form in front of him. He passed by Roger's right with a quiet comment, "Going right." With just those two words he jogged up the now damaged stairwell.

Roger's aim drifted to the left as he scanned. He saw a movement of black in the dusty interior and immediately squeezed the trigger.

Daniel hunched down in position with an expletive. "Shit, did you get him?"

"I don't see any more movement, but I can't really see all that well."

"I'll check," Eddy vowed as he approached Roger from behind. He stopped and squatted down. "Where was he?"

"Upstairs to the left. Be careful up there. I'll watch your back."

Eddy slapped Roger's shoulder. "I know. You be careful too," he said as he got up and made his way up the ruined staircase. A few moments passed before both Daniel and Eddy's voices cried out. "Clear!"

A loud stomping came from the staircase. A powerful blast shook the foundation below them and caused a small crashing noise inside as well.

"What the hell was that? You okay, brother?" Daniel asked.

"I'm fine, just have that funny feeling inside again," Roger said in a quiet tone. "I just kind of tripped when I heard that explosion is all. Let's keep going," he said, now between the two men at the top of the stairs.

"I'll take point," Daniel said. "Rog, you're behind me. Eddy, you'll cover our flank. Got it?"

Eddy began the process of reloading. "Give me a sec and we're ready boys."

Roger flipped open the chambers of the weapons in his hands and did the same. "Let's be sure we're prepared first. When's the last time you reloaded?"

"Don't need to," Daniel fired back.

"Just check why don't you? I don't want your laziness to be the end of us."

"I only fired three rounds, I have thirteen left in this magazine. That's it. Now let's go already. Our boys are being slaughtered while we piddle around."

"Good point," Roger said.

The three men lined up single file in front of the door. Daniel reached for the handle and turned.

A few minutes earlier...

Elizabeth hovered over Tanya's shoulder. Her right hand reached out to the screen and pointed. "Does that say they're making their way inside now?"

"Yes," Tanya said in a low, even voice. "Now if you'd please stop blocking my view, I could tell you more."

"Fine, Ms. Snippy." She crossed her arms in front of her under her chest. "Besides, shouldn't I be the one to be worried here? It's my brother and boyfriend out in that."

"Maybe, but I'm the one who has to watch all of it, including watching our boys get blown up outside. Since we didn't get proper time to prepare and had to go purely on schematics, we walked right into this one. Forgive me if I'm not in the best of moods."

"I guess you're probably worried about my brother too. I didn't even think of that."

"Danny can take care of himself," Tanya immediately said. Her index finger tapped the front of her laptop.

"Of course he can."

"Not to tell you how to do your job, but shouldn't you be

more concerned with the manpower being slaughtered in droves out there?" She raised a hand to her mouth as she gazed at the monitor. "Oh good God. All that's left of that one is his boot."

"Me?"

"Well, you're the one technically in charge of this op, aren't you?"

"My brother and his group are inside the building now, right?"

Tanya tapped the mouse pad in front of her with her finger. The picture zoomed in on the front door of the compound. "As you can see, they're no longer outside. I'm not sure that's much safer, but yes, you're right."

"If they're inside, they'll get the job done."

"You hope so anyway."

"What's that supposed to mean?"

"It means it's mighty convenient that you'll get the credit and you're back here at the back lines."

Elizabeth's hands balled into fists. "I'm going to chalk that one up to stress. They volunteered for it anyway."

"Whatever you say," Tanya said under her breath. Her left ring finger reached across the keyboard and slammed on the tab key. Her right hand danced around the touch pad and pushed down, resulting in several clicks. A picture of the building's blueprints popped up. "Okay, now according to these schematics, you need to go through the foyer door leading upstairs and at the end of that hallway hang a right. It'll be the second door on your left. Murtagh is in there. At least that was the intel the boys gave me as soon as this war started. He may have moved, so be on your guard in there."

Tanya leaned back in the van's backseat. Her head fell back, and she rubbed her eyes. "I'm supposed to be raiding right now."

"You are raiding," Elizabeth said. "I mean, helping to raid a rival organization's headquarters has got to count for something, right?"

"Wrong kind of raiding," Tanya muttered. "Talk about progression raiding though, at least I'm used to being raid leader." Her eyes widened as her focus fell back to the screen. Her finger slammed down on an altogether different push to talk button. "Hold your position! I repeat, hold where you are!" She grunted and lifted her arm up before slamming it down onto the arm rest beside her.

"What's happening?"

"The men are fleeing for their lives. We'd better hope they're chased too, because otherwise all those defensive units are going to be headed back into the building." She looked up and looked deep into Elizabeth's eyes. "Our boys are in there alone right now with no distraction."

21

Three men walked single file down a dark corridor. The leader spoke softly. "We're almost there," Daniel said. "Get ready now. After this we're high tailing it out of here. Simple, right?"

Tanya's manic voice interrupted their approach. "You all need to get out right now."

"Negative," Daniel answered. "We're right outside the door."

"The men outside have abandoned the three of you. You need to get out while the extraction window is still open. The McCrane's manpower outside is flowing back into the building. Get out while you still can, Danny." She paused before an almost incoherent word followed. "Please."

"I get it already. We'll be back before you know it. We're going now and will be running out afterward. Good enough?"

"It better be," Tanya's dry voice said over the coms.

"I think she's worried about you," Roger said.

"That's sweet and all, but it's go time. I'll take point. Rog,

I want you on the right. Eddy, I want you on the other side of the door. As soon as Rog opens that damned door, we all unleash hell. You got it?"

The men nodded without a word and got into position around the door. Roger holstered one of his revolvers, pulled back the hammer of the other in his right hand, and reached for the doorknob with his left. He grasped it and looked at his friend in front of him.

Daniel laid down on the floor in a prone position with his handgun pointed in front of him. He looked at Roger and mouthed, "Go."

Roger, right hand holding his firearm, traced the pattern of the cross over his chest. He exhaled before twisting his left hand and swinging the door open.

Eddy pointed his pistol into the doorway and squeezed the trigger, causing a veritable hail of gunfire to enter the room. Roger's one revolver did its part along with Daniel's handgun, bouncing in his grip with every muzzle flash, until a series of clicks and a deafening silence overtook the men again.

"Did we get him?" Eddy asked.

"We certainly got somebody," Daniel said with dry wit. He stood up and started the process of reloading his pistol. "Cover me. I'm going to go confirm the kill."

"Right behind you, brother," Roger said while busy reloading his six shooter. He flicked his wrist to the right causing the chamber to shut. "Ready to go."

"Eddy, you cover our exit."

"They won't get past me," he said with a wide smile revealing a gold tooth. He ejected the clip at the bottom of the handgun and inserted another. He stood watch just outside the door craning his neck left and right periodically.

Roger moved behind Daniel and pulled out his second revolver. He tapped Daniel's shoulder with the butt of one. He extended his arm and pointed to the right.

Daniel moved with his pistol in front of him at the ready. As soon as he cleared the doorway he pivoted to the left and scanned the room. A large window sat behind the only bed, with a high powered rifle pointing out of it on a tripod completely abandoned.

He moved forward toward the bed and gazed at the body laying before him.

"This isn't him. It's the little bastard Michael."

"What?" Roger asked. "That can't be. We took him down."

Roger's attention flew to the right side of the room. A lone desktop computer sat on the only desk in the room. He walked over and shook the mouse. "No password on startup. Either someone was confident in their security, or they didn't care if someone saw," he said out loud.

"They could have left in a hurry too, right?" Eddy asked from the hallway.

Daniel leaned into the still body. "It looks like they've bandaged him up pretty good." His left hand reached down toward the man's throat and placed his index and middle fingers on the exposed flesh. "He's dead, and we didn't even hit him from the looks of it."

"Murtaugh probably didn't want to give up on his nephew and brought him back here is my guess," Roger said.

"You're probably right." He straightened up his posture, turned back to the doorway, and walked. "No time to sit here and theorize though. We have a job to finish."

"Just a second," Roger begged. "Come here." He pointed

at the screen as soon as he heard Daniel's footsteps come up behind him. "See this? According to this still in session browser, Murtaugh was receiving emails from someone with the screen name of "xXMercyKill69Xx. Real original handle," Roger quipped. "The last message was at ten p.m." He paused. "That was after our little briefing, in time where they could still set up an ambush." He looked over his left shoulder. "This could be our rat." His free hand reached for his phone, flicked the screen, and input his password. He tapped the phone and held the phone up to the screen before tapping again with a faint noise. "I got a screenshot at least. That should help track him down if we can get it back to Tanya."

A series of gunshots along with Eddy's voice caused Daniel and Roger to duck and seek cover behind the bed. "You want me you sheep fuckers? You ain't getting in here." More gunfire erupted. "Shit!" A small thud interrupted his tirade. "You think one little bullet will stop me? You're not getting my boys in here. It'll be over my dead body." Eddy fell back into the room and crawled back behind cover.

They crouched behind the bed and angled their firearms toward the door, trying to cover Eddy.

A loud voice emerged over the loudspeaker above the door. "That can be arranged."

Yet more bullets flew. The thin doorframe Eddy held up behind had holes appearing beside his head. He angled his firearm around the corner and squeezed off more rounds. "I'll kill all of you overgrown leprechauns. Mark my words!" Another hole appeared mere inches beside his temple. "You only nicked my ankle. You think this is over?" The last of the hail of gunfire erupted and Eddy's head slumped forward with a fresh hole apparent in the back of his head.

"Eddy?" Daniel asked. "Eddy, don't tell me..." he trailed off.

No answer came from the other side of the room. Only Eddy's still open unmoving eyes could be seen beside the door.

"Eddy?" Roger called out. He looked in front of him to see Daniel's head poking up over the bed's frame. He shook his head.

A low, growling, but unmistakably Irish voice came to life along with some white noise, and echoed across the building. "I'm afraid he isn't going to answer, boys. He's got an acute case of lead poisoning in his brain matter at the moment, courtesy of yours truly. I don't recommend stepping foot outside that door unless you want the same."

"I think the mission objective just went from assassination to survival," Roger said in a dry voice.

The voice roared to life over the building's intercom again. "I'd listen to your somewhat intelligent friend if I were you, Morris. I have the advantage here, and we both know it. You two fell for the trap - hook, line, and sinker."

Daniel spoke in a loud, clear voice. "Maybe we did, but you using your own nephew as bait, that's stone cold."

"When you're dealing with the infamous Daniel Morris you'll take advantage of anything available. Now be good, boys. Throw your weapons into the hallway, and we'll let you live. We may even give you back after a little ransom, if you're lucky."

Daniel stood up and swept his neck across the room. "Well with us huddled in here, why don't you come get us?"

"So I can waste precious men? No, we're not as cheap with lives as the Morris family apparently is. Thanks for letting us get some target practice in by the way. We hadn't had a chance to use that ordinance yet. Only problem is all the body parts we're going to have to clean up. There's always a price for new toys being deployed after all."

Daniel knelt beside Roger and whispered into his ear. "They don't have cameras in here. Find a way out while I keep him busy."

"Got it," Roger said. He stalked his way to the window. He squatted low when he got near the paneled glass. He poked his head above the bottom of the frame and looked out. He also looked straight down to see a wall of ivy and a wooden trellis lining the outside of the manor. Bushy hedges lined the outside of the building below him.

He ducked and took cover back behind the bed. He reached into his back pocket and his thumbs typed once the screen lit up. "SOS. Need distraction of any kind. We have plan, need chance to use it. Keep them away from north side." He hit send and started typing once again. "Didn't see anyone outside." He turned to Daniel. "The girls know. Now we stall until they give us opportunity." He held the screen up facing Daniel.

Meanwhile back in the van

A low vibration interrupted the tranquil quiet of the cabin. Elizabeth retrieved her phone from her pocket. "I swear this better not be spam. Oh God," she gasped.

"What? Is it a malware infected file or something?" Tanya asked.

"Take a look for yourself," she said as she shoved the phone into the backseat into Tanya's field of vision.

Her eyes veered left and right a few times as she looked

at the small screen. At the end she uttered only two words. "Of course." She typed at an accelerated pace.

Elizabeth placed her phone back in her pants pocket. "That's it? We need to do something."

"I'm working on it. It looks like you'll be involved in this after all." She looked up from the screen. "I have a plan, but you're probably not going to like it."

"What I don't like is my brother and Rog being trapped in there with the enemy while I'm sitting on my ass out here. Lay the plan on me already. I'll do anything."

"Are the windows in this thing bulletproof?"

Elizabeth spared a glance toward the front windshield and back at Tanya. "Oh shit. Yeah, they are."

"We know the explosive on their roof is pointing north and has a low launch angle, so it can't hit close to the building. That machine takes a long time to reposition; so, if we hurry this should work. We're going to drive this thing right up to the front door and lob another grenade through said door. That should get them scurrying to defend the south side. While they're busy playing catch up, we'll circle around the north side and hopefully pick up the boys. What do you think?"

Elizabeth blinked before turning to Axel who was sitting in the driver's seat. "Where are the grenades?"

He looked at her. "I believe they're in the back, but are you sure we should-"

"This isn't a debate. We're going." She climbed into the backseat beside Tanya. She got onto her knees and reached over into the large back chamber. She grunted and leaned forward. Her right hand crested over the seat holding a green, round shape. "Got it!"

"Do you even know how to use one of those?" Axel asked, causing the two women to look at him. "You can't just pull the pin and throw one of those sons of bitches over-handed like a baseball you know. You have to toss those underhanded for safety reasons."

"Why not?" Elizabeth asked.

"That's how you get a whole squad blown up, because some idiot lets go of it too late. At least that's what my old CO told me during training. In this case, it'd be us and the vehicle. I know this, because there's no way you'll be able to toss that from a sitting position in this cramped space."

"Huh," Tanya grunted. "Today I learned."

"You want me to toss a grenade out of a moving vehicle's window underhanded while sitting down. How exactly?" Elizabeth asked.

"I, uh," Axel hesitated. "We never had training on throwing them from a vehicle before. It was always on the practice field in BT. I guess you may have to open the window, stand half out of the vehicle, and toss it that way?"

"I guess we're improvising then because I'm not getting shot if I can help it, which I would if I did it your way," Elizabeth said. "Signal the boys that we're starting our run and to get outside on the north field in a few minutes." She transferred the explosive into her left hand and rested her right beside the window controls to her side.

"Just give me the damned thing." Axel held an open hand out. He saw Elizabeth glare at him. "No offense, but I know I can make this work. I don't trust someone who's never handled explosives before."

"Oh yeah? And how are you going to do that as the driver?"

"When I stop, I'll reach out my window and lob it over the car onto the porch area. Think of it like a hook shot in basketball. I know I can hit that big of a target. You? I don't trust so much since you've never thrown one. It's harder to throw than it looks."

"So be it." Elizabeth handed the ordinance over to Axel and watched him place it on his lap."

Axel made sure the grenade was secured. "Then we're ready to go."

Tanya exhaled. "So much for being safe on the back lines. I mean, this is as improvised a plan as you get. I hear that's a great idea in a war zone," Tanya muttered as her thumbs danced across her phone.

"A little less negativity please," Elizabeth sang in a sugary sweet voice.

Axel ran his hands over his chest before sighing with a smile.

"What are you doing?" Elizabeth asked.

"Just making sure I was wearing my vest for this. You guys do know bullet proof windows are more like bullet resistant, right? I mean, some do get through if they keep their spread tight."

"They do?" Tanya asked in a higher pitch than before.

"Calm down. You can hunker down behind his seat." Elizabeth looked out the window to her right before muttering, "I'm the one up front."

A low electronic beep prompted Tanya to speak up. "Message sent. They should be making their way outside if they can."

"We'd better pray they can. We won't be able to stay out there long," Axel said.

"They'll be there," Elizabeth said with resolute determination in her voice.

"We hope," Tanya chimed in. "If they're not..." She trailed off. Her right hand reached up and wiped a solitary tear away. "Never mind, they'll be there. They have to be."

"Hope really works in combat situations in my experience," Axel said under his breath with a sarcastic edge. His right hand reached up and hovered over the key hanging in the ignition. "Everyone ready?"

He received no response except for an ever so slight 'Go' from Elizabeth.

He grasped the keys and twisted...

22

Daniel angled his hand around the door corner and fired off two more rounds in a blind fire down the hallway. He ejected the magazine and investigated the bottom before inserting it again. He held up two fingers in Roger's direction.

Roger climbed over the bed and made his way over to Daniel. He stopped beside him, shoulder to shoulder, when he felt a familiar rumble in his back pocket. He fished his phone out and his eyes widened. He held up the screen in front of Daniel.

"Get outside on the north side? What the fuck? What good will that do?"

"Do you hear that?" Roger asked. He raised an index finger up. "Shh, I hear something. It sounds like a car engine. Oh no don't tell me they're going to-"

A loud explosion and a rumbling caused them both to stumble. "No time to second guess. Let's go!" Roger called out. He made a break for the window and climbed out. His left foot reached down and kicked a foothold through the wooden lining. He made his way down at a controlled pace and then heard a grunt above him. He looked up to see Daniel following suit. He hopped off the lattice and looked around him. "Hurry up. I hear an engine again. I think they're nearly here."

"I'm going as fast as I can," Daniel barked. "Just watch the damned window. They may start getting curious."

"Good point," Roger agreed. He drew a lone revolver and leveled it above his friend toward the open window. A head poked out and looked down at Daniel. A spark and a crack to his right caused him to fall screaming back inside the building.

"They're outside on the ground. They climbed down the ivy. Get out back now before they get away."

"Damn, I missed," Roger muttered. He raised his voice with a hand cupped around his mouth. "Hurry up, for God's sake. Just jump. You're like three feet off the ground at this point."

Daniel hopped off the structure and turned around. "I'll be glad to never do that again." He saw Roger still aiming above him and suddenly heard his friend call out, "Move!"

Daniel lowered himself closer to the ground and made a mad dash toward Roger. Another loud crack fired off into the night, except this time a dull thud and the crunching of grass followed it. He turned around to see a body behind him, face down in the grass and dirt. "Good looking out. There's our ride coming now," he said with a point over Roger's shoulder. He watched them swerve through the grass around the corner of the manor.

The van screeched to a halt beside them and the back-seat door slid open immediately. Elizabeth's voice welcomed them. "Get in."

The two men didn't hesitate and jumped in, Daniel first. Roger backed up with his revolvers still trained on the building until Daniel reached out with both hands and dragged him further in. "Go." He reached over Roger and slammed the door shut. They both fell over backwards as the vehicle gunned it and made a turn on a dime. The roar of the engine was soon replaced with yet more gunfire being leveled in their direction. This only lasted a few moments until the pitter patter of a gravel road beneath them indicated they were finally away from the compound. The van finally turned onto the local highway.

"You two get closer while you were away?" Tanya teased the two entangled men by her feet.

Daniel immediately pushed Roger away. "I was just saving him is all. The dingus here was just standing there." He scrambled to get up and into the backseat beside Tanya.

"Says the guy who I saw shaking after he climbed down two stories. Besides, you were the one who told me to cover you, so I did."

Tanya elbowed Daniel in the side. "Aw, is the big guy afraid of heights? I thought you weren't scared of anything."

Daniel crossed his arms. "Of course not. I just saw that shillelagh hugger coming toward the window ready to shoot me. It's a common reaction when you're unarmed and exposed like that is all."

"Whatever you say," Tanya slurred. Her head leaned to her right and fell on Daniel's shoulder.

Elizabeth angled her head around her seat to look back at her brother's predicament. "Aw, that's cute," Elizabeth whispered. She looked to her left at Roger. "We were worried you know."

Roger ran a hand through his short, straight hair. His voice came out quiet. "Yeah, it was looking dicey as hell. I'm sorry to say we lost Eddy."

"Big fricking loss there," Elizabeth quipped.

"Show some damned respect." Daniel pointed at his sister. "He was a great brother in arms that gave everything so that we could escape. You'd best remember his sacrifice when you two are spooning tonight, because he helped get your boyfriend home."

Elizabeth glanced at Roger's nodding face and back to Daniel who was still staring daggers at her. "Alright already, I get it. If he helped bring you two back to us, then I'll miss him. Happy?"

"I'm never happy when I lose friends, especially under my watch," Daniel muttered too quietly for her to hear.

Tanya smiled and her left hand moved to his left leg.

"Looks like someone's not really asleep," Elizabeth teased.

"No, I'm asleep. Look somewhere else with your wild, slanderous, conspiracy theories," Tanya said.

"Yeah, how silly of you, dear," Roger said with a smile that didn't quite reach his eyes.

"Silly am I?" Elizabeth asked. She looked back behind her toward the windshield and saw that they were stopped at a red light. She climbed into the back seat, eliciting an annoyed grunt from Axel in the driver's seat. "I'm not the one who walked into the enemy base and got trapped, am I?"

"No, you're just the three lunatics who somehow managed to get us out of there I suppose. My bad."

"That's right, we are. You two had best remember that." She dropped into a sitting position on Roger's lap and faced him. She leaned in close to his ear and barely spoke. "You're mine. I'm not letting anyone take you away, not even those damned Irish. Got it, honey? You're not getting rid of me that easily."

Daniel grimaced and turned away from his sister. His

eye caught Axel's face in the rearview mirror looking at his sister with a prolonged stare. "We really have to get you a girl, don't we, Axe?"

"I certainly wouldn't complain, sir."

Daniel felt Tanya nuzzling into his shoulder. He reached up with his right hand and rubbed the back of her head. He turned to her and whispered. "I'm fine. Rog made sure of it."

"Mm," she grunted and shook her head again.

He turned away from her ear and in a louder voice said, "Take us home won't you, Axe? It's been a long night, and it'll be a hell of a day tomorrow."

"Got it."

Back at the apartment

"What a night," Roger said with a push to the front door. It creaked open as he pushed. He entered and held it open behind him.

"If you think tonight was bad, tomorrow will be far worse," Daniel grumbled loud enough to be heard.

"Worse? How could it be much worse?" Tanya asked at Daniel's side.

"It won't be as physically violent, true," Daniel admitted with a shrug. "It will be a very different story when it comes to politics. Someone's going to have to take the blame for the bodies dropped. Not to mention we couldn't complete our objective."

"No offense, honey, but I am not looking forward to talking to your dad this time," Roger whispered to the woman glued to his side.

"Which is precisely why you won't be," Elizabeth said.

"It'll be just his children explaining all of this, for your own good."

"I'm taking first shower while you all do whatever," Axel declared and ducked into the bathroom.

Daniel trudged toward the lone sofa straight ahead and sat down with a loud sigh after grabbing the remote control. Tanya sat to his left, Roger and Elizabeth scrunched together to his right. He pushed the top left button and the television roared to life. A woman sitting behind a large desk appeared. The box above her left shoulder showed a large woodland area with police lights flashing. "This is channel three news tonight. Intrigue abounds in the local Harriman State Park. Four apparently recently desecrated bodies were found near a local camping site. Local police are suspecting foul play as the bodies have been tampered with." The ladies voice cut off as Daniel muted the screen.

"Oh, fuck me sideways," Roger muttered out loud. "Unmute it. Who the hell were they?"

Daniel pushed down his thumb and the sound returned. "Only two victims have been identified so far due to a lucky break. Investigators found a wallet nearby containing identification of one Lenny Ramone and presumably his girl-friend, Charlene Cooper. The bodies were found buried next to a nearby camping ground."

The room fell quiet except for the occasional shuffling feet on carpet. "She didn't just say Lenny Ramone did she?" Roger asked. "Oh shit, that's why we didn't put it together. The kid has the surname of the mother. Come to think of it, I think I remember hearing Lenny was dating a single mother. Ah fuck. Oh shit. Oh my God. That's what he meant," Roger said with hands covering his nose and mouth. "He told me he was out there 'because of us' before I finished him off. He must have been sent as backup even if he was supposed to be on vacation. That's why his family was there. They must have just decided to go camping since he was ordered there."

"You mean to say..." Tanya trailed off. "You all accidentally killed a family member along with his woman? It just gets better, doesn't it? Why does it rain shit around you people so much?" She leaned forward and glared at Elizabeth. "Liz, what the fuck? I sent you a text telling you I was ordered to send Lenny. I even told you how the idiot insists on using a gps system? Remember that message you never read? I assumed you dealt with it in a better way than this. Besides, how did you not recognize him? He's one of your dad's favorite men." Her cheeks puffed out and her head fell onto Daniel's shoulder with a loud sigh.

"It was a little bit of a trying time. Besides, Daddy sent that guy away when I was a small child. He was put in charge of a branch. We hadn't seen him in decades. So sue me. I didn't recognize him," Elizabeth said.

"So not only do we have to explain a failed mission, a rat in the organization who sold us out, and numerous dead men under our command, but now we have to convince your father that we had nothing to do with Lenny?" Roger asked.

"When we did," Elizabeth said.

"Yes. Thank you, dear," Roger said with lifeless eyes. He leaned forward, placed his hands on the sides of his head and stared at the floor between his feet. "I'm dead. When it comes out that I was the one who-"

"We're not hopeless yet. We do have one advantage here," Daniel declared.

"You mean besides the fact that your old man now thinks the Irish didn't chase us and probably suspects we killed one of his favorite lieutenants?"

"He has no proof the McCranes didn't follow us there. All anybody knows is that Lenny is dead. The Irish could have been there, and he and his wife fell in a blaze of glory while defending us. We managed to repel them of course and get vengeance."

"So we lie? That's our plan?" Roger fell back and leaned his neck back on the couch.

"Would you rather lie and live, or tell the truth and be cut out?"

"I hate that term your old man coined. 'Cut out' is a polite way of saying you get a nice dirt nap."

"Those are our choices, and I for one am not going to die in such a stupid manner. I didn't survive all those battlefields to die for politics, nor did you. Now if you're done panicking, I'm going to come up with a way to salvage this." He turned to his left. "Your laptop still holding much of a charge?"

Tanya moaned and grumbled before picking her head off his shoulder. She reached down over her side of the sofa. She lifted the device onto her lap and cracked it open. "It should have about three hours of charge left. What do you need me to look up?"

"We have an email address and screen name I need you to look up. Rog, do you remember the details?"

"Yeah, I took a screenshot with my phone. Let me get it." His right hand dug into his pants pocket and fished out his phone. He pulled it out, leaned forward, and passed the phone to Tanya.

"Alright, what am I looking at here?" she asked as she rubbed her eyes with the back of her hands.

"That is who we believe sold us out. Not 'TrueIrish2', the other screen name."

"Obviously," she scoffed with a roll of her eyes. "Okay.

Assuming you're right, which is a huge assumption by the way, I guess I'll run a search through our dark net mailing list. It's not likely they were so stupid as to use the same email address, but we do have one thing in our corner."

"What's that? Roger asked. "It sounds like a long shot."

Tanya giggled. "Not everyone is as good with tech as you. Especially folks like the guy sitting next to me. If he thought the email server was secure, which it wasn't..."

"It wasn't?" Roger asked.

"Oh you poor naive fool, very few 'private' email services are actually private. Once almost any government agency finds them, they either shut them down or require them to share the transcripts of their contents. Which is precisely why we all learned how to encrypt text."

"That doesn't seem very legal for them to be forced to do that," Daniel said.

"Thank God you're not a lawyer, because it is. It's also slimy, opaque, and more than a little corrupt if you ask me. They cry it's for 'security'. It's a load of shit. They just want to spy on us so they can know every little thing about our lives. If they can prosecute the local population, all the better.

"Are you done with your little political rant?" Daniel asked.

"Sorry. I was an amateur hacktavist before I joined the Morris family you know."

"So bottom line, assuming the name is in there, how long will the searches take?"

Tanya brought a thumb up to her lips. "Our list isn't that big. I'd say about ten minutes tops?"

"Good, then I'm going to go do some laundry," Daniel said. He stood up and walked behind the couch.

"You know how to do laundry?" Tanya's neck fell back and looked at Daniel's now upside-down frame.

"You think I cleaned his clothes or something? No ma'am," Roger answered.

"Oh this I have to see. Rog, be a dear and watch the search, will you? Come get me if it gets a hit."

"Will do. Have fun."

Daniel continued his way to the back rooms followed by Tanya, leaving Elizabeth and Roger all alone on the seat.

Roger was the first to speak. He grabbed Elizabeth's hands from her lap and gripped them tight to his chest. "You've been quiet."

She refused to meet his gaze or even look at him.

"You're worried, right? I don't blame you."

"Yes, alright, I'm worried. I was worried I'd lost you earlier tonight. Then what do I hear next? Tomorrow my own father might finish the Irish knobs' work. I'm afraid. Is that what you wanted to hear?"

"Not really," Roger said with a flippant edge.

She finally looked at him. "What's that mean?"

"It means I don't want to hear that from you, obviously."

"Well, what do you want to hear?" she asked with her voice growing louder.

He gave an unabashed, warm smile. His eyes softened as his hand stroked the back of her hands. "That you're happy. It's always been what I wanted."

She tore her hands away from his grip. She turned away and laughed out loud. The solitary laugh soon escalated into a cackle. "You are too damned corny. Sorry, but that won't happen until after all this is settled."

"Look at me," Roger said.

She looked over through the corner of her eye.

"No, I mean really look at me," he said. His right hand reached out. His index finger touched her chin with gentle strokes and turned her head to face him. He stared straight into her eyes. His left hand cupped her cheek. "Then I guess I'll have to figure a way to get out of this and get you smiling again, won't I?"

"My hero," She laughed through the tears now dripping down her cheeks. "Unfortunately, life rarely goes like the fairy tales, my Prince Charming."

"I never base a decision purely on the odds. So don't tell me."

Elizabeth giggled. "I think you screwed up that movie quote. Danny would be so disappointed."

Roger leaned in. His forehead brushed up against hers. "Let him be. It wasn't for his benefit anyway."

Elizabeth bit her lip and averted her gaze before locking onto his eyes and lunging forward. She wrapped her arms around him and squeezed. "I can't lose you," she whispered into the crook of his neck.

"I've no intentions of dying, honey," he whispered into her ear.

She looked up at him now with her mascara running. "I love you."

Roger tilted his head and leaned in. His right hand rose to cradle the back of her head. Their lips met for a moment before he pulled back a few scant inches. "I love you too. Now let's figure a way out of this mess, okay?"

Meanwhile...

Daniel threw a shirt from the nearby pile into the machine. "I wish we had a damned machine in the apartment. Going to the basement every time is a real pain."

"Aww, look at them," Tanya cooed from his side.

"What?" Daniel asked. He leaned to his side and peeked over her shoulder at her phone. "You don't learn, do you?"

"Excuse me?"

"I mean you caught an eyeful before, and yet you still watch them. That must mean something. You a voyeur? I didn't know you were so freaky."

"It's my job, thank you very much," she replied with a huff. Her hands fell to her hips as she spoke.

"How nice of you to have your hobby be your job too," he said with a toothy grin.

"You're so mean," she said with a weak back handed slap to his shoulder. Her eyes fell to his hands. "Gross. No wonder you said you needed to do laundry. Hold up a minute," she ordered. She looked to her right and leaned over to pick up a nearby tissue. She spit on it and dabbed Daniel's dust covered cuff.

"You don't have to do that," Daniel said with a scratch at his nose with his free hand.

"Be quiet. It annoys me to see dirt is all," Tanya said with a growing crimson hue spreading across her cheeks.

"Is that right?" Daniel asked. He looked at her eyes as she continued cleaning his shirt cuff. "Say, I've been meaning to ask you something."

"I'm not doing your laundry for you."

"Good, because I had no intention of asking that yet."

"Yet?" she asked. She brought her eyes up to his with the question.

"I was hoping you might change your mind if we got married, maybe?"

Tanya's hands froze. She took two steps back before staring wide eyed at the man. "Excuse me? Did you just ask me to-?" She cut herself off. "No, that's too crazy."

"Is it?" Daniel asked.

"This is not the time to be focusing on this at all." Tanya shook her head. "That's all there is to it."

"Is that what you really think, or what you think you should be saying?" Daniel asked. He took a step forward. She mirrored his movement and took a step further back.

"This is no life to bring a kid up in. Just look at the past week for God's sake," she mumbled toward the floor.

"Maybe, but we won't always be here you know."

"Like I want to be married to the future Bernard."

Daniel sighed with a shrug. He turned and tossed a few more garments into the machine before closing the door. He kept his back to her and placed his hands onto the machine in front of him before asking in a quiet voice. "I'm only going to say this once, so pay attention. Okay?" He turned around and marched right up to her. He looked down at her as he spoke. "I know I'm not the greatest catch. I'm a jerk, not always the smartest, and probably not all that much to look at. But I look out for those close to me." His arms reached out slowly and placed a hand onto her shoulder. "I may not act it at times, but you're important to me. I also know that if anything happened to you, I would lose it. I don't know if it's love, honestly. I just can't imagine the rest of my life without you." He turned around again and pressed the start button causing the washer to whir to life. "That's all I have to say."

"I don't know what to say," Tanya admitted. "I need time to think about this," she blurted out before leaving the room.

He looked up at the ceiling and shook his head. He crossed his arms and leaned back against the now active machine. "Why did I have to push it?" Daniel asked himself. "Damn it all to hell!" he cursed. He kicked back into the nearby machine. An audible beep came from the washing machine. "Aw, shut up," he scolded the beeping machinery. "I'm the one who just screwed up big time." He looked to the right. Tanya's phone sat on top of the nearby dryer. "Well at least you're having better luck with the ladies, my friend," he grumbled as he watched his friend and sister cuddling on the couch.

Back in the apartment later.

"You said all that?" Roger asked Daniel who sat beside him on the sofa. "No wonder she came in here and dragged Liz away in a hurry."

"What's that mean?"

"Don't you get it, brother? You must have shocked her something fierce." Roger laughed out loud. He reached up with his right hand to stifle the noise when he saw his friend's glare at his side. "I'm sorry, but this might not be a bad thing you know."

"It sure felt bad just being left there after laying it all on the table."

"I know, buddy. It's funny, isn't it? You never tremble, even when in the middle of a hellish fire- fight, but here you are confiding in me because of a woman."

"I'm not confiding anything," Daniel snapped in an instant. He paused before continuing. "I'm just looking for advice is all. You seem to be better in that department."

Roger snapped his fingers and pointed at him. "That right there, what you just did, probably doesn't help. Look man, women like feeling wanted, protected, and loved. Right?"

"I think anyone sane does, yes."

"Denying it like that out of pride probably doesn't help. It just sends mixed signals that can be confusing to interpret for her. I know it would perplex me if your sister started acting like that."

"Men do it too, eh?" Daniel asked out loud. "This is fricking complicated."

"Welcome to love. Why do you think people still make songs about it?"

"I always imagined it had something to do with their record companies forcing them to do it for money, honestly," Daniel answered.

"It was a rhetorical question, but thanks for playing," Roger's sarcastic voice fired back with an ever so slight rising at the side of his mouth.

"Enough about me. How long is it going to be until we're legally brothers?"

Roger faced away toward the television. "Well to start with, I have to get out of this alive and well. I figured I should probably deal with that first before thinking about proposing, unlike some people's sense of timing. What do you think?"

"I think you should just do it now since you're going to be fine."

"I wish I had your optimism," Roger said.

A beep interrupted the discussion. Roger looked to his left to see the laptop no longer scrolling down a list. One entry was highlighted along with an address to its left. "Looks like we got our lead on the rat."

"Where is it?"

"The address looks familiar," Roger spoke with narrowed eyes. "This looks like Bruce's home address."

"How the hell do you know his address?"

"Well, I was just going by the registered address field

right there beside it. It says it's his house. I mean, we all filled out these when we registered for our dark net mail email address so we could get emergency emails. Don't you remember?"

"Smart ass," Daniel chuckled. "Still, Bruce is the rat? That doesn't make sense. The man's a horse's ass, but I never pegged him for a traitor."

"He was second in command. He may have just wanted a promotion."

Daniel picked up the remote control and turned off the television. "It looks like we're going to go see. Gather everyone, and I'll get the van started."

"Got it," Roger said as they both stood up from the couch.

23

"We're really just going to go to his apartment, bust in, and accuse him of ratting in the middle of the night?" Tanya asked from Roger's left.

"No, of course not," Roger answered. "We're going to go looking for evidence, and then accuse him. All we have now is his name on a list."

"He's lucky. If Dad heard this, he'd be dead already. He's not too keen on due process as we all know. Threats are dealt with immediately," Daniel said from the front seat.

Roger added, "Lucky for him, we have a thing about executing potentially innocent men."

"So I've seen with your little massacres," Tanya sarcastically muttered.

Roger became quiet and looked to his right. His gaze fell on Elizabeth.

"Are you still harping on that one room? For God's sake, girl, it was our boys or the Irish," Elizabeth said. She grabbed Roger's right arm and pressed it between her chest.

"That argument would work if they'd at least shot them

in the front, not the back." Tanya crossed her arms in front of her and looked out the window to her left.

"Oh, like you're Little Miss Innocent sitting back there," Daniel snarled from the front.

"Excuse me?"

"I've witnessed you threatening a man's family and using it against him, along with God knows what other cyber crimes you've committed. Don't try taking the high road with us now. The incident you're referring to was under my orders. It was them or us. You want to know how I know this?"

"Yes, please explain how shooting them in the back was self-defense. I want to hear this rationalization," Tanya fired back.

Daniel turned around and leaned forward, coming within a few feet of her face. "You ever been in a battlefield before? If one of any number of things goes wrong, someone doesn't come home. If the door had creaked louder they'd have more than likely sent a hail of bullets through it, and us along with it. So to mitigate the risk, I decided to neutralize the potential danger. Simple, right?

"You're oh so convincing with this 'more than likely' crap."

Daniel's voice became low and even. His eyes narrowed as he spoke. "I'm going to teach you something. There are no absolutes in battle. This is no video game where skill always gets you through. While aim will undoubtedly help, the plain and dirty truth is it's mostly luck. You play the odds the best you can to get everyone home alive. It's not pretty, fair, nor is it moral at times. I almost always get everyone home exactly because I'm willing to do what it takes to protect them." He reached his right hand out and flicked her nose. "That includes you, little missy," he finished before turning back around in his seat.

"Dick," was Tanya's only retort. She shifted her position so she could face the window and still balance her ever present open laptop. She pulled one of the many thumb drives out of the side of it. She reached to her side past Roger and dropped it on Elizabeth's lap. "Just plug this into his computer, and I'll run a sweep."

Silence reigned in the cabin until the screeching of the brakes interrupted the tense atmosphere. "We're here," Axel said.

"Rog, you and Liz are with me. Axe, I need to talk to you in private before we head in." Everyone besides Tanya exited the van. Roger and Elizabeth walked into the apartment complex. Daniel motioned Axel over some dozen yards away from the vehicle in a nearby alley. "You protect her with your life. You understand me?"

"One more thing." He looked left and right, reached up to his ear, and pushed a button before leaning in and whispering. "You did clear up that mess in the park, right? There's no evidence linking us?"

Axel followed suit and whispered back. "Yes, sir. We liquidated the kid's body. Thankfully, the boys got to the four bodies in time before police found them. Thirty minutes to be precise. With those chemicals they used, along with burning them, they won't get any evidence pointing to us. That wallet was a mistake though. Can't do much about that. The world knows it was Lenny, I don't look forward to that fallout."

Daniel gave a rare grin. He slapped Axel on the arm. "Good man. I'll take care of the blowback. You keep up this good work and you'll go far. I'm putting in a good word to Father for your hard work when this all blows over."

Tanya's voice burst into their ears. "Hey Jackass and new guy, you went mute. Check your hardware, would you? It'd be a real shame if I didn't have to hear you."

"Boy, she gets pissy awfully quick, doesn't she?" Daniel said with a chuckle. He shook his head. "You want my advice, Axe? Find you a good woman who'll do anything for you. The crappy thing is that those are usually bitchy in their own ways." He stared at the immobile van. "Still, that's usually just a sign they care," he scoffed. "Listen to me sitting here sounding like a pussy. You just remember what I said."

"Not to worry, sir. I'm always strapped." Axel lifted his shirt to reveal a handgun pushed down the front of his pants.

"You just remember to clean your pieces whenever you get the chance. It'll keep you and those around you alive longer."

Roger's voice came alive through their earpieces. "You almost done out there, brother?"

Daniel reached up and pushed a button on the earpiece. "Yeah, buddy. I'm on my way."

Axel nodded as he unmuted himself and made his way back to the van, leaving Daniel alone.

He ducked out of the alleyway and marched toward the building Elizabeth and Roger had entered.

Inside the apartment complex

"That took a while," Roger said. "Everything okay out there?"

Daniel marched up the stairs toward them with his jaw

set, his teeth gritting. "It's nothing to worry about. Let's get this over with already."

Roger turned to his side and gestured toward the door with an upward facing palm. "Be my guest."

Daniel slipped between the two and stopped in front of the plain door. He raised his right hand and banged his fist on the white wood. "Bruce? Open up, would you?"

"He might not be home," Roger said.

"He's home alright," Daniel said.

"How on earth do you know that?" Elizabeth asked.

"His car's outside in the lot. Did you two not see it? You need to sharpen your observation skills." He resumed his knocking. "Come on, Bruce. This is on orders from my father. Open the damned door."

Unintelligible yelling from inside was their only answer.

The three looked at each other and waited. Slow footsteps soon replaced the voice coming from inside. They stopped, and after a few seconds the sound of sliding metal and a click were all that could be heard.

Daniel moved to the side quickly. Roger wrapped his arms around Elizabeth and pulled her toward the opposite side, eliciting a grunt from the woman. He placed his body between hers and the door.

The door opened, revealing a disheveled looking Bruce rubbing his eyes with the back of his hand.

The three released a deep breath, and Roger released Elizabeth.

"What the hell are you doing at my home at this time of night? Aren't you late for your failure debriefing? You know, for nearly getting all of us killed tonight?" Bruce asked.

"The orders from on high are to search your place," Daniel said.

"I'm sorry?" Bruce asked. "Are you having a laugh here or something? The last I heard was that your father wanted to see your little posse as soon as possible after our little Irish assault."

"No joke, unfortunately. Why do you think he wanted to see us? He wanted us to hunt for the damned rat. For what it's worth, we don't think you're involved. We're here to prove you knew nothing," Roger said.

"What in the rancid piles of hell are you talking about?"

"You don't know?" Daniel asked. He turned to Roger. "You may be right. He might not be part of this."

"Part of what?" Bruce asked.

"We're not at liberty to discuss that quite yet. After we prove you're cool, we'll explain everything. Deal?"

Bruce stepped back further into the room. "Yeah, sure. Just hurry it up. I want to sleep."

Daniel led the group through the doorway, followed by Roger and finally Elizabeth.

Roger tapped Elizabeth's shoulder. She looked toward him to see him pointing further into the apartment toward a lone desktop. "We just need to check something on your email. Then we'll be on our way."

Elizabeth took the lead and inserted the drive, while Daniel and Roger remained near Bruce.

"My email? You really must be bored to go looking through my encrypted messages."

"Did you get any weird emails lately?" Roger asked.

Bruce's eyes wandered up and away. "Not to my knowledge. I mean, besides the usual spam. What is this about exactly?"

Tanya's voice came over their headphones. "This is not the origin of the messages. It was forwarded from a different ip address. I'm running a trace now. It looks like Brucie was supposed to be a fall guy for our rat."

"Good news, Bruce. You're not the rat," Daniel said.

"Rat? Hell, I could have told you that."

"Yeah, but the rat forwarded his correspondence with the McCranes through your darknet email address."

Bruce reached up and rubbed his mustache. "What? The only people who know my personal address are the boys."

"Boys? You mean your group?" Daniel asked.

"That's right. Unfortunately, most of them are dead now." He glared at Daniel.

"Who's still breathing?" Daniel asked.

"Jared's still alive last I heard. Though I've no clue where he's holed up now. He tends to go get blackout drunk after an operation. You know, he just falls off the grid."

"Perfect alibi for a traitor," Roger said. Bruce's glare moved to him. "Hey, I'm just saying."

"The kid's always been a little money hungry, but I figured that was just because the government pay checks dried up from the dishonorable discharge."

"He needed money bad, did he?" Daniel asked.

"The kid didn't talk much about himself, but I remember the one time he did in the middle of a job. He went on about how he had alimony and child support payments piling up. He also had a bad habit of buying another rifle every so often, come to think of it."

"Motive, means, and no alibi huh?" Roger asked.

"You don't really think Jared had anything to do with this?" Bruce asked.

"Someone ended up getting your boys and Eddy killed. We have evidence from Murtaugh's own computer. So we're not ruling anyone out due to sob stories," Daniel said.

"Understandable I suppose," Bruce said. He looked back to Elizabeth still standing by his computer. "How long are you going to be here anyway? I'd like to sleep sometime tonight."

"In a hurry to get rid of us, hm?" Daniel took a step closer to Bruce and came face to face. "Are you nervous about what we'll find if we stay?"

"Grab him by the ear." Tanya's voice came over Roger's ear piece.

Roger brought a finger up to his ear piece. "What? Why?"

"Just do it."

Roger reached up and grasped Daniel's ear and pulled hard.

Daniel turned to face Roger and stomped his foot as he held his ear with his hand. "Ah God damn it. What the hell, man?"

Bruce and Elizabeth burst into laughter.

Roger's shoulder rolled into a shrug, and his hand pointed to his ear.

Tanya's annoyed voice met his ears. "He's not responsible, as I said, Danny. Grilling him more isn't going to accomplish much except waste time. Maybe you should listen to me more."

Daniel stared at Roger with narrowed eyes for a few seconds before turning back to Bruce who was stifling his laughing. "At least tell us where Jared's place is."

"He will get a fair shake, right?"

"Of course. It's not like the group here would allow for much else." Daniel stole a glance at Roger.

Bruce walked over beside Elizabeth. "If you'll excuse me." He turned to his side and shimmied past her into the corner. He got into a squatting position and reached behind the large desk. He grunted as his arm disappeared behind the obstruction. "Here we are," he said. He stood, bringing his hand up, and revealing a piece of paper. He walked back to Daniel with his hand extended, offering the paper. "This should have all the boys' addresses they were using when they signed up with the family and were assigned here. Fair warning, I don't know if he's still there."

"Thanks," Daniel said as he snatched the paper. "We'll let the big man know how cooperative you were." He looked at his sister and then back at Roger. "Let's go." He turned and walked toward the exit.

"There's one more thing before you go, Mr. Morris," Bruce said.

"What?" Daniel asked. He stopped in his tracks and turned in place.

Instead of words, Bruce started into a jog in Daniel's direction. He balled his right hand into a fist and launched a right hook into Daniel's jaw, knocking him to the floor. "That's for all the friends I lost tonight. Now we're even, you overconfident jackass."

Daniel reached up and rubbed his chin. He spit blood onto the floor with a smirk. "Fair enough." Without more words he got up and resumed his exit.

Elizabeth immediately came to Roger's side. They both looked at Bruce just standing in the middle of the room now.

"Get out now," Bruce's quiet voice said. His hands were shaking at his side. His hair fell over his face as he looked down at the floor.

Roger's hand reached around Elizabeth and patted her back. She moved toward the door first, leaving Roger behind. "For what little it's worth, sorry about tonight. The only reason we got out was Eddy." Without further words he followed his friends and turned toward the door before Bruce's voice interrupted him.

"Sounds like him alright." Bruce looked up. He took a step toward Roger and grabbed his collar. "You find the son of a bitch responsible and put him down like the rat he is. You get me?"

"That's the plan," Roger said. He reached up and brushed off Bruce's grip. "Try and get some rest, brother," he said before turning around and heading toward the twins waiting at the doorway. He passed through the arch and closed the door behind him. The three made their way down the nearby flight of stairs.

"What did he say before we left?" Elizabeth asked the man beside her.

"Just to catch the one responsible and end him," Roger said.

Elizabeth leaned against him as they neared the bottom of the stairwell. "Yeah? Well, he didn't have to throttle you. I nearly lost it you know."

"I'm a big boy, dear. I can take care of myself. Besides, I can't let you assault a member because of me, can I?"

"Let me? Did I hear that correctly?"

"Shut your feminist crap up. He's right, and we all know it. You could say adios to your own squad if you had." Daniel pushed the door open and held it open behind him. "Let your boyfriend look out for your best interests. It's what good ones do."

"My, I didn't know you had experience with men, Brother," Elizabeth said. Her lips widened into a smile watching her brother's reaction.

Daniel gave a sideways glare but remained quiet. His

right hand fell to his side and raised a solitary finger in his sister's direction. "We have a bigger problem you know. You heard Bruce. Father is looking for us. The longer we're out, the worse it's going to get. We'd better make sure to get it done before we head back, since we're already so late."

24

"The kid lives here?" Axel asked. He turned into the nearby parking lot. "Seems like a shady area."

"We're shady people, if you hadn't noticed," Daniel said with an elbow into Axel's side. He looked straight out the windshield. "Still, you do have a point. Why would the kid choose to live in this ghetto and not near his group?"

"We won't find the answer sitting out here," Roger said. He reached for the car door at his side.

"Wait a minute," Tanya said. "You all are just going to go up to a guy who we suspect sold us out? You realize if he catches a whiff of that, it's going to go down, right?"

"If you have a better plan, let us know. I don't relish the thought of trying to take down a military trained marksman," Daniel said.

"I'm just saying if we're right, he's already proven he's not afraid to use force against us." Tanya looked down at the floor and shuffled her feet in place.

"So?" Daniel asked. "Armed men are nothing new. We appreciate your concern, but I'm still not hearing a better plan. Let's go." Daniel opened the door to his right. "Same plan as last time, everyone."

"You stubborn idiot. Hold your horses for a minute," Tanya said.

"I'd like to sleep tonight. Make it quick," Daniel said.

"I can't remote hack into his computer. There're far too many different people here. I'd be here all night trying to find the right wireless network. On the flip side, if he's tech literate he should be using the surveillance cameras for his own benefit. He'll see you coming."

"Okay, and what do you suggest?" Daniel asked.

"How much do you know about fuse boxes?"

"Oh, I see," Roger said. "We cut the power to the whole building and catch him by surprise. No one notices the power going out at three in the morning."

Daniel shook his head. "You want us to try and navigate a huge ass apartment complex in pitch black?"

"Of course not. You'd end up breaking your neck on the stairs as clumsy as you are. I can, however, get the floor plans for this building with a little quick searching. You'll have to trust me."

"It's settled then," Elizabeth said from Roger's side. "Where is the fuse box?"

"That's it?" Tanya asked.

"Yes. I," Daniel paused. "I mean we, trust you with our lives." Daniel looked to the side and coughed. "So where is it?"

Tanya angled her head with a few audible clicks. "It shows there are surveillance cameras on every side outside of the building except for the north side. You'll have to shimmy around the corner and stay close to the wall. After you turn the west corner, some stairs leading down will be about ten feet in front of you. I'll walk you through deactivating it after you get there if you need it."

Roger looked up at the car interior's roof. He lifted a finger and pointed while his mouth was moving.

"What are you doing, stud?" Elizabeth asked from his side.

Daniel turned around in his seat. "Yes, what the hell?"

"I was trying to figure out which way was north."

"Use the north star, you stooge," Tanya said with a smile which was illuminated from the screen in front of her.

"Who the hell knows where the north star is in the twenty-first century?" Roger asked.

"I think the military teaches it in survival training," Daniel said.

The three in the backseat stared at him for a few seconds.

"He's right actually." Axel's voice fell to a mutter. "God, that week sucked," he said from the driver's seat.

"We're off track. Let's get started already. The sooner we start, the sooner we're done," Daniel said. "Keep your ears open." He looked at Tanya. "We're counting on you in there." He looked at the other two occupants in the back seat. "Let's go, same groups as last time." Elizabeth opened her door and stepped out of the vehicle.

"Which is north exactly? No one ever elaborated," Roger said.

Tanya pointed. "It's that way. Be careful not to be seen getting into position. Keep in mind I'll be recording everything that goes on in there for a confession. Do try not to kill him right off the bat, will you?"

"Thanks," Roger said and took off into a light jog to catch up with Elizabeth. The pair started heading north and stopped a distance away.

"Hey wait a sec, Mr. Morris," Tanya said. She reached out and grabbed his cuff as he took a step out of the vehicle.

"Give us a second, bro," he said with a pat on Axel's shoulder.

He nodded and exited the van, joining the group a dozen yards away.

Daniel climbed into the back seat and sat beside her. "Yes?"

"Were you serious before?" she asked with her voice barely above a whisper.

"Yes," he said without pause.

"I'll say yes if you'll say yes to a question of mine," she said with a look up at his eyes.

"What's that?" he asked.

"Would you leave this life and settle down? I don't want a child to be brought up in this down and dirty life. I mean, look at your childhood. Is that what you want for your future kid?"

Daniel's mouth fell agape. "You want me to ask for an out from Father?"

"It's the only way I'll say yes. It's not negotiable, Danny."

He closed his mouth and looked down at the floor for a full minute before looking back into her eyes. "I need to think about this for a little while." He lifted a hand to her cheek and cupped it. "You understand, don't you?"

She raised a hand and placed it over the one on her face. "Take all the time you need. I'll be waiting here if you say yes." She used her other hand to place the laptop to the side.

He attempted to remove his hand and felt her holding it in place.

"There's one more thing," she said looking back at him.

"Hm?"

Her now free hand reached around the back of his

neck and pulled his head forward. Their lips crashed together. Her tongue licked his lips. He opened his mouth and it shot inside. Their tongues entangled together into a dance.

She pulled back and removed her hand from his head. She wiped her mouth with a smile. "If you die in there, I'll kill you. Got it, Mister Morris?"

Daniel stared blankly at her. He blinked. "Yeah," he said. "I got it."

"Then get going, you bum." She raised a hand to his chest and pushed him. "Let's get this last ordeal over with."

A smile appeared on his face. "Yeah, okay." He scooted over to the opposite door and grasped it. He turned back to her. He saw her placing the laptop back onto her legs. "I don't think I've said it yet, but you really should know."

"Don't."

"Why?"

"If you say it now, I'm afraid it'll be the last thing you ever say to me."

"Sadly, I'm not as considerate as Roger, so I'm going to say it anyway because I want to. I'm selfish like that. I love you," he said with a wide, tooth filled grin. He immediately opened the door and slammed it behind him.

She lifted her computer back onto her lap. "You dummy. You weren't supposed to say it," she said to herself.

The driver's side door opened, and with a grunt Axel sat down. He closed it and looked into the rearview mirror. "Everything go okay?"

Tanya reached up to her lips and her tongue licked them. "Yeah, you could say that."

Axel laughed. "Good. It's about time you two got on the same page."

Her foot reached out and kicked the back of his seat.

"You're a jerk." She leaned back and saw Axel's closed mouth smile in the mirror.

North side of the building

"What do you think is taking him so long this time?" Roger asked.

"If I had to guess, it's probably his girlfriend," Elizabeth said. She curled into Roger's side. "It's so cold out tonight."

Roger reached an arm around her shoulder and rubbed up and down. "You're probably right. You know he asked her to marry him earlier?"

Elizabeth gasped. "You're shitting me. Danny did? No wonder she dragged me away. She never told me why. Just that he was an ass."

"She didn't tell you?"

"No, all she did was complain about how he never thinks anything through. She always did love playing hard to get though. I think it was her version of girl talk."

"That's a mystery to all mankind right there."

"What?" Elizabeth asked.

"That girl talk thing. We took bets on what transpired in there. It sounds like neither of us won."

A loud thunk of a car door interrupted their conversation. The pair turned to the van to see Daniel jogging toward them.

"It's about time you got out here, bro. We were freezing," Roger said.

"Sorry about that. You know how it is when a lady wants to talk."

"She turn you down?" Elizabeth asked.

"I'll have you know she said yes. Well, she kind of said yes," Daniel said.

"I don't know what that means, but let's hurry up and get into that basement. Okay? It's got to be warmer than standing out here," Roger said.

"It should be right over there." Daniel took lead of the group and brought them to the outside of the large apartment complex. The group inched along the outside of the structure until they came to the corner. "It should be right around this corner. Remember, stay close to the wall."

"Yeah?" Roger asked. "Wait a minute. Turn around for a second."

"I'm cold, hon. Can't it wait?" Elizabeth pawed at his side.

"Just a second." His index finger pointed at Daniel's face. "You have something on your mouth. Yeah, what is that?"

"What?" Elizabeth leaned forward toward her brother. "Why, dear brother, I do believe you either applied that hot pink lipstick yourself, or something happened in there."

"Oh Lord, you're not a minute man are you?" Roger asked. He laughed at his friend's expense.

Daniel brought the back of his hand up and rubbed his lips. "You jackass. Can we focus on the job here?"

"Whatever you say, Romeo," Roger said.

Daniel looked back and traced his thumb and index finger across his lips. "Zip it already." He peeked around the corner and angled his neck to look up. He ducked back around the turn. "The camera's right above us. Just stick to the wall and we're set."

"Is it unidirectional?" Roger asked.

Daniel shrugged. "It wasn't moving, if that's what you're asking," Daniel said.

"Good," Roger said. "Let's go then."

Daniel flattened himself against the wall and shuffled around the turn. Roger and Elizabeth followed. They were directly below the camera when Daniel hopped down. He grunted when he reached the bottom. "Careful, it's a good drop down," he said.

Roger sat down on the ledge and scooted over much slower than his friend. He then looked up and saw Elizabeth doing the same. He widened his arms and caught her as she fell. "There we are," he said. He turned to the door. "Now let's get out of this cold, shall we?" he asked. He reached out to the knob and twisted with a click.

He pulled open the door and gestured inside, allowing the other two to go first. He followed and shut the door behind them.

"It's a little warmer," Elizabeth said to Roger. Her hands went to her arms and rubbed up and down.

"We have a little bit of a bigger problem here," Daniel said behind her.

"What?" Roger asked. He walked up and wrapped his arms around Elizabeth. He came up alongside Daniel. "Oh, that's right," he mused, looking at the row of fuse boxes laid out on the wall in front of them. "Most apartment complexes have one box for each floor, so tenants can reset their own." He reached up to his ear. "Any clue which floor our target is on?"

"He should be on the fourth floor according to Bruce," Tanya said.

Roger gave a sideways glance at Daniel. "Easy enough." He unwrapped his arms from Elizabeth and strode forward to the fourth box, flipping it open. "Anyone have a flashlight? It'd be even better to find the overhead light switch. I can't read in this darkness. It could be the fourth or the tenth floor for all I know.

Daniel scoffed and headed back the way they came. "It's almost always by the door." He groped the wall. "Found it." He flipped the switch and the lone bulb hanging above flickered to life.

"There we go," Roger said. "This is the ticket." He turned to face the twins. "Flip them all, or only his room?"

"Blacking out the whole floor would be less suspicious," Elizabeth said.

"Yeah, but you raise the risk someone comes down here after we leave and turns them all back on. Then there we are. If there's a night owl on the floor, we're fucked," Daniel said.

"It's your decision, honey. What'll it be?" Roger looked straight at Elizabeth.

Elizabeth raised a balled fist in front of her mouth. She lowered it to reveal she was biting her bottom lip. "We flip them all. If he exits his room and sees everyone else's power on, he'll know something's up. At least this way he'll just figure it's a power outage."

"That's assuming he's awake," Daniel said.

"Hey, at least we'll be able to see until we get to the fourth floor. We have to look on the bright side," Roger said. His hand flipped the entire row of switches beside the tape labeled four. "There, the whole floor's blacked out. Now we're good to go." He turned around and walked toward the two. His right arm extended out to his side. Elizabeth pounced into the opening and walked with him. Roger turned to his friend, still looking at the fuse box. "You coming, brother? We're on a timer. You said so yourself."

"Yeah, sorry about that." He shook his head and followed the two. "I was just preoccupied is all."

"Well get your head out of the clouds. We need you here," Elizabeth said.

Roger pushed open the door and led the group back outside. "We don't need to be careful about the cameras now do we?"

Tanya's voice entered his ear. "Jared can't see anything unless he looks out a window, so no. Just stay clear of the west side and you'll be fine. You do remember which side north is, don't you? That helps figuring out west."

"Ha ha." Roger gave a fake laugh. "I think I remember. We'll just circle around this way and enter the main doors then."

"Not that way. That's west."

"It is?" he asked.

"Nah, I'm just messing with your head." Giggles became audible over the earpiece.

Roger's voice fell to a mere mutter. "Oh, for God's sake." He looked down to see Elizabeth's smiling face. He leaned close as they walked. "That's what I wanted to see. A smile on that face brightens up any of my days."

"Keep it in your pants, you lovebirds," Daniel said with his nose crinkled up at the display in front of him.

"What's the matter, big boy? Jealous?" Tanya asked from his ear piece.

The group entered the building and ascended the stairs. "I don't know what you're talking about."

"What?" Roger asked without turning around. "Did you say something?"

"They can't hear me, Danny. The new guy is standing watch outside. Don't worry. It's just us on this channel," Tanya said. Her voice cooed into his ear.

"No, nothing. I thought I heard something," he said to Roger as they walked.

"Oh, okay then," Roger said. "I just hope you're not going crazy. It'd be unfortunate if you started hearing voices."

The group ascended to the fourth-floor door and stood outside. "This is it," Daniel said. He reached up to his ear and pushed a button. "Which room is he in exactly?"

"According to this, he's in 407. If you're at the stairwell entrance, it should be to your right last door at the end of the hallway. Got it?" Tanya asked.

"Everyone ready?" Daniel asked. He reached down the front of his pants and removed his pistol. He ejected the magazine and peered into the bottom before reinserting it. "I'm good."

Roger and Elizabeth followed suit with their revolvers. "I'm ready," they said in unison.

"Is it possible for you two out there to pull around to this side of the building?"

"Why?" Tanya asked.

"In case he decides to make a break down the fire escape? It's the most obvious route a person would use."

"I never even considered that," Tanya said.

"Is it possible without being seen?"

Axel's cutting voice said, "We could probably park on the other side of the street without pulling attention, but it'll be rough to stop him from that distance without putting him down."

"Try not to, but if it's you or him, light him up."

"Understood, sir," Axel said. The faint sound of an engine started up over the intercom.

"Give me a minute while we wait on them to move." He moved down a flight of stairs.

"Overwatch?" Daniel asked. "You there?"

"Are you referring to me?" Tanya asked.

"Yes. Look under Axel's seat."

"What the hell am I even looking-" A loud squeal caused him to cringe. "Danny, I don't want this."

"Be careful with it. Never put your finger on the trigger unless you intend to kill. I want you to keep that close. If Jared gets away from us and past Axel, I want you able to defend yourself."

"Danny, I-"

"This isn't negotiable," Daniel said, his voice soft. "It's loaded already, so just pull back the hammer and squeeze the trigger after pointing it at him. You can do this. You're a big girl now."

"I hate this," Tanya said in a huff.

"I hear that we all do things we hate for those we love."

"Do you mess up all movie quotes or just the ones you quote me?"

"Only for you, darling."

Tanya sighed into his ear. "I guess a girl has to take what she can get."

Axel's gruff voice followed a brief burst of white noise. "We're in position."

"Understood," Daniel said. He walked back up the stairs toward the two cuddling against the wall. "Time to disentangle yourselves. It's go time."

Roger and Elizabeth took a step apart and readied their weapons.

"Do you want me to take point?" Roger asked.

Daniel reached out and placed a hand on his shoulder. "Nah, I got it, buddy. You back me up. Besides, the boss would kill me if I did let you." He looked over at his sister with a grin.

"Damned right I would. I don't want you near that piece of shit traitor."

"It's fine for your own brother though?" Roger asked.

"He'll be fine. He's too stubborn to die."

"I'm not sure it's a matter of stubbornness."

"You heard the boss. Let's go." Daniel removed his hand from Roger's shoulder and turned back to the door. He readied his weapon in front of him in his right hand and reached out for the knob with his left. He looked over his shoulder. "Let's deal with this piece of shit."

He pushed the door open and stalked into the dismal, shadow covered hallway. He snapped to his right and pushed forward.

Tanya's voice talked as they moved forward into the blackness. "It should be the fourth door on your right."

Daniel moved forward. He transferred his pistol into his left hand and placed his right hand onto the wall to his right. His hand came across a smooth cold circular object. "That's the first door," he whispered.

The group passed three doors in this manner until his hand came across the fourth, smooth, freezing object. He stopped in place causing the two behind him to bump into his back. He leaned forward, and his right hand shot out to the floor now in front of him to steady himself. He looked back with a glare, without saying a word. He stood back up and whispered to the group.

"This is it." Daniel took position in front of the door. "I don't guess anyone knows another way to enter a locked door besides busting it down?"

"What time is it?" Elizabeth asked.

"What? It's like three thirty in the morning now," Roger said.

"I got this." Elizabeth stepped past the two men. "Get ready. He's not going to be happy." She reached back with her right hand and slammed it into the door.

Roger shook his head and pulled out his other revolver.

"Dammit, who the hell is that?" a voice called out from within the apartment.

"Hello, sir," Elizabeth started in a chipper voice. "I have something urgent to speak with you about."

"What in the world is that, pray tell?" the voice asked.

"Do you have a moment to talk about our Lord and Savior, Jesus Christ?"

"Oh for fuck's sake. I told you peo-" Jared wrenched the door open and went silent, except for two words escaping his mouth. "Oh shit."

Daniel shot forward and tackled the man into the apartment. The two men tumbled backward leaving Daniel on top with his knee atop Jared's neck. The group moved into the room and closed the door behind them.

"Don't worry, Jared, you'll be meeting Jesus soon enough. Just relax and start praying." Daniel's growling voice pierced the relative silence. "First, you're going to explain just why you turned traitor."

"You can ask all you like, but I've no clue what you're talking about, Morris." A smug grin stared up at Daniel.

Roger took a few steps forward and brought his shoes above Jared's outstretched hand. "Is that right? I might suggest thinking harder, unless you want a more challenging time squeezing the trigger from now on."

"Screw you. You'll just kill me anyway."

Roger shrugged. "I think this one's in your wheelhouse, brother." He holstered his weapons and reached down to Jared's side. He patted him down. His search stopped, and he reached inside his pants and pulled out a lone handgun. The lights above roared to life, causing everyone to cover their eyes. He held up the piece to the light. "Nice piece of hardware you've got here. It'd be a shame if you lost it."

Tanya's voice interrupted. "According to cameras, a tenant reset the box. So you'll have to be quiet getting out."

"Hey, Sis, do you think this place is sound-proofed?" Daniel asked, his eyes never leaving the man below him.

"It's not," Tanya's voice said.

"I don't know, Danny. We might have to do it quietly. I'll go look for some duct tape or something." She wandered around the apartment opening random drawers and looking inside.

Jared's eyes widened.

"What's the matter, Deadeye?" Roger asked. "Have you heard of my associates' reputations with information extracting? Yeah, I don't blame you. I'd be panicking too, if I'm honest." He shivered. "I can't watch it though. Good luck. Hopefully you'll last longer than the last guy." He paused and grimaced. "Actually, I hope you don't. That was some medieval shit."

"Alright already. I get it. I'll talk. I didn't want to do it, okay? Orders are orders."

"What in the world are you talking about?" Roger squatted down beside the two men.

"Look, some new guy, on orders from your girl over there, came by Eddy's and asked for a few men. He sent me and a couple more of the boys. We took care of the job."

A gasp echoed across everyone's ear buds.

Elizabeth ceased her search and came up on his other side. "Stop lying."

"What?" Roger asked. He glanced over at Elizabeth and back to Jared. His voice raised. "What does that mean? What did you do?"

Jared's head rolled to the side to face Roger. His voice became low and quiet. "We took out that kid. Afterward we dug up a half assed grave and cleaned the bodies up too. You're welcome, by the way. We got rid of all the evidence.

Only thing we missed was that little wallet that fell in the bushes."

Roger stood up and backed away from the group. He stared at Elizabeth. He shook his head as he spoke. "You did this?"

She stepped toward him. "Baby, he's lying. He's trying to turn us against each other."

"Bullshit," Jared said. "You got us to clean up your mess. We did it well, I might add. Your boy Axel was the one to put them down. I didn't even have to do it myself. He was a real trooper."

He took another step back. "You ordered that child's death under my nose?" Roger asked.

"She sure did, man." Jared looked up at Roger with an even smile. "She probably saved you decades of prison time too, from what I understand. You should thank her. Not many girls would do that for their man."

Daniel's right hand clenched into a fist and shot forward into Jared's nose. A light dribble of red dripped down. "Stop lying right now."

"Good God almighty." Roger raised a hand in front of his mouth. "He was a baby, for Christ's sake, and you had him murdered? For who? Me? I'm going to be sick."

"Bathroom's right over there." Jared nodded his head to the side.

Roger took off in a jog in that direction and barreled inside. Loud retching could be heard throughout the room.

"Your boy's a bit of a pussy, isn't he?"

Elizabeth circled around behind her brother. She reached down and grasped both of Jared's feet. She held them up and spread them. "Hold him down," she told her brother with a pat on his shoulder.

Daniel extended his arms, placed his hands on Jared's shoulders, and kept him pressed into the ground. "Go."

"Maybe he is, but you won't be getting anymore in your short existence." Her leg lifted off the ground and rocketed forward between the man's legs, resulting in a loud crunching noise.

A loud high-pitched squealing escaped from Jared's mouth, along with only two coherent albeit high pitched words. "Piss off."

Elizabeth reached to her side. With the sound of metal sliding and a giggle she said. "You're going to have trouble with that the rest of your life unless you tell him you were lying before."

"You're bluffing."

"You think Daddy didn't teach me how to neuter bulls when I was a girl? Oh, I have the know-how and the will. Trust me on that. Now you're going to tell him you were lying, or I'm going to cut not only your sack off, but your dick along with it."

"She's not kidding man," Daniel said. "I learned the same lesson. She was a little more squeamish about it though." He glanced over his shoulder to see her scowl. He turned back to the man below him. "I don't think she will be with you though." He leaned closer to his face and whispered. His eyes were wide and crazed as he spoke with a wide toothy smile. "You will tell him you were lying one way or the other."

"The rumors are right. You twins are fucking nuts."

A door opening interrupted the group as they turned to Roger holding his stomach. "Just one more question. Why did you sabotage the operation?"

"Why? Money of course. The old penny pincher they

call father hardly pays me what I'm worth. I've got bills, man. They're much bigger than some shitty apartment."

"Ah, that's it? You killed those men for a larger check?"

"You're damned right."

"Have fun with them then." Roger emerged from the bathroom. "I'm done. I'm out." He trudged toward the door with his head hanging down.

"Rog, wait a minute." Elizabeth turned around and reached out.

He stopped in his tracks and turned around. His eyes stared past her as he spoke. "I thought I knew you. Did I ever really?" he asked before continuing his trek out the door. "I'll run interference on the night owl. You three have fun." He exited, leaving the three alone.

Elizabeth lowered her hand. Her focus snapped back onto the man below them. "This is all your damned fault!" she screamed. She yanked on his ankle eliciting a groan from Jared. "Cover his mouth."

"Got it." Daniel lifted a hand over Jared's mouth.

"You won't need to walk at this point, right?" She twisted with all her might causing a loud snap along with a muffled scream. "Now let me go find some tape. We're not done yet. Not by a long shot." Her empty voice echoed her blank stare. She looked to her left and walked into a tiled room.

"Looking for something, Sis?"

"I just need a gag and a new steak knife. You know how it is. I like preparing the meat myself."

"I got it." He looked back down at Jared's now swelling face. "You have no idea what you just did, do you? There's a good reason people don't screw with her. Worse than that, you hurt those closest to me, so don't expect me to stop her."

"You're just going to kill me like this?" His head rolled over toward the nearby footsteps. He looked up.

Elizabeth was brandishing his biggest knife in one hand and a roll of duct tape in the other. She stared down at him with empty eyes. "Rats don't deserve better. You know that." Her feet came closer with every step, until her shoes were right beside his eyes. "More than that, you just made this personal."

Jared looked up at the twin's faces. The one on his left grinned, while the one on the right simply stared through him while fondling the knife in her hands.

Jared struggled against Daniel's iron grip, but ultimately remained still.

"What's the matter, buddy?" Daniel asked. "Did you just realize there is no escape? No one is coming to save you. Your life is over, and it's going to end in this little apartment in the next ten minutes."

Elizabeth kneeled. "More than that, since you decided to dabble in my personal affairs, I figure it's only fair I do the same."

"What the hell does that mean?" Jared asked with a shaky voice.

"I hear you have alimony and child support." She brought the blade up to her mouth and licked it.

Jared's voice grew more desperate. "No. They did nothing. They knew nothing about any of this."

"Roger didn't either, but you pissed on that."

A blast of white noise caused the twins to wince before Roger's steely voice came across. "Elizabeth Morris, you're not going to do that unless you kill me first. Bluff it if it'll help you feel better to scare him. As God is my witness, no harm will come to them. Do you understand me?"

Daniel gave a glance toward Elizabeth.

A growl escaped her throat. Her mouth contorted into a smile that didn't reach her eyes, and a sweet voice emerged from her mouth. "I understand." She looked back at Jared. Her voice fell several octaves. "Now as for you, I guess it has to be quick." She ripped a piece of the duct tape off and placed it across his mouth. She stood up and circled around until she disappeared behind her brother.

Jared's legs lifted and he felt his pants being pulled off his bottom half. He shook his head and yelled into the gag.

"Sorry, man. I wasn't joking when I said you were getting neutered before you die. There has to be a sign for others to never do this. You understand? Also, let's face it. You deserve worse than this since you helped kill one of my best friends, along with dozens of my brothers in arms. You think about that in hell."

Back in the van...

The door to Tanya's right opened. She kept her gaze focused down onto her trusty laptop and remained silent.

Roger scooted over into the middle to sit alongside her. He looked into the rear-view mirror. His flat voice asked, "Axel, leave us for a second, would you?"

The man nodded and, without a word, left the car.

Roger kept his eyes on him the whole while as the man moved to near the building he'd just exited. He shifted positions so that he faced Tanya. "You didn't know, did you?"

She looked down at the monitor and shook her head. Her tremulous voice quivered. "I went with Lizzie to see the kid. It looked like a regular family camping trip for them." She turned to Roger, her mascara beginning to run. "Then we just left for some 'privacy' and talked on the way back to the van." She looked down and kicked the seat in front of her. "That quiet creepy guy must have taken them out then." She lifted the laptop off her, set it onto the floor, and turned back to him. "I can't believe she'd do something like this." Her right hand reached up and wiped away tears.

"It's not that hard to believe, if we're being honest," Roger said. He leaned forward and placed his elbows on his knees. "She always gets what she wants, right? It doesn't matter what anyone else wants. It's always everybody else that has to give in. God, why didn't I see it? Looking back the signs were there, but I was blind."

"At least he's with his parents now?" Tanya asked with a weak chortle. "Ok, that's not helping is it?"

"It does to me." He turned away from the floor and gave her a sidelong look. "I don't know about your beliefs, but it brings me some measure of peace. I robbed him of his parents, and she sent him to them." He paused. "Of course killing a child," he shook his head and sniffled, "that's not justification or anywhere near okay."

"A silver lining, if you will?"

"That's as good as it gets, isn't it?"

Tanya reached an arm over and patted him on the shoulder. "Such is life for people like us."

Half an hour later...

"Here they come." Roger snapped his attention away from the window and back to Tanya. "You did what I asked about the audio file? We can't let the whole thing go to the brass."

Tanya reached up and swiped her forehead with her forearm. "Yeah. I feel like I shouldn't have though."

"I know the feeling."

All three doors flung open in sequence. The cabin shook with each person entering.

Roger looked to his right to find Elizabeth staring at him. He looked forward toward Daniel and leaned to his left. "I assume he's gone, so how are we dealing with the left-overs? I sure hope you didn't just leave him in there to rot."

Tanya's voice was somber as she spoke. "You'll be happy to know that no one called anyone, including the cops. You kept him quiet. You succeeded."

Elizabeth slid further over toward Roger. "I took care of it. A team is on their way. They'll be here in a few minutes, wet vac, bleach, and all."

"Yeah, apparently you always do - with or without my input."

Daniel barked from the front seat. "Hey, we're not done yet. We still need to find Murtaugh and finish this."

"Isn't that a bit overstepping our boundaries?" Roger asked.

"You want to survive this, right? What better way to get in the old man's good graces than to end the war we started and deal with the rat in the same night?"

Roger scratched the back of his neck. "That's great and all, but we have no clue where he is."

Elizabeth came shoulder to shoulder with Roger and turned to face him. She leaned in and rested her head on his arm. "Jared was willing to part with some information on an Irish pub he likes hanging out at."

"What?" Tanya asked. "I never heard anything over the comms."

"Yeah," Daniel said. "We muted it, since we didn't think you two would want to hear that portion."

Roger looked to his left past Tanya out the window.

"You're probably right about that part. My stomach's a bit upset after tonight's revelations."

"You'll have to suck it up, bro. We're ending this tonight, and I need your help to get it done."

Roger felt Elizabeth rubbing her face against his arm and glared forward at her brother. "Yeah sure, whatever. I'll get it done, don't worry. I'll even come up with the plan this time." His left hand reached over and fell over Elizabeth's. He leaned down and rubbed his cheek on the top of Elizabeth's head. "Is the boss okay with that?"

"Whatever you say."

"Good." He looked back at Daniel. "Tell Axel where we're going then. I'll handle the rest."

"You want to let the rest of us in on your little plan?" Daniel asked.

"No, I figured I'd surprise you. It's only fair, right? Don't worry, I'll let you know the plan before I head in there. Fair enough?"

"It's fine," Elizabeth rushed out. "Right, Danny?" Her head turned toward the front seat and glared.

Daniel rolled his eyes and shook his head. "It's not like I have much of a choice. You're the boss."

25

The car came to a stop a few blocks up from a building with a four-leaf clover and a beer mug on the sign above the door. "We're here," Axel said.

Daniel pivoted around and faced the back. "Tell me already what this plan is."

Roger reached inside his coat pocket and extracted his revolvers. He flicked them open with both hands and looked inside. "The plan is nice and simple, but I don't think you're going to like it."

"Spit it out already."

"Alright. So that place is full of micks, right?"

Daniel nodded. "Yeah, so?"

"So you're too well known to waltz in there."

"Oh no."

Roger gave a thumbs up. "That's right. This is going to be an old school assassination."

Elizabeth wrapped her arms around his right arm and squeezed. "Those never work too well for the perpetrator, honey. You're going to be surrounded afterwards."

"Which is precisely why I wasn't done yet, if you people would let me finish."

Tanya focused entirely on the monitor in front of her as she typed. "That's right. Clear communication is key here. He's going to head in and get comfortable near our target. After he gives the signal, a small group needs to head into the back and subdue any security personnel."

"To what end exactly?" Daniel asked.

"At this time of night, they're likely all soused to the gills. Well, if we go with the old favorite of cutting the power, they'll be unlikely to piece it together, since Roger here will leave immediately after his shot."

"You're going to shoot him in the middle of the dark?" Daniel asked with an arched eyebrow.

"The hope is that I'll be able to get close enough so it won't be an issue."

"Sorry, man, but that's a really bad plan," Daniel said with a frown. "You can't be serious."

"The only other way is if someone has a syringe handy with some poison." Roger looked left and right. "Anyone? No?"

"We can do it smart, where no one here is stranded behind enemy lines."

"Fine," Roger said. "What's that? Don't even say to just shoot a hail of bullets through the window either. There are too many potential innocents in there."

"Nope." Daniel grinned. "It's simple and effective, while marginally less dangerous than yours. We have someone go in, order a drink, and locate him. Right?" He looked around to see nodding heads. "They leave and come tell us where he is. We go in and immediately shoot and leave."

"So basically, a smash and shoot?" Elizabeth asked.

"It's a better idea than Mr. John Wilkes Booth's plan."

"Screw it," Roger said with a clap. "I'm up for it. Who's going in to scout? I'll volunteer if no one wants to."

"No offense, but a guy in a suit is going to stick out like a sore thumb." Tanya looked up. "It has to be me when you look at it logically. Elizabeth here is too well known. A blonde girl in jeans and a kiwi shirt won't stand out nearly so much."

"I don't like it," Daniel said. He pointed past Axel. "Do you know what they'll do if they figure you out?"

"They'll ask me to leave. I'm just some girl wanting a drink for her insomnia. I'm not even armed."

Roger raised his hand out of Elizabeth's clutches and placed it in his pants pocket. "She's right. If they killed every girl entering, they'd never stay in business."

Tanya reached forward and tweaked Daniel's nose. "I'll be fine, Danny. I'll be back to safety before anything happens." She leaned back, "It'll be a nice change to be out of this van for once."

"You're not ready for field work," Daniel said.

"I'm just ordering a drink, and then after I'm done, I leave. Stop worrying so much. Now you need to get your little assault ready, I assume, so we can finally be done with this ordeal."

Roger removed his arm from Elizabeth's hold and turned around to look in the back. "It's a good thing you brought your shotgun. We'll need some real shock and awe for this party."

Daniel pointed above Elizabeth's head. "Hand me my baby, would you? Look beside him if you want. I brought a couple of grenades, if you really want some fire power."

Roger climbed up over the chair and disappeared behind the seats. "I'd rather not commit mass civilian slaughter. Thank you though. Where are your damned shells? Oh, there they are. Why in the hell were they by the door? Those will fall out one day you know."

"You won't need many. I mean, you're just after the one guy, right?" Tanya asked over her shoulder.

"It depends," Daniel said. "I want at least enough shells for two full reloads though. You know, just in case."

"Watch your head." Roger's voice came from the back. A hand holding a long rifle moved forward above the ladies' heads.

Daniel reached forward. He stashed it, barrel down, beside the passenger door.

"Here, pass this will you?" Roger's hand appeared above Elizabeth's head.

She reached up with a smile. "Of course. Anything for you." She caught the shells he dropped and handed them to her brother.

Daniel tucked away the shells into his pants pockets. "We're ready I guess."

"Look at the big grumpy Gus." Tanya again reached forward and pinched his cheek with a radiant smile. "I'll be right back, you big worry wart." She placed her hand on the door handle beside her and pulled down before stopping and looking back. "What should I even order? I don't drink."

"Oh my God." Daniel's head fell into his hands.

Tanya stuck her tongue out. "Just kidding." She craned her neck to her left and looked behind her, then opened the door and exited. She walked down the street toward the establishment.

Daniel followed her form as she walked.

"She'll be fine," Elizabeth said.

Inside the "Irish Pride" Pub...

Tanya pushed open the glass door and stepped inside. Her nose crinkled up. She coughed and waved a hand in front of her face. "People still smoke?"

"Remember to look tired for your cover," Daniel's voice entered her ear.

I think I have that covered. Lord, my eyes are probably still bloodshot from all the sleep I've lost the past few days, she thought. *At least I reapplied my makeup after I ruined it earlier, or I'd be a right mess.*

She walked forward and scanned left and right throughout the room. It was half full of sleeping patrons, headfirst on tables. The bar in front of her had a few empty seats at the end beside a colossal man who was snoring. Her eyes fell to the man's lower back. A metallic shine poked out of the man's pants. *He's armed,* she thought.

"Did she hear me?" Daniel asked.

"Yes, I'm sure she did," Roger's voice said. "She's under-cover right now, bro. She can't exactly answer without raising suspicion, now can she? I know you care about her, but don't worry so much. She's just getting a drink is all."

I didn't hear any denial there. She skipped forward toward the bar and climbed onto a stool.

A large man behind the bar looked over to her side of the bar and approached. She brought a hand up to her nose. A loud voice in front interrupted her. "You're just in time for a last round, miss. What'll you have tonight?

She fidgeted in her seat. "A screwdriver please."

He nodded and grabbed bottles and glasses from behind the bar.

"What's this then?" The man beside her lifted his head off the bar with a slur. He rubbed his eyes and let loose a massive yawn. "I'm bushed," he muttered. He looked to his side eyeing her up and down. "I'm sorry for making a cute little bit of fluff see me like that."

A glass was placed in front of Tanya. She picked off the lemon wedge and placed it on the napkin. She brought the glass up to her lips and gulped the yellow drink. "I envy your ability to sleep anywhere, honestly. It's always hard for me to relax without a little help."

"You're here for a nightcap, eh?" He slammed his hand down on the bar. "Put hers on my tab."

She gently moved her glass, causing the liquid inside to swirl around. "I appreciate that, Mr.?"

"Murtaugh. My name is Murtaugh, my little blonde blade."

She could hear Roger laugh. "Dude, I think he's hitting on your girl in there."

"I'm Tanya."

"That's a lovely name for a dreamy lass like yourself." He placed his left arm on the bar and leaned on it. "I don't remember seeing you around here before."

Daniel's tense voice growled into her ear. "He just hits on anyone, doesn't he?"

She took a swig of the drink. "Yeah, it's my first time here. A friend from work said this place had the best drinks and real men that don't drink shirley temples. It's also within walking distance."

"Ha," Murtaugh laughed. His boisterous outburst caused many patrons to grumble and shift positions. "They're right." He raised a huge arm above his head. "Get me an old fashioned slammer."

Her eyes widened and she set her drink down. "What's that?"

"Something only real men drink. I'm not surprised you

haven't heard of it in your glitzy uptown bars, with your soy boys all over the place."

The bartender came back with a glass and two shot glasses filled with dark liquid. He placed the larger down and with great care dropped the smaller glasses inside.

"What in the world?"

Murtaugh brought the glass up to his mouth and tilted his head back. He drank the whole thing in one go. He placed the glass back on the bar with a roar. "That's the stuff." His right hand came up to his forehead. "Ooh, I might have had a little too much tonight."

Daniel's voice hissed. "Get out of there already."

Tanya upended her own drink. "Thank you, Murtaugh. I guess I'll be seeing you around soon. Hopefully when we're both at our best," she cooed with a wink.

He pushed the stool back on the hardwood, causing a loud screeching and more than a few angry grumbles around the room. "Would you allow me to walk you back to your home, Tanya?"

Tanya stood up and tilted her head to the side. "Sure, I guess so. It could be dangerous out at this time of night."

"What?" three voices simultaneously asked.

"That's right. No one around here will mess with you. I'll make sure of it." He extended his arm toward the exit in an exaggerated pose. "After you."

She walked side by side with him toward the door. She raised a dainty hand to her mouth and giggled. "It's not often you run into such gentlemen at this hour."

"If there's one thing you'll learn from me it's that I'm anything but ordinary." He erupted into a loud belly laugh. He pushed open the door in front of them. "Ladies first," he said.

An altogether feminine chuckle helped Tanya smile at

Murtaugh as she walked forward. Elizabeth's voice met her ears. "She's calling an audible, boys. We'd better get ready."

She pointed right, down the street toward the van. "I live just over there." They walked down the sidewalk underneath the lights. "So what do you do, Mr. Murtaugh?"

He looked up at the stars. "I'm in..." he trailed off. "I guess you could say I'm in HR."

"You're in charge of hiring and firing? That must be a lot of stress."

Murtaugh stuck both his hands folded under his arm pits. "You wouldn't believe me if I told you. Why just earlier tonight I had to dismiss - it had to be over ten people. I'd never seen such incompetence. I'll tell ya, I have no clue how they got where they were."

"That sounds like a lot of work." She sidestepped to get right next to him.

He reached a hand up and snubbed his nose with his thumb. "Ah, it was nothing for me."

She looked up at the man on her right. She placed her left hand on his chest as she spoke. "You're also very confident, aren't you?" Her right hand reached around his back. She leaned into his side, plucked the pistol out of his pants and stuck it down the back of hers.

He jabbed a thumb into his chest. "Why wouldn't I be? I'm good at what I do, and everyone knows it."

She pointed across her body. "My building's right over there. The two faced the street and looked both ways before jogging across.

"If you'd like I could walk you to your door?" he asked.

A car door slammed behind him.

She placed her arms behind her and shook her hips with a wink. "I guess that'd be okay."

A gruff voice came from behind Murtaugh. "Hey, asshole, get away from her."

Murtaugh's face went blank. He spun around only to be knocked to the ground with a blow to the head from the butt of a rifle.

Daniel held the pump action up. He signaled toward the van. "Come on already. Let's get him inside and cuffed."

Axel and Roger hurtled out of the back of the vehicle. They bent down and carried the unconscious man into the open back of the van. He turned back to Tanya.

Her hands emerged from her back and held out Murtaugh's firearm. "It's a gift. Aren't you glad you're with a girl with quick hands who's smart enough to choose a place with no cameras?"

26

R oger pulled the billowing red curtain at the large window to the side and stood staring out at the trees.

"Calm down. You're making me nervous. Dad probably just decided to hear what happened from our leader first. At least we're not the ones getting barked at," Daniel said. He rocked back and forth in the black leather recliner. He looked around the room. "Can you believe the ostentatious taste of my dad? All these paintings and marble busts had to cost a fortune. You have to imagine there was a better use for all that dough."

"Did you know?" Roger asked.

"What? You have to be a little more specific than that."

Roger spun around. "Did you fucking know about the child?"

Daniel stopped rocking. "No, I didn't."

"I'd like to believe that." Roger's voice fell to a brittle intensity.

Daniel stood up and walked up to him. "Look at me."

Roger looked down and away with a shake of his head.

Daniel slapped him across the face. "You look at me."

Roger brought his attention up.

Daniel pointed at him. "I'm telling you I knew nothing about it, man. I wouldn't go behind your back like that. We're brothers here, remember?" He placed a hand on his shoulder. "Brothers don't lie to each other. How many times have we saved each other's asses over the time we've known each other? All of a sudden you think I'd betray you?" He shook his head. "Your head's all twisted right now. I get it, but I'm not my sister. Do you trust me?"

Roger broke eye contact and looked down at his sneakers. "Yes," he said in a quiet voice.

Daniel patted his shoulder. "That's right. What she did was a piece of shit move no doubt. You don't kill kids. You know that's one of my rules."

Roger looked up. A small smile adorned his face. "Yeah, I don't know why I doubted you. It was my bad, dude."

"Don't worry about it. I'd be twisted up inside too. Maybe one day you'll forgive her."

"I wouldn't get too crazy now. I mean it's like she doesn't even realize I'm pissed at her. She just acts like everything's normal. It's infuriating. I mean, have you ever had a dog before?"

"I know you're not making the comparison I think you are."

"It's like when you're potty training your dog, right? Have you ever had it where they'd go in the house and sit by it smiling at you? Obviously this is on another scale, but yes, it's like that. You don't want to scream at them because they love you, but they need to learn. Well dude, she doesn't seem to learn or pick up on nuances I'm throwing."

Daniel circled around and threw his arm around Roger's shoulder. "It's just the opposite, bro. I think she's playing the perfect girl right now because she knows how mad you are."

"It's not working."

"It's all she knows how to do. I'm just saying, as her brother, I do hope you two can patch it up eventually."

Roger looked up at Daniel. "I wouldn't hold my breath."

Daniel removed his hand and stepped back. "They say time heals all wounds. I never understood that saying. Emotional problems just get worse the longer they linger. Still, I hope they were right and just smarter than me."

"It'd be different if she even showed the slightest bit of guilt, but it's just business as usual with her. That's the scary part. Do you understand?"

"I don't see how that would help, but I get it. She's always been sure of herself, so you may be waiting a while to hear 'sorry'."

"I wonder who she gets that from?" Roger asked.

Daniel brought a hand to his chest. "Surely you're not implying it's from me?"

"It's either you or your father. Come to think of it, I don't think I've heard any of you ever say sorry."

"Sorry doesn't solve much in this line of work."

Roger exhaled. "Just because that's true, it doesn't make it right."

"Wait, what? My head hurts from that statement."

Roger chuckled. "That does not surprise me."

Daniel jabbed at Roger's shoulder. "Watch it now."

Creaking, along with the sound of a throat clearing, caused both men to look back at the entrance. Bruce stood there in the marble doorway. "He's ready for the both of you. Follow me."

The two men fell in step behind Bruce as they left the room. They came to the stairwell leading both up and down. This time they descended.

"We're not going to his office?" Roger asked.

"Sure you are. It's just not the office you usually go to," Bruce said.

Daniel let his hand glide down the hand rail. "He's probably questioning his guest, if I had to guess. You'd better steel your nerve, buddy. If you think my questioning methods are bad, you've seen nothing yet."

The group reached the bottom of the stairs to the concrete floor beneath them. A musty smell permeated the whole floor. Bruce spit and smeared it with his heel as they walked. "Whatever the boss does to that Irish dog isn't enough, if you ask me." The group approached a decrepit wooden door. The sounds of impact and grunts were emanating from within. Bruce sidestepped and turned. "Here we are. Have fun." He turned and walked past them back up the stairs.

Daniel reached and knocked on the door.

Moans of pain met their ears, along with a loud Brooklyn accent. "I'm ready. Get in here."

Daniel opened the door

All both men could see was a wife beater clad Bernard standing with his back to them. His hands dripped with blood at his sides. The smell of iron overwhelmed the tiny room. "Get in here and close the door.

Both men entered the small room. Daniel closed the door behind them. He moved forward and came shoulder to shoulder with his father. "Get anything out of him yet, Dad?"

Bernard's right arm rocketed forward into the gut of the man sitting before them, causing a cough of blood. "Not yet, but we're close to a breakthrough, aren't we?" He leaned down to the restrained man's face. A few strands of his graying hair fell in front of his face. "Don't leave us right when company arrives now. Do you Irish have no common courtesy?" He cracked his knuckles and threw a left hook across Murtaugh's jaw.

His head rolled to the side and his eyes closed.

"I guess not." Bernard turned around to face Roger. "This isn't why I invited you down here anyway, boy." He walked over to the only other seat in the room and plucked the towel draped over it. He wiped his face. "I know what you all did. Did you really think you'd get away with it without me knowing?"

"What are you talking about now?" Daniel asked.

"Do not interrupt me, you bumbling fool." Bernard's voice fell low and even. "Did you think I wouldn't find out about Lenny, his poor lady and kid?" He tossed the towel onto the ground. "If this was anyone else, you know what would have to happen."

Daniel stared down at his shoe tops. "They'd be dead."

"At least you're not as clueless as I initially thought. Thankfully for you, that won't happen."

Daniel looked up with widened eyes.

"That doesn't mean it's overlooked, Son."

He stepped past Daniel and came face to face with Roger. "You're the main reason this happened. Isn't that right? While my boy here was injured you were put in charge, or so the story went."

"Where did you hear that?" Daniel asked.

"A member more loyal than you in your circle of friends, as a matter of fact. It doesn't matter who," Bernard said. He still locked eyes with Roger. "You're the one who killed a family member. You know what that means, right?"

Daniel reached out and placed his hand on his father's shoulder. "Wait a minute. You can't be serious."

Without further warning, Bernard knocked Roger down to the floor with a right cross. "We don't take betrayal lightly here." He pulled his foot back. He landed a kick into his ribs. "That's for the man's family, you low life piece of shit."

Roger rolled away with a cough.

Daniel wrapped his arms around his father's neck and clamped down. "Let's all just calm down now."

Bernard reached up and scratched at his son's sculpted biceps. "Get off of me, or you'll share his fate."

"What fate is that? You're not going to kill him, are you?"

His father's voice was strangled. "No, I wasn't."

Daniel released his father who stumbled forward.

Bernard hunched forward and placed his hands on his knees. He gasped for a few moments along with hacking coughs. He recovered and again regained his posture. He turned to face his son. "He's being fired with the under-standing that if I ever see him again, I'll kill him." He walked to Roger's still form. "If he ever touches your sister again, I'll kill him after cutting his sack off. If he so much as crosses our organization's path again, and I find out about it, I'll kill him." He knelt beside the gasping man. "Is that easy enough to understand for you, Mr. Johnson?"

Roger's voice was low. He gasped before answering. "Yes, sir."

Bernard stood up. He marched up to his son. He looked down at him and sneered. "What should we do with you? I heard you wanted to leave us for a little bit of blonde snatch. Is that right?" Bernard circled around him. "You wanted to have a little white picket fence and a family, right? Was that the dream you've been harboring, my boy? Did you think you'd get a job and earn a straight living? You're just going to have a kid and live happily ever after with her?" Bernard chortled. "That's rich coming from the boy who rejoiced when the men came up with his nickname."

"I want to be with her."

"Even at the cost of your family?"

"If it has to be that way. I want to try."

Bernard laughed and turned to the door. He opened it and looked back inside. "It'll never work, Son. I know. It never works for men like us." He looked down at the floor for a moment. "Fine, you can go play good boy." He locked eyes with his son. "Just don't ever expect any help from us. You're on your own. Do not try to operate near our AO. Stay away from us, and we'll do the same. After all, it'd be a shame if something happened to that petite, button nosed lass of yours." He left and slammed the door behind him.

Daniel rushed over to Roger and helped him into a sitting position against the wall. "You okay?"

"It's just a few bruises. Nothing major," he said. His hand moved to his chest and rubbed in a circle. "Your dad packs quite a kick for a guy over fifty." He reached a hand into his coat pocket and brought a joint to his mouth. He flicked downward, causing a flame to jump forth from the lighter. A puff of smoke exited his mouth before he snuffed the end and extinguished the flame. He shoved it back into his coat pocket with a cough.

Daniel waved his hand across in front of his face with a cough. "Seriously? You do that at a time like this?"

"Bite me," Roger said. "It helps the pain. Now hurry up and help me up. I get the feeling we won't be welcome here for much longer."

Daniel reached down, threw his friend's arm over his neck, and lifted him up. "I'm wondering how the old coot even got that intel. Who told him?"

Roger pushed the door open in front of them. "It was probably Axel, if I had to guess. Your sister wouldn't out me. At least I'm pretty sure she wouldn't."

"There's no way in hell she would," Daniel said. The pair

hobbled down the hallway. "God help whoever did once she finds out."

The pair climbed the stairs from before. "I'm more shocked at you. I never imagined you'd give up the life. You're actually going to get married?"

"Yeah, she said the only way she'd say yes is if I quit."

"I can't believe you said yes."

"Sometimes a man has to sacrifice for his woman to be happy. Right? There are more important things than what I want. Some fool once taught me that."

Roger laughed. "I wonder who that was."

The pair stopped in front of large oaken double doors. Roger unhooked his arm from Daniel and stood without help. "I've got this. I don't want the last thing the boys see is me being hauled out." He straightened up and removed his hand from his ribs.

Daniel nodded. "I get it. Let's go then." He opened the door and held it open.

Roger entered the main room, and it went silent. He could feel glares piercing his body as he strode forward. A few furtive glances and hushed whispers were all that could be heard, apart from his and Daniel's footsteps. He looked up toward the stairs to see a row of maids watching from the balcony. One raised a hand and waved at him with a warm smile. He nodded in her direction and kept walking.

Crashing rapid steps rang out in the room. All eyes moved to the stairs to see Elizabeth sprinting down towards the two, with Tanya behind her carrying a large bag. "Oh my God, what happened?" She stopped in front of Roger and raised a hand to his blackening eye.

"Your father dismissed me from his service in his trademark manner."

"Yeah," Daniel said. "He also threatened to kill him if he touches you again. Back it up, Sis."

Elizabeth took a step back. Her face darkened into a scowl. "He did what?"

"He made it clear in no uncertain terms that I was to disappear. Come on. I'll explain away from prying eyes as we get ready to leave." He used his left hand to point toward the front door. He ambled forward, with Elizabeth jogging to catch up and eventually falling into lockstep beside him.

Tanya eventually reached the bottom of the stairs. Daniel moved forward and extended a palm. She placed the bag in it and snuggled beside him as they walked. He snapped his attention to the nearby sofa. "What are you boys looking at?" He received no verbal answer. "That's what I thought. Mind your own business." He snaked an arm around her shoulders.

They made their way outside. A lone beat-up station wagon awaited in the driveway. A man leaning against the driver's door kicked off and approached the group. He tossed a ring of keys at Daniel. "Here you go, Mr. Morris. Good luck. I'm supposed to tell you that this is all the help you're ever going to get. If you'll excuse me." He gave a polite bow of his head and pushed past them back into the safe-house.

"I guess we'll go get settled. Just let us know when you're ready," Daniel said. He and Tanya moved around the back and opened the rear door. He threw in the bag. Tanya got onto her tip toes and planted a chaste kiss on Daniel's cheek. She skipped around the car and got inside the back.

Roger felt Elizabeth's hands reach his shoulders and turn him around. She looked deep into his eyes. "Now you tell me what happened. You're not leaving right now."

"Someone told your father that I was the one responsible for Lenny."

Elizabeth's eyes ballooned. "Who? I'll kill them myself."

Roger reached up and caressed her face with the back of his fingers. "That's not what's important. They were right. There's something more important we need to talk about before I go."

She looked up at him with quivering lips and leaking eyes. "What's that?"

"I wasn't lying before when I said I loved you." He shook his head. "The problem is, you never trusted me. You never told me your plans. You need to grow up before we can even think of trying this again. Do you understand? You killed a child. That's not okay. I don't care if it saved me from the clink. Can you just try to imagine if someone did something as unspeakable in your name?"

"It sounds romantic to me," she said through a steadily growing torrent of tears dripping down her face.

"Just look at your brother." He stepped to the side and pointed at the car. "You see that? That's real love. She wants what's best for him and their future family. She pulled him out of this life for a chance at something better. Contrasted to you, who just made me a party to something so much worse. Don't you get it? I have to live with that, and I didn't even get the choice. My freedom was bought with his blood."

She moved forward and, without warning, enveloped him in a hug, smothering him in a tight embrace. She spoke into his shoulder. "I just didn't want to lose you is all. I was afraid."

"I know." Roger backed away. "That's why, if you do learn from this, I'm not opposed to maybe giving you another shot down the line if I'm still single. You understand? I'm still here. The main problem would be that your dad promised to end me. I believe him with every ounce of my being and don't intend to test him."

Her voice fell to a shaking whisper. "He won't live forever you know."

He raised a hand and gave a light tap on her head with a finger. "No, that's a bad girl. You're not going to do that. You need to reflect on what I've said. Do not eliminate the hypotenuse. Talk to the man if you think it'd help, but no more senseless culling. Promise me."

She backed up. "I get it." She pursed her hands in front of her. "I promise."

"You be careful. Don't do anything I wouldn't do."

"I have just one last thing I need to do before you go," Elizabeth said between sniffles.

"Yes?" Roger asked.

She took an unsteady step forward, brought her hand up behind his head, and coaxed his head forward until their lips met. She stepped back and wiped her lips. "That was for the road." She gave a small wave before turning and running back inside with a hand over her mouth.

Roger stood there and brought a hand up to his mouth. A metallic slapping noise broke his reverie. He saw Daniel reaching out the driver's side window and slapping the door with his palm. "Hurry up, Romeo."

He entered the passenger's side and closed the door. "So, where we going on this merry adventure?"

"I hear Chicago is lovely this time of the year," Tanya said from the backseat. "It's far from the Morris family, and it's a clean start."

Daniel turned the key and the engine roared to life. "Chicago it is."

Meanwhile inside on the second-floor balcony...

"The old man said he'd kill him?" Ana asked. She whistled. "Damn, that's rough. I guess you'll have to give up on him huh?"

"You're not thinking of the long game. The old man won't live forever you know."

"I'd be careful talking like that around here."

"Besides, I'm getting my own group soon. It's probably some stupid way of 'trying to make it up to me'. Guess who's getting out of here."

Ana's usual stoic face lit up into an unrestrained smile. "You mean?"

"That's right. We girls are going to make our mark here, one way or another."

Ana pumped a fist in front of her chest. "That means we'll have some power around here?"

"We'll have more than that. You just watch." Her gaze went back to the front door. "We'll all get what we want by the time I'm done..."

THANKS FOR READING!

The adventures of Roger and the Morris family continue in Any Means Necessary available now. If you'd like to support this work, please consider leaving a review on Amazon. Have a great day!

ABOUT THE AUTHOR

Alex J Fischer has been writing for close to a decade and has won five National Novel Writing Month challenges in a row.

Alex grew up in a small town in Ohio and still resides there. Hobbies include writing, video games, and watching crime shows.